June 2014

P9-CRC-094

THE
LAST HEIR

THE LAST HEIR

A Jack MacTaggart Mystery

CHUCK GREAVES

MINOTAUR BOOKS
A THOMAS DUNNE BOOK NEW YORK

A THOMAS DUNNE BOOK FOR MINOTAUR BOOKS.
An imprint of St. Martin's Publishing Group.

THE LAST HEIR. Copyright © 2014 by Charles J. Greaves. All rights reserved. Printed in the United States of America. For information, address St. Martin's Press, 175 Fifth Avenue, New York, N.Y. 10010.

www.thomasdunnebooks.com
www.minotaurbooks.com

Library of Congress Cataloging-in-Publication Data

Greaves, Chuck.
    The last heir : a mystery / Chuck Greaves.—First edition.
        pages cm
    ISBN 978-1-250-04556-0 (hardcover)
    ISBN 978-1-4668-4432-2 (e-book)
    1. MacTaggart, Jack.   2. Heirs—Fiction.   3. Inheritance and succession—Fiction.
    4. Murder—Investigation—Fiction.   5. Napa Valley (Calif.)—Fiction.   I. title.
    PS3607.R42885H45 2014
    813'.6—DC23

                                                                      2014008318

Minotaur books may be purchased for educational, business, or promotional use. For information on bulk purchases, please contact Macmillan Corporate and Premium Sales Department at 1-800-221-7945, extension 5442, or write specialmarkets@macmillan.com.

First Edition: June 2014

10 9 8 7 6 5 4 3 2 1

For Pati,

whose memory we cherish

PROLOGUE

"Five minutes!"

The gnome in the radio headset raised a hairy little hand with all five digits splayed, in case we'd failed to hear him shouting at us in our earpiece microphones. As I reached to adjust mine—it felt like I'd fallen asleep at my computer and awoken with the mouse lodged in my ear—Terina Webb, our panel moderator, gently took my arm.

"Quit fidgeting."

"What?"

"I said, stop fidgeting. You act like you've never done this before."

"I told you I've never done this before."

"I know," she said, "but don't *act* like it. I told my producer you were a pro."

We were seated at a raised horseshoe podium, its surface gleaming Lucite, its swivel chairs done in chrome and black calfskin leather. Behind us, a curving video screen carried a live feed from the civil courthouse in Van Nuys, California, where day one of this year's trial of the century had just recessed for lunch. Arrayed before us were four television monitors on which we'd been following the morning's proceedings from the relative comfort of the cavernous CBS News soundstage in Studio City, less than ten miles from the courthouse.

At the other end of the horseshoe, presently engrossed in whispered conversation, sat a pair of tassel-loafered Beverly Hills divorce lawyers who, had they been on the meter, would have been billing Channel Nine Action News a combined five grand per hour. Today, however, they—along with yours truly—had been dragooned into providing expert trial commentary for the over five million Southern California housewives, shut-ins, and unemployed actors with nothing better to do on a hazy Monday in June than curl up with some popcorn and pray for the second coming of O.J.

"Four minutes!"

The trial in progress was a so-called palimony action brought by Rosemary "Randi" Tandy, a former adult-film actress, against the widow of legendary Hollywood media mogul Lew Rothstein. Mrs. Rothstein—Betsy to her friends—was the executor of Big Lew's billion-dollar estate. She was also, it seems, the last of her gilded social circle to learn that her octogenarian husband had—according to the now-undisputed DNA evidence—fathered three teenage daughters with the erstwhile thespian.

One can safely assume that most fortysomething starlets whose career apogee was a bachelor-party standard called *Randi Does Richmond* would have been content, if faced with the same situation, to sign a confidentiality agreement and receive a quiet million dollars in child support from the Rothstein estate. But then, most porn stars would have lacked the perspicacity to hire Maxine Cameron—the Pit Bull in Prada—as their lawyer. Just as most lawyers would have lacked the requisite something—let's call them clanking brass balls—to sue for half the Rothstein fortune on the enterprising theory that Big Lew had verbally promised as much to his blushing young paramour.

"Three minutes!"

Since jury selection and opening statements had concluded last week, the morning's televised proceedings had begun with Maxine Cameron's direct examination of her client. Ms. Tandy had dressed for this solemn occasion in leopard-print spandex with matching high heels, and she'd teetered to the witness stand with a Kleenex box in her bejeweled hand—always a harbinger of good television to come. She'd then, under her counsel's machine-gun questioning, described with the exactitude of an Army quartermaster every gift, trifle, and bauble Big Lew had lavished upon her during their twenty-plus years of quasi-connubial bliss.

It was an impressive inventory that ranged from furs to diamonds to six Mercedes-Benz automobiles.

"Two minutes!"

Once Big Lew's generosity had been firmly established, the plaintiff next chronicled for the jury the many exotic vacations the couple had taken together, from Maui to Gstaad, Lake Como to Phuket Island. I was running a tape in my head, and by the time the judge had called the noon recess, I'd put the total of Big Lew's largesse at around six and a half million dollars.

My telephone vibrated, earning scowls both from Terina and the gnome in the headset.

"Talk to me."

"I just left the clerk's office downtown." Regan Fife, my office investigator, had to shout to be heard over the rumble of L.A. street traffic.

"And?"

"And you were right," she said. "There's nothing in the file."

"Okay, thanks."

I powered down the phone and slipped it into my pocket. By now the makeup girl had reappeared on set and was moving down the line with her little powder-puff thingy.

"One minute!"

Terina shoved back from the podium, the better to deliver a final pep talk to her trio of expert panelists.

"Okay, listen up. I'll do a short intro, then turn it over to you. We'll go from stage right to left, starting with Marv. Just touch on what you thought were the morning's highlights, and then we'll go to commercial. Ten minutes total. That means you'll each have up to three minutes to talk." To me she added, "Remember to look into the camera with the red light showing. And stop doing that thing with your ear."

Marvin Broadman, the most famous divorce attorney in all of Beverly Hills—a town with more family lawyers than parking meters—leaned in my direction.

"Maybe you'd better just stick to the sizzle," he said, "and let us handle the steak."

He then sat back and cleared his throat and smiled into camera two.

"Ten seconds!"

A pharmaceutical commercial was running silently on the monitors— floating butterflies carried a harried young housewife to bed after a day of domestic drudgery—when the light blinked red on camera one, and the video feed cut to Terina Webb in medium close-up.

"Welcome back to Channel Nine Action News' live and in-depth coverage of the blockbuster Beverly Hills Bigamy Trial. I'm Terina Webb, your studio host, and I'm joined today by three of the biggest names in the L.A. legal world: Marvin Broadman, Tom Schwartz, and Jack MacTaggart." Terina did a half turn to her right. "We'll start with you, Marv. First impressions, what did you think of what you heard in court this morning?"

On the monitor, superimposed beneath Broadman's grinning yap, were his name and the tagline "Divorce Lawyer to the Stars."

"Well, Terina, you know that whenever you have Maxine Cameron in a courtroom, you're going to see fireworks, and today was certainly no exception. She effectively established three things right up front that are critical to her theory of the case. First, that the relationship between her client and Lew Rothstein was a close one. Second, that Big Lew's generosity toward Ms. Tandy knew no bounds. And third, that they traveled the world together, often holding themselves out to the public as husband and wife. It remains to be seen whether Maxine can make the leap from those key facts to proving a promise to leave half the Rothstein estate to Ms. Tandy, but I think she's off to a heck of a good start. And given her track record with juries, I wouldn't want to be betting against her."

"Tom?"

A decade younger than Broadman, Schwartz had leading-man looks and a Faustian reputation as the go-to guy in Hollywood for challenging prenuptial agreements. He was said to have every tabloid and gossip-rag editor in the country on speed-dial. He was also rumored to be on monthly retainer by the Celebrity Centre of the Church of Scientology.

"I'd have to concur with my friend on all counts, Terina. We've both litigated against Maxine Cameron, and I'm sure Marv will agree that when Maxine takes on a client's cause, she makes it personal. She also has an uncanny knack for proving what might, at first blush, seem highly improbable. We saw that this morning with her opening gambit of establishing the kind of close relationship between Ms. Tandy and Lew Rothstein that could easily have led to the promise we'll soon be hearing about. I'd look for more of the same this afternoon, ending with a bombshell at around four-thirty that will jolt the jury awake and send them home with an entirely different view of her client and her client's case."

Terina squared some papers as she swiveled to my side of the podium. "Jack?"

The light on camera three blinked red, and I stared into the lens. I was, I'll admit, at a momentary loss for words, given that Schwartz and Broadman—both supremely confident in their analyses—were reputedly among the best in their specialized field.

"Say something!" barked the headset gnome, his klaxon voice echoing deep in my cochlear canal.

I cleared my throat and swallowed.

"I guess I have a slightly different take on Ms. Cameron's performance this morning than my esteemed colleagues." I glanced down the podium at Broadman and Schwartz, both of whom were frowning back at me. "I'm not a family lawyer, but I did do a bit of research before I came down here today, and one thing I noted is that the California Family Code gives an innocent spouse up to three years from date of discovery within which to recover for the community estate any unauthorized gifts made by the other spouse during the marriage. Also, I had my investigator check the probate file downtown, and it appears that there was never a creditor's claim filed by Ms. Tandy against the Rothstein estate within the four-month statutory deadline."

Terina's brow had furrowed. "The significance of all that being . . . ?"

"That unless I'm mistaken, Maxine Cameron just proved up an air-tight reimbursement case against her own client, under oath, to the tune of around seven million dollars. And if she never filed a written claim in the probate action, then I'd say her palimony case against the Rothstein estate is dead in the water, barred by limitations."

Silence fell over the set. Schwartz and Broadman shared a glance, with Broadman muttering something that sounded like "Holy shit."

Terina, herself at an uncharacteristic loss for words, swiveled back to the camera.

"Uh, why don't we come back to explore these fascinating new developments after a quick word from our sponsors?"

My nascent career in punditry proved, alas, to be short-lived, since the first day of the blockbuster Beverly Hills Bigamy Trial was also the last. Betsy Rothstein's motion for a directed verdict was granted after the first day's lunch recess had ended and, a week later, the Rothstein estate sued Randi Tandy to recover some eight million dollars in luxury goods and services. Which, in the finest American tradition, Ms. Tandy sought to recoup by filing a legal malpractice action against her lawyer, Maxine Cameron.

On the whole, it promised to be another banner year for the Beverly Hills Bar Association.

But the affair was not without a silver lining, as, perhaps ten days after my appearance on television, the phone rang in the law offices of Mac-Taggart & Suarez, and an elderly gentleman introduced himself as a friend of Betsy Rothstein. He asked, in a courtly French accent, whether I'd be willing to consult with him on a matter that was, as he put it, of "some delicacy."

When he offered to pay for the consultation, travel time included, I was favorably disposed toward his request. Then, when he offered to send his private jet to fetch me up for a weekend in Napa Valley, I had no choice but to agree.

I

They called it the French Laundry, but I hadn't seen a steam iron or a sweating Chinaman all night. We were on our seventh or eighth food course, none of them larger than a nine-volt battery, and I for one was still hungry after two hours at the table.

The wine was another story. Six dusty bottles of Château Giroux Private Reserve Cabernet Sauvignon lay at anchor before me like galleons in a sea of crystal glassware, all of it rocking and swaying in the gentle swell of my incipient intoxication. Commanding this ambrosial armada, his silver personage outfitted in a blue blazer and paisley ascot, was the owner of the eponymous winery whose dark nectar I'd been imbibing—the winery generally acknowledged, or so I'd come to learn, to be the crown jewel in the glittering tiara of California's storied Napa Valley.

"Here," Philippe Giroux said, reaching for another bottle. "Let's try the sixty-one."

A waiter, noticing movement, sprang into action. He intercepted the bottle and walked it around to my side of the table where, cradling it like a premature newborn, he measured three inches of purple liquid into my glass.

He then did the same for my prodigal host.

The Frenchman raised his glass, turning it slowly in the half light, and gave it a swirl. He passed his sharp Gallic beak over the rim and inhaled. Eyes closed, he took a sip and made a bubbling noise with his mouth, then spit the wine back into the glass.

Again.

"Black currants," he pronounced, dabbing at his lips with a napkin. "Tar and licorice and wet pebbles."

I took a slug. Like the others before it, this bottle was aces high.

"Tell me something. Why is it always plums and cherries and notes of old-growth cedar? How come wine never just tastes like grapes?"

Giroux brightened. "Ah. Therein lays the artistry. In the hands of a great winemaker, each vintage is a precise expression of the soil and the climate from which it is born. The soul, if you will, of the grape itself. What we French call the *terroir*."

"We have the same thing here in America. We call it Beechwood Aging."

He chuckled, setting down his glass. "I'm the luckiest man in the world, Mr. MacTaggart. For over thirty years, if ever I came home to dinner and *didn't* reek of wine, my wife would say, 'Philippe, what mischief have you been up to?'"

He chuckled again, and this time, so did I. He was a charming old rooster—a *boulevardier* of the Maurice Chevalier stripe, all raffish twinkle and easy warmth—and you couldn't help but like the guy. I'm sure he'd sold a lot of wine over the years.

"Let's try the ninety-four, shall we? That was an excellent vintage."

I placed a defensive hand over my glass just as the next phalanx of waiters arrived from the kitchen with steaming plates of braised chinchilla testicles in *buerre blanc*. Or something very much like it. Another thing I hadn't seen all night was a menu.

"Maybe we should get down to business while a part of my brain is still dry. You spoke on the phone about a matter of some delicacy?"

Giroux's smile faded, a shadow passing behind his eyes. He lifted his napkin again and dabbed, stalling for the waiters to move out of earshot.

"Very well then, to business. I have two sons, Mr. MacTaggart. Or had, perhaps."

He reached into an inside pocket and handed me a slip of newsprint. It was an article clipped from a back issue of the *San Francisco Chronicle*, bearing the headline VINTNER'S SON CLAIMED IN AVALANCHE.

I read the story. It described a heli-skiing mishap somewhere north of Lake Tahoe from which Phil Giroux, age thirty-nine, had been rescued, but his brother Alain, age thirty-eight, had not. The incident had occurred in mid-February of this year.

"By the time he was found, my son Philip had lost three toes to frostbite. Alas, he was the lucky one."

"I'm terribly sorry," I said, returning the article. "But you said 'perhaps' just now. Does that mean Alain's body was never recovered?"

"Correct." He folded away the clipping and patted his breast pocket. "There was a rock slide, apparently. The body could easily have been buried. That's what the authorities say."

"But you don't believe them."

He thought about that, lifting his glass again and gazing into the wine. As if peering into some rose-colored past.

"Do you have children, Mr. MacTaggart?"

I showed him my left hand. He grunted.

"Perhaps I'm just a foolish old man, but something here"—he tapped again at his heart where the clipping was folded—"tells me that Alain did not die. That if he were dead, I would know it. That I would *feel* it."

"I hope you're right about that. But I don't see how I'm in any position to help."

He set down the glass and took up his fork, his eyes falling to the steaming plate before him.

"Indulge me, if you will, in a bit of family history. My father came to this country after the Great War. He was Bordelaise. He grew up as a field hand, an *ouvrier*, working for some of the great châteaux of the Médoc, planting and pruning and harvesting. Then, once the war had ended, he set out to buy a vineyard of his own. But not in France. Not after all that carnage. So he did a bit of research, and he learned of a sleepy little valley in a place called California where German and Italian immigrants were already making wine. There, he said, is where I will raise my family. He married my mother in 1918, still in France, and together they bought twenty-five acres of land here on the eastern edge of Napa Valley, sight unseen, through a farm agent with whom he'd corresponded by mail. That was in May of 1919. The price was quite reasonable, you see, because his research was not very thorough. He bought just in time for Prohibition."

Giroux smiled ruefully as he sampled the braised whatever, his eyes closing to savor the culinary moment.

"But still they came. Instead of planting vines, they grew vegetables. For ten years, nothing but vegetables. All the time making contacts and connections with the very best restaurants in San Francisco. Connections that would pay off handsomely when, in 1933, they finally planted their first fifteen acres of Cabernet Sauvignon, plus a few odd blocks of Cab Franc and Merlot and Petit Verdot. They were, as I said, Bordelaise."

I tried the cooling dollop on my plate, for which so many chinchillas had sacrificed. Then I tried the rest.

"In order to consecrate the new vineyard, or so the story goes, my parents conceived a son. Their only child, as it turned out, since my mother died in 1937 of complications from pneumonia."

I nudged my empty plate aside, the better to resist licking it. "So you inherited the family business from your father when he died."

"In a manner of speaking. Here is where you come in, if I may be so presumptuous."

He reached into another pocket and produced a different piece of paper. It was a three-fold brochure, the kind you'd find in a rack at the airport, printed on glossy paper stock. It promoted something called the Napa Springs Spa and Golf Resort.

"By the time my father died in 1979, Château Giroux had grown to a hundred and fifty acres. Today it includes the original stone château, the vineyards, the winery, four other family residences, and a new visitor center run by my daughter, Claudia."

"You also have a daughter."

He nodded. "Our youngest child. Or mine, to be precise. Marie, my beloved, passed in 2003. It seems to be a curse of the Giroux men, to outlive their wives."

But not Alain, I thought, as Giroux leaned sideways in his chair and produced a wallet from his pocket. From it he removed a color photo of a real looker—a twentysomething blonde with notes of ripe apricot and vanilla spices. She had her father's nose, and what appeared to be Kate Moss's body.

"You'll meet Claudia tomorrow. She is the spitting image of her mother. She too is a lawyer, although she's never actually practiced. Instead she manages all aspects of our hospitality—the tasting room, the winery tours, our wine club. In many ways, she has become the public face of Château Giroux."

"And this Napa Springs Spa?"

The shadow returned. He reached to pour me another drink, and this time I let him.

"My father and I were never close, despite the many years we worked together. Or because of them, perhaps. He was a stern man, *très severe*, with what you might call an Old World point of view. To him, the wine business was just a business, like selling vegetables, or vacuum cleaners. No public tours for him, no tasting room. It was a source of conflict between us. We were estranged, you might say, by the end of his life. When he died, all of Château Giroux became part of a trust for the benefit of his grandsons, my male heirs."

I nodded. "It's a common estate planning device, called a generation-skipping trust. Although the male part is unusual, in this day and age."

"As I said, his views were quite old-fashioned. According to the trust document, I have control over Château Giroux only until the youngest of my sons reaches the age of forty years. After that, it passes to them outright, as equal beneficiaries."

"And the resort?"

He glanced at the brochure again and sighed.

"A bit more local history, I'm afraid. In 1990, Napa County voters passed an initiative limiting the conversion of vineyard properties to nonagricultural uses. I personally helped to lead that effort, and provided much of the funding. Its purpose was to prevent urban sprawl from gobbling up the most storied vineyard acreage in all North America."

"I'd call that sound public policy."

He nodded. "But you must understand that Napa Valley is more than just a wine-making region. It has also become an international vacation destination, with tourism accounting for over a billion dollars per year in local spending. Tourists, of course, need restaurants and hotel beds. So the developers hired lawyers, and the lawyers hired lobbyists. Soon loopholes were exploited, and resorts like that"—he flicked a finger at the folded brochure—"were permitted to move forward. It's a monstrosity, I can assure you, and it borders Château Giroux to the south. The owner is a man named Clarkson, Andy Clarkson. He and Alain were schoolmates."

Foggy though I was, the picture was coming into focus.

"Now Clarkson wants to expand, but your vineyard is in the way."

"Correct again. He wishes to build a second golf course. A course he cannot complete without fifty acres of my prized Cabernet!"

Heads turned at the neighboring tables. I leaned forward, lowering my voice.

"And if Alain is dead, that puts exclusive ownership of Château Giroux in your son Phil's hands when he turns forty."

"Just so. Two-and-a-half months from now, on the thirtieth of August."

"Is Phil willing to sell out to Clarkson?"

Here the old man hesitated. "That I cannot say. He denies it, of course, and I prefer to believe him. His wife, however, is another story."

A hushed murmur rippled through the restaurant as a large, florid man in a chef's white jacket and toque appeared at our table. He and Giroux spoke in fluent French, the chef obsequious, beaming and bowing at what I presumed were Giroux's expressions of gastronomic approval. Giroux filled a glass—I think it was the ninety-seven—and watched as the chef did the old swirl-and-sniff routine.

Like me, he was a swallower.

"Jack MacTaggart, meet Lucien Moreau. Lucien is America's greatest sous chef."

The big man bowed in my direction, then bid a reluctant *bonne soirée* to Giroux as he continued on his rounds, taking the wineglass with him. Giroux watched him depart before resuming his story.

"My son Philip has filed a legal action to have Alain declared dead. Merely to clear title, he says, to Château Giroux. But I know that Lourdes, his wife, is the one behind it. She cares nothing for the vineyards, nothing for the wine that is our family legacy. She cares only for the thugs and criminals who would drive us into bankruptcy!"

"Thugs and criminals?"

"The United Farm Workers. A terrorist gang of extortionists that she, in her misguided naiveté, both idolizes and enables."

As Giroux's trembling hand lifted a bottle and filled an empty glass, I recalled my college Tolstoy—that all happy families are alike, but each unhappy family is unhappy in its own way.

"Why are you telling all of this to me? I'm sure there are plenty of excellent lawyers in the area, and certainly in San Francisco."

Giroux nodded. "There is a firm in the City of Napa that we've used for many years, called Melchior and Moore. Perhaps you've heard of them?"

I had not, which wasn't surprising, since there are nearly two hundred thousand lawyers in California alone. As my late uncle Louis once observed, two lawyers can make an excellent living in a town that can't support one.

"Thad Melchior is the senior partner there," Giroux continued. "He tells me that, having represented Château Giroux in the past, his firm would have a conflict of interest taking sides in any personal dispute between Philip and myself."

"So you plan to oppose Phil's action."

"Yes, of course. And when Betsy Rothstein told me about you, I was intrigued. She'd spent a small fortune on attorneys' fees, not to mention a year of sleepless nights, and yet the answer to her problem was right there, staring her in the face the entire time. I value an agile mind, Mr. MacTaggart, and I value tenacity. I take it that estate planning is not your field of expertise?"

"No. I'm strictly a trial lawyer."

"No matter. I've checked up on you. You're exactly the kind of lawyer I need."

Which was good, because Philippe Giroux was exactly the kind of client every lawyer needs—a worried millionaire. I poured myself a glass of the ninety-seven, and I raised it in his direction.

"All right, you've got me. But in this case, agility and tenacity won't be enough. If we're going to disprove that Alain is dead, we'll need more in the way of evidence than a gut feeling from his father."

The twinkle had returned to the old man's eye as he leaned across the table to grab hold of my sleeve. "We *have* the evidence, Mr. MacTaggart. Solid evidence. And I'll show it to you in the morning."

2

My suite at Auberge du Soleil had a balcony overlooking a swimming pool and, beyond its turquoise oblong, vine rows that unfurled like wales of plush corduroy across the valley floor. The setting was woodsy—the hillside resort lay nestled amid live oaks and native brush—with the virid geometry of the distant vineyards broken by up-thrusts of poplar and Italian cypress flagging Tuscan-style estates, all of it backset by purple mountains that formed the valley's western rim.

It occurred to me that I was about as far from the asphalt lattice of East L.A., where I'd grown up, as you can get without showing a passport.

I sat on the shaded balcony in a thick terrycloth robe and lingered over my room-service Belgian waffle, which, this being Napa Valley, had come with a warm Cabernet-grape compote. From the in-room *Visitor's Guide* in my lap, I learned that Napa Valley is roughly thirty miles long and five miles wide, runs northward from the City of Napa, includes the storybook towns of Yountville, Oakville, Rutherford, St. Helena, and Calistoga, is home to more than four hundred wineries, and receives over five million visitors annually.

Since most of those visitors come here to imbibe, I figured Napa Valley was also the drunk-driving capital of North America, although I couldn't find any mention of that in the *Visitor's Guide*.

The *Guide* did, however, include a small real estate section, where I discovered that you can buy a modest two-bedroom, two-bath fixer-upper on a quarter-acre lot in Yountville for a mere $799,000. Like Marshall at Sutter's Mill, Philippe Giroux's father had clearly stumbled onto a gold mine.

I refilled my coffee and punched up Mayday on her cell phone. Marta "Mayday" Suarez is my protégé and law partner, not to mention most of the brains and all of the tact behind the law firm of MacTaggart & Suarez, and I knew she'd be eager to learn the details of our new client's case.

"How'd it go?" she answered before I could get to hello.

"The sacrifices I make for this firm," I told her, sounding aggrieved. "Cramped airplane, crappy food, and now this fleabag of a motel."

"I happen to know that you're in a suite at a Relais and Châteaux resort, and that your room rents for two thousand dollars a night, which I hope the client is paying. An incidentals charge came through this morning on the firm credit card. By the way, what movie did you watch last night?"

"Never mind that. I have a life-threatening hangover, I overslept, and our new client's limo is picking me up"—I glanced at my watch—"in thirty-five minutes."

"I like new clients with limos."

"Then you'll love Philippe Giroux, although his father apparently didn't, and the jury's still out on his kids. He has two of those, by the way, or possibly three. That's what we've been hired to determine."

"When did you say you stopped drinking?"

"We've been retained to oppose an action to establish the death of an heir," I told her. "You'll find it covered in the Probate Code somewhere. And if you'd be kind enough to research the subject and give me a call back in the next half hour or so, then I can sound like I know what I'm talking about, and the client will sleep better at night. And so will I, although the Belgian chocolates they leave on the pillows here are extraordinarily rich."

"Why do I suddenly feel like Cyrano de Bergerac?"

"Because you've been a very nosy young woman. *Au revoir*."

I shaved, showered, and donned a clean dress shirt. I found the Advil in my toiletries case and swallowed three. Since it was already eighty degrees outside, I left my tie and jacket in the room and headed over to the lobby with my shirtsleeves rolled. There I waited for Larry, Philippe Giroux's personal chauffer, who'd picked me up at the Napa County Airport and had, I presume, dropped me off last night at the hotel, although I wouldn't swear to the last part under oath.

It was only after we'd exited the resort property and turned downhill toward Silverado Trail—the two-lane country road skirting the eastern edge of the Valley—that Larry the Driver addressed himself to the rearview mirror.

"Sleep okay?"

"Like a baby. Every two hours, I woke up crying."

"Hah. You did seem a little tipsy last night."

"Just trying to blend in with the local tourists."

Larry promised a short drive to Château Giroux, and then delivered it in discreet silence, leaving me to contemplate the wrath of grapes. We traversed sun-kissed vineyards to the west and low foothills to the east furred by oak and native pine whose shadows dappled the windshield as we glided past. Not more than a mile farther on, a large and garish billboard marked the gated entrance to a driveway. The sign read NAPA SPRINGS SPA AND GOLF RESORT, and below that, MEMBERSHIPS AVAILABLE.

I made a mental note of the location.

After another quarter mile we forked off of Silverado Trail onto an unmarked county road that climbed and wended over an oak-studded hill and deposited us, a half mile later, into an idyllic little side valley. The first driveway we encountered had an open double gate that bore amid its black iron filigree the iconic gold fleur-de-lis of Château Giroux.

Larry slowed and signaled.

Ancient olive trees lined the long and landscaped driveway, which led us to a paved visitor parking lot in which a dozen or more vehicles already basked like cats in the low morning sunlight.

"Pretty quiet for a Saturday," Larry observed.

Most of the vehicles appeared to be rental cars, but they included a cherry-red Porsche and, in a striped-off area by the Visitor Center entrance, a white stretch Hummer that was longer than a Quentin Tarantino film festival.

Larry glided to a halt. "Bachelorette party would be my guess," he said, following my gaze to the Hummer. "We get a lot of those in June. They're probably taking the tour."

My phone vibrated. It was Mayday, calling in the nick of time.

"California Probate Code section two hundred," she began without preamble. "'If title to or an interest in real or personal property is affected by the death of a person, another person who claims an interest in the property may commence proceedings pursuant to this chapter to establish the fact of death.'"

"Cliff Notes, *s'il vous plait*. They're waiting for me inside."

"Okay, bottom line. Jurisdiction is in the Superior Court of the county in which either the property is located or the decedent resided."

"The alleged decedent."

"Right. The action is commenced by the filing of a petition. Notice of the action must be mailed to interested persons not less than fifteen days before the hearing. Evidence is by affidavits, which, and here I'm quoting again, have 'the same force and effect as if the petitioner and the affiants were personally present and testified to the facts set forth.'"

"That's it? No evidentiary hearing?"

"Not per the statute. But I'd imagine if there are disputed issues of fact, you could ask the court to take live testimony."

This was what I had feared. It meant that Phil Giroux and his lawyers had weeks or even months in which to assemble their paper case, while we'd have only ten days to rebut it. Less, depending on when and how the petition had been served. Moreover, it meant that a probate court judge could decide the case while sitting in his chambers with his feet up on the desk eating a ham sandwich, all without any cross-examination of the affiant-witnesses in open court.

"Burden of proof?" I asked her, which prompted the sound of riffling pages.

"The statute doesn't say, but I'd presume it lies with the petitioner, and that death need only be established by a preponderance of the evidence."

"Please tell me there's some good news."

"The good news is that a judgment rendered by the probate court creates only a presumption of death. So if any post-judgment evidence should come to light—"

"Like the dead man limping into court?"

"Good example. That would rebut the presumption, and the issue could then be re-opened for adjudication."

I saw Larry the Driver checking his wristwatch, and I did likewise. I was already five minutes late.

"Okay, new subject. What do you know about the economics of growing wine grapes?"

"Everything there is to know. As long as it's on Wikipedia."

I smiled. "I could use a crash course, for which I'll call you later. Oh, and you might want to start clearing the decks down there. I have a feeling we're going to get busy."

The glass double-doors to the Visitor Center were flanked by potted topiary trimmed into the same fleur-de-lis shape as had adorned both the driveway gates out front and the Château Giroux wine labels I vaguely recalled from last night's dinner. Stepping through the doors was like entering the lobby of a modern luxury hotel, complete with furniture groupings, floral arrangements, and a huge sectional rug covering most of a gray flagstone floor. The perky young redhead at the reception desk straightened and beamed at my approach.

"Good morning and welcome to Château Giroux. How may I be of assistance?"

"Jack MacTaggart to see Philippe Giroux. I have a ten o'clock appointment."

"Yes, sir." She made a check mark in her appointment book as she lifted the telephone. "Mr. Giroux asked if you'd be so kind as to wait for him in the tasting room. It's just that way."

She gestured toward an open archway, through which a peal of drunken laughter gusted into the lobby. I was heartened to know that someone was feeling festive this early in the morning. I knew for sure it wasn't me.

The tasting room was configured like an upscale restaurant bar from which all the barstools had been removed and the table area replaced by a boutique gift shop. The bar itself was over thirty feet long and besieged at present by customers standing two-deep. The mob included what looked like a Kappa Kappa Gamma rush party—a dozen or more debutantes in colorful sundresses, some wearing cowboy hats and boots, all of them chattering like grackles as they swirled and sniffed their breakfast beverages.

I guessed it was five o'clock somewhere. Possibly in Bordeaux.

I didn't see the old man, so I killed time in the boutique, which offered everything from hundred-dollar wineglasses to golf shirts and ball caps at forty bucks a throw, all of it embossed with the ubiquitous gold fleur-de-lis. I was eyeing a wine-country cookbook for Mayday and Regan—who share what is known nowadays as a domestic partnership—when a girlish giggle interrupted me from behind.

"Excuse me, sir. Could we all ask you a question?"

I turned to see three lushly coiffed brunettes holding wineglasses. They weren't blitzed, exactly, nor were they rock-steady on their feet. One of them—the one in the middle, with the white lace veil pinned to her hair—appeared to be standing in a rowboat.

"You certainly may."

"It's about my friend's boots," said the giggler, gesturing toward the bride-to-be's tooled crocodile footwear with the inlaid orange cow skulls.

"What about them?"

They shared a conspiratorial look. "Well. We all were wondering if you think they make her breasts look too big."

They doubled over laughing, hands to mouths, the bride spitting her wine.

"Mr. MacTaggart?"

Philippe Giroux stood at an open door. He wore a different blazer this morning, this one paired with a mustard-yellow ascot, and his appearance caused a minor stir at the bar, where several patrons snapped photos of him with their cell phone cameras. I excused myself and crossed the room to join him.

"Sorry to keep you waiting," he said, offering a hand. "At least you found a way to amuse yourself."

He led me down a carpeted hallway to a door near the end on the left. The office within had mullioned windows overlooking a courtyard, comfortable chairs and sofas, and a Louis XIV desk with long, finely shaped legs. As the door closed behind us, a woman rose from her perch on the edge of the desk.

For my money, her legs were nicer.

This version of Claudia Giroux had a few years on the winsome girl in the photo, and maybe she'd put on a few pounds, but she'd put them in all the right places. She wore a white silk blouse and a snug navy skirt with sensible blue heels. Her golden hair, long and straight in the photo, had been cut to shoulder-length and swept backward in a way that displayed the diamond studs in her ears.

She put the hyphen in high-class, as would befit the new public face of Château Giroux.

"Mr. MacTaggart," she said, her handshake firm, her sapphire eyes assessing. "My father has told me so much about you."

"But me so little about you. We'll have to remedy that."

"Be careful what you wish for," she said, circling to her swivel chair and pressing her palms on the desk. "I'm afraid you'll have had quite enough of me before this is through."

I bit hard on my tongue as Philippe and I took the client chairs facing his daughter, where we waited in polite silence as she sifted through some paperwork on her desktop. When she found what she was after—a nine-by-twelve envelope—she handed it across.

"It arrived on Wednesday," she said. "It came with the regular mail delivery."

The document inside the envelope was a pleading that bore the case caption *In re Estate of Alain P. Giroux, Deceased,* and the title "Petition to

Determine Death of Alain P. Giroux." It had been filed by a lawyer named Rubenstein. The proof-of-service form at the back confirmed its deposit in the U.S. Mail on Monday, the thirteenth day of June. A hearing date had been rubber-stamped on the face page by the clerk of the Napa County Superior Court. That date was July 6.

"We'll want to ask for a continuance," I said absently, flipping to the supporting affidavits.

Philippe half-turned in his chair. "Are you sure? Don't forget Philip's birthday. If we wait too long . . ."

He didn't finish the thought, but he didn't have to. If we were to wait too long, and if Alain were declared dead by the probate court, then under the terms of the Giroux family trust, Phil would own everything as of August 30. What effect might an appeal have after that? Or the discovery of new evidence that reopened the question of death? What if Phil sold part of Château Giroux to Andy Clarkson, the owner of Napa Springs Spa, while an appeal was pending? Or what if Phil dropped dead at his birthday party, leaving Lourdes, Philippe's insurrectionist daughter-in-law, in control of Château Giroux?

Philippe was right—time was of the essence.

The supporting Declarations—the affidavits referenced in the statute—were from the Petitioner, Phil Giroux, and from a man named Brent Vroman, who headed up something called the Tahoe Nordic Search and Rescue Team. Both Declarations described the circumstances of the avalanche that, to the declarants' best knowledge and belief, had claimed the life of Alain Giroux.

"Well, what do you think?"

I returned the petition to the envelope and set it on Claudia's desk.

"Your father mentioned some evidence that Alain might still be alive. That would come in handy right about now."

Father and daughter shared a look, and Claudia rose and crossed to a file cabinet on the wall directly behind her, where she bent to open a drawer. Philippe's voice brought my attention back to the business at hand.

"Château Giroux employs over twenty full-time staff, but it remains a family enterprise. The board of directors consists of myself and my three children. Each of us, along with a few key personnel, is issued a company credit card. Alain had his card with him when he disappeared. We know that from Philip. Also from the fact that Alain's wallet was found in their hotel room in Tahoe with the credit card missing. Also from the last charge processed on the card on the day Alain went missing, to a firm called Alpine Heli-Guides."

Claudia returned to her desk with a folder. She passed it to her father, who opened it and handed me an American Express credit card statement for the month of February.

"We requested a copy of the charge slip," he said, passing me another sheet. "Here it is."

The photocopied receipt showed the time of the Alpine Heli-Guides credit card charge—9:12 A.M.—and bore the cardholder's signature, *Alain Giroux.*

"What time did the helicopter depart for the mountain?"

Philippe again looked to his daughter. "We spoke to the pilot. His flight log shows skids-up at eight-twenty A.M."

"That means Alain paid for the flight while they were en route to the mountain, or shortly after they'd landed. If his wallet was still at the hotel, then he must have had the credit card with him."

Philippe nodded. "The card and some cash. That's what Philip told us."

"All right. But what's the significance of all this?"

Philippe passed me another sheaf of AmEx statements from the file.

"These are the statements for Alain's credit card for the months of March through May. For *after* he disappeared."

As expected, the statement for March showed no activity. For April and May, however, there were charges to the account. I counted seven transactions in total.

"Did you—?"

"We did." Philippe handed me the final pages from the folder— photocopies of the receipts that corresponded to the seven credit card charges. Five of them bore signatures, and I compared those signatures to the one on the Alpine Heli-Guides receipt.

They were a perfect match.

3

Philippe returned his papers to the file. "Perhaps now, Mr. Mac-Taggart, you understand my position."

I did, and a whole lot more.

In a contested court proceeding—the kind with pretrial discovery and live witnesses and cross-examination—Philippe Giroux's position might prove less tenable than he believed. There were, in fact, several plausible explanations for the evidence he'd assembled. Alain's credit card might have been lost or stolen before the avalanche, and the thief may have copied his signature off the back of the card. Or, Alain's remains might have been found post-avalanche by a felonious hiker. Plus there are bad guys who can, as I understand it, create credit cards from scratch using stolen electronic data.

"What about his cell phone?"

"He carried a company phone," Philippe said. "It too was found in the hotel room, along with his wallet."

If this were a criminal matter, in which a prosecuting attorney must establish Alain's death beyond a reasonable doubt, then Philippe's credit card evidence would probably suffice to raise a reasonable doubt, much like O.J.'s shriveled leather glove. But this wasn't a criminal prosecution.

As the petitioner in a civil action, Phil Giroux's burden of proof was merely to establish his brother's death by a preponderance of the evidence—a scintilla greater than fifty percent. In that forgiving context, and before a probate judge rather than a jury, Philippe might need more in the way of evidence than those pages from his file.

Then again, he might not. It was a pretty close call.

"Does Phil know about these charges?"

"No," said Claudia. "Nobody does. When the April statement arrived, I showed it to Father. He asked me to order copies of the receipts from American Express, which we've done every month. We thought it best to keep this in confidence between the two of us."

Which was good, because the fast-track, stripped-down nature of a probate proceeding would now, strangely enough, work to our advantage. Given time and resources, Phil and his lawyer might find a way to blow holes in our credit card evidence, and meet their modest burden of proof. But under the current timetable, our opposition to Phil's petition would be due on June 23, five days hence, and nine court days before the hearing. Phil and his lawyer would then have only six days—or until June 29—within which to file a reply. Which left them precious little time for hole-blowing.

"Do we know this lawyer, Mark Rubenstein?"

Philippe nodded. "He's an estate-planning attorney in Napa. A sole practitioner. I'm told he's competent, but no Clarence Darrow."

"When he sees this evidence," I told them, nodding to the file, "Phil might be the one to request a continuance."

"Not if Lourdes has a say in the matter. That little Judas can't *wait* to get her hands on Château Giroux."

"Now, Father—"

"She probably has union meetings scheduled for the Visitor Center already. No, she'll oppose any continuance, and by God, so will I. I don't want Philip turning forty with the ownership question unsettled."

"Very well," I said, rising from my chair. "Then I have work to do. Those receipts don't just waltz into evidence. We'll need a foundational declaration from a records custodian at American Express. Also"—and

here I turned to Claudia—"we'll need a declaration from you as to issu-
ance of the credit card, receipt of the account statements, and the authen-
ticity of Alain's signatures."

"Not a problem."

"And please remind me, to whom did Phil describe the events of the
accident? The part about Alain leaving his wallet and phone in the hotel,
but taking his credit card?"

"Me," said Philippe.

"Both of us," said Claudia.

"Good. I'll also want copies of the receipts and statements, a copy of
Phil's petition, and a ride back to L.A. as soon as possible."

Philippe rose in protest. "But what about our dinner? It's essential that
you meet Phil and Lourdes in person. Beard the lion in its den, as the saying
goes. If there's one thing I've learned, Mr. MacTaggart, it's that you can't
make exceptional wine without first observing the grapes on the vine."

"I don't think—"

"But you must." Claudia was on her feet now, circling the desk. "I agree
with Father. We can scan the documents here and have them e-mailed to
your office this afternoon. I think you'll find an evening at the château to
be rather edifying."

Well, since she'd put it that way.

"The problem is, we can't discuss the case in front of Phil or Lourdes,"
I told them. "That would be unethical. Nothing whatsoever about Alain's
death, or the trust, or the pending petition."

"Of course not," said Philippe, "which is why I've told them that our
dinner guest is a new Los Angeles food critic. Mrs. LaBoutin, my private
chef, has planned something quite special, and I can assure you that you
won't be disappointed."

While Philippe certainly meant well, his proposal was fraught with
peril. It's an absolute no-no for an attorney to discuss a pending matter
with an opposing party he knows to be represented by counsel. And since
this case at its core involved the family and its business, that narrowed
the permissible scope of dinner conversation to the unholy trinity of food,
weather, and politics.

"How about this for a compromise? I'll come for cocktails, say hello, then make an excuse to leave early. That way, no one can later accuse me of impropriety."

Philippe frowned, but eventually nodded. "All right, if you think it best. I'll send the car for you at six."

Claudia moved to the door, and I followed.

"Oh. There's one more thing I've been meaning to ask," I said, turning back to Philippe. "Was there an insurance policy on Alain's life?"

The old man shook his head. "Alain didn't believe in insurance, Mr. MacTaggart. Alain didn't believe in death."

That, too, he must have inherited from his father.

I was on the phone with Mayday, swapping information and updates, when the garish billboard again rose into view.

"Turn here," I told Larry, who checked his mirrors and signaled.

"You sure about this? These people can be assholes."

"Don't worry. That makes them my kind of people."

The driveway leading to the Napa Springs Spa and Golf Resort was steep and shaded, and it leveled off at a parking lot with a wooden sign that read BAG DROP. I rang off with Mayday just as Larry dropped his baggage—me—at the curb, where he offered to park and wait.

"Thanks, but I think I'll stay for a spot of lunch. Maybe check out the facilities. I'll see you at the hotel at six."

"Be careful," he told me.

"You be careful. The roads out there are full of drunks."

I got as far as a large central courtyard just beyond the entrance arch before I was accosted. The courtyard was landscaped with small, orderly plantings smothered in redwood mulch, the kind you'd find at a suburban McMansion in a new Orange County subdivision. It lay central to four Italianate buildings that housed, according to their signage, the Pro Shop, the Spa, the Clubhouse, and something called Pilate's Trattoria. As for the accoster, he was neither small nor orderly, but he may have been Italian. He wore a rumpled blue blazer with a white plastic name tag, and he carried a walkie-talkie radio in one hand and a Styrofoam coffee cup in the other.

The name tag read MARCO.

"Excuse me. Can I help you?" Marco wanted to know, and I gave him my brightest smile.

"I do hope so. I'm a new Los Angeles food critic, and I was hoping to speak with the general manager about sampling your luncheon cuisine."

"This is a private club, you know."

"Excellent. One can't be too careful nowadays."

Frowning, Marco stepped far enough away that I only caught a word or two as he spoke into his handheld. I heard "some guy" and "food critic" and "cuisine." Possibly "hide the body," but maybe I was being paranoid. He kept his eyes on me for the whole conversation, which he ended with a "ten-four" and a gesture with the radio antenna toward a shaded bench.

"You can wait here. Mr. Clarkson will be with you in a minute."

Yahtzee. I sat and crossed my legs, still smiling at Marco as he sipped his coffee and lurked by the entrance arch, pretending to ignore me. I saw golfers coming and going—silver-haired foursomes in pastels and plaids—gumming about that birdie they'd almost made on seventeen. After five minutes had passed, I saw Marco straighten and nod in my direction as a handsome guy of about my age and size—thirty-seven and extra large—strode forward under the arch. He wore khakis and loafers and a blue dress shirt. As he drew closer, I saw that the shirt matched his eyes. His hair, thick and licorice-black, most certainly did not.

"I'm Jack MacTaggart," I said, standing to greet him. "You must be Andy Clarkson."

"That's right."

I handed him my card. "I'm an attorney representing Philippe Giroux. I wanted to ask you a few questions about his son Alain."

Clarkson eyeballed the card, and then he eyeballed me. He glanced at Marco, still loitering under the arch. Marco raised his cup and smiled.

"I'm on duty," Clarkson said, "but I guess I can take an early lunch."

"I'd appreciate that."

"Good." He gestured in the direction of Pilate's Trattoria. "That way we can both sample the luncheon cuisine."

The restaurant staff scrambled to accommodate what I surmised to be an infrequent appearance by the boss. We were led through the nearly empty dining room—faux Tuscan decor, trompe l'oeil murals, brick-oven fireplace—to a table on the outside patio, a curved concrete expanse with matching balustrade that resembled nothing more than the massive prow of a ship.

A white marble statue—a woman in flowing robes—presided over the patio. Positioned by the balustrade, she faced outward toward the golf course, her right hand raised in benediction, her gaze peering off into the future.

Our Lady of the Perpetual Slice.

Her view encompassed an emerald fairway and a small artificial lake with water spraying upward from its center. Golf carts buzzed to a stop in the fairway, and four aging linksters alighted and rummaged for their clubs. One of them looked up and saluted the statue.

The waitress adjusted our umbrella before leaving us to our menus.

"Unusual name for a restaurant," I told Clarkson, breaking the ice. "I'm guessing Heil Hitler Haus was already taken?"

"Pontius Pilate was a respected Roman prefect, for your information. Legend has it that after his death, his body was submerged in the Rhône River, turning the water to wine."

"No kidding. I'll bet you have a sign in the restroom telling employees to wash their hands."

Oblivious to my sparkling repartee, Clarkson glanced at his menu before setting it aside. I cleared my throat and soldiered on.

"I've heard you described as the owner of this place, and now as the general manager. Which one is it?"

"The club is owned by a partnership, of which I'm the managing general partner. We're relatively new, and still shaking out the bugs, so I try to be hands-on."

"Pretty quiet for a Saturday afternoon."

He nodded. "Quiet is how we like it. Not to sound snooty, but when it comes to membership, we favor quality over quantity."

"And yet I hear you're planning to expand."

He smiled at that, just as the girl returned for our orders. Clarkson asked for the usual. I said "the same," since he didn't strike me as the pineapple-and-anchovy type.

"We'd like to expand, that's no secret. If you represent Philippe, you must know that."

Below us, the Four Coursemen of the Apocalypse had played their shots and moved on, and a new pair of carts had entered stage right, disgorging another quartet of retirees.

"I've been wondering about those expansion plans. The economics, I mean. I don't know what you charge for a membership, but I've priced some local real estate, and I suspect vineyard property fetches a premium in this neck of the woods. In fact, I had my partner look into it. She says that vineyards in this area produce around four or five tons of grapes per acre."

"It depends, but something like that."

"She also says that five tons of grapes will make around 3,500 bottles of wine."

"I wouldn't know," he said, shifting in his chair. As though it had grown a little less comfortable. "That sounds about right."

"So let's do the math, shall we? That juice at Château Giroux goes for over a hundred bucks a bottle, right? Which means those vines must generate around four hundred grand per acre, year in and year out."

"So?"

"So that's a lot of green fees. Especially if you multiply it by fifty, which I'm told is how many acres you'll need to build a new course."

He made a noise that was intended to approximate laughter.

"You're forgetting a thing or two. Overhead, for starters. Do you have any idea what it takes to turn grapes on the vine into wine in a bottle? And that's under perfect growing conditions, never mind things like spring freeze and autumn rain and phylloxera. But for a golf course"— and here he nodded to the old duffer addressing his ball below us, who, as if on cue, chunked it fat and dribbled it into the lake—"all you need are lawnmowers and a whole lot of water."

The waitress returned bearing not, as I'd hoped, two large pepperonis with extra cheese, but rather two tall glasses of viscous green liquid. She set them down and then speared them each with a straw. I caught a telltale whiff of kale.

"Tell you what," said Clarkson, scraping back his chair. "You wanted to talk about Alain. Let me show you around the club. We'll drink as we walk."

Which could, I thought, be a new marketing slogan for Napa Valley. I stood and followed his lead, back through the still-empty restaurant and into the central courtyard.

"We were prep school classmates, Alain and I, at Justin-Siena. I went on to Stanford, and he went to Davis. That was his father's idea."

"The enology program."

Clarkson nodded. "Best in the world. Only Alain didn't want to make wine. He was an artist, did you know that? A painter, and a damned good one. But the old man wouldn't hear of it. The Giroux family tradition, and all that bullshit. Alain despised him for it."

Which was, I believe, another Giroux family tradition. "Did you stay in touch with Alain after college?"

"Sure. My dad was a contractor in Napa. Residential construction, mostly high-end stuff. We got into real estate development. That was back in the nineties, when things were really booming. Alain, meanwhile, went to work for his dad, who put him in the tasting room. Can you believe that? Here the guy had a degree from U.C. Davis, and his prick of a father had him tending bar for tourists."

We'd crossed through the courtyard and descended a short concrete staircase. At the bottom lay another, smaller courtyard framed by an outdoor bar, a glass-fronted health club, and another Italianate building with the word SPA scribed in stone over its arched entrance doorway.

It all seemed eerily deserted. The girl behind the bar stood up for the boss, or maybe her ass was just getting sore. She had a dazzling smile under a pile of brunette curls. I left my green-algae beverage in her custody.

"I had the impression that Philippe and Alain were fairly close."

We were moving again, circling below Pilate's Trattoria on a path that followed the undulating contours of the fairway. Clarkson waved to a passing golf cart.

"Close? That's a laugh, but it is classic Philippe. For him, image is everything. His airplane, and his limousine, and his phony French accent. To the outside world they're one happy family, all dancing to Philippe's magic flute. But if one of them should ever fall out of step . . ."

The path rose again and joined with a service road. We followed the road as it curved around to the front entrance of the Clubhouse, which could have passed for a Medici palace if not for the golf bags huddled like Parthian refugees under its shaded front portico. Here Clarkson stopped and turned to face me, again checking his watch.

"I don't know if I've answered all your questions, but I have an appointment at one. I trust you can find your own way back."

"Just one more, if you don't mind. About Alain."

"Shoot."

"Have you talked to him lately?"

This time, the laughter was genuine.

"I'd call that wishful thinking, MacTaggart. Don't tell me the old man's got you bamboozled, too."

And with that he turned and strode toward the Clubhouse entrance, pausing only to raise his empty glass in my direction before pushing through the heavy wooden door. I watched it close behind him. I gave him the finger.

Only then did I hear the melodious lilt of distant voices.

With my afternoon open and my curiosity piqued, I followed the sound across a lawn and around a hedge and through an iron gate. There a large outdoor swimming pool shimmered in the noonday sun, its coruscating ripples reflecting on my old friend Marco. He stood staring with bovine longing toward my side of the pool deck, where a dozen Kappa Kappa Gammas, now in various stages of undress, crowded an open bar and a smoking barbecue grill.

I skirted their perimeter, looking for signage that might lead me back to the main entrance, when through a gap in the hedge I caught a fleeting glimpse of a blue-skirted female hurrying toward the Clubhouse on sensible high heels, her golden hair luminous in the sunlight. As I turned to look again, one of the debutantes stepped backward and, perhaps blinded by her lace bridal veil, turned into my path.

We collided face-to-face.

"Fuck," she said, spilling half her margarita. She sported a burnt-orange bikini now, and a sunburn whose apposition of pink and pumpkin hues approximated, in the fleshy depths of her cleavage, the view from the south rim of the Grand Canyon.

"I'm terribly sorry," I told her, brushing her drink from my shirtfront. And then, "By the way, nice boots."

4

It was still daylight at 6:30 P.M. as we rolled to a stop before a small medieval castle, turreted and ivy-covered, like something lifted from the graveled bottom of a giant goldfish bowl. We'd bypassed the Visitor Center parking lot, gated at this hour, and we'd followed instead a narrow side road marked PRIVATE. Now Larry the Driver turned to face me in the backseat, where I gathered up the flowers we'd stopped to purchase at a grocery store in Oakville.

Claudia Giroux, I'd told him, was the kind of girl who needed to receive flowers.

"Mr. MacTaggart, you shouldn't have," spoke the devil as the door swung inward and Claudia stepped backward, beckoning me into a spacious foyer.

"It's Jack. And they were Larry's idea. I was thinking six-pack."

I'd gone with the old-school jacket and tie, which, judging from Claudia's little black cocktail dress, had been the right call. She accepted the flowers, closing her eyes and lifting them to her face.

"Well then, I'll have to thank Larry for being so thoughtful. Not that a six-pack wouldn't have been equally welcome."

I followed behind her in the slipstream of her perfume, past a polished wooden staircase and into a long, wainscoted hallway. The house was a treasury of delicate French antiques and dark oil paintings, none of which I really noticed, focused as I was on the porcelain perfection of Claudia's bare shoulders. We emerged into a kind of sitting room whose open doorway, I ventured to guess, no six-pack had ever darkened. Philippe Giroux struggled to his feet, a champagne flute sloshing in his hand.

"There you are. As you can see, we've started without you." With his free hand he lifted a dripping green bottle from a silver bucket on the coffee table. "You'll have some catching up to do."

"I was afraid I'd be the last to arrive," I said, accepting a glass of chilled bubbly just as Claudia rang a little brass bell and returned it to the table. Within moments, an aproned servant arrived with canapés on a silver tray. She traded the tray for the flowers, and as she turned to leave, Philippe's voice stopped her at the door.

"Frederique, this is our guest, Mr. MacTaggart. Mrs. LaBoutin has been my personal chef for . . . good Lord. Has it been ten years?"

"Oui, monsieur." She was ringlet-haired and bug-eyed, like a lemur, or maybe a ferret-faced extra from *Les Misérables* in her black dress and white peasant's head-kerchief. She did an awkward little curtsy in my direction; awkward because of the flowers, and little because she also appeared to be around six months' pregnant.

Alone again with only our wine and canapés for company, Philippe shot a cuff and frowned at the face of his wristwatch.

"Typical of Lourdes," he muttered.

"Father, be fair. I'm sure Phil's the one who's at fault."

The old man grunted. His ascot this evening was periwinkle blue, approximating the color of his daughter's eyes that watched circumspectly as I studied the gallery of framed photos and mementos on the wall. It included a row of glossy magazine covers—*Wine Spectator, Gourmet, Bon Appétit, Food & Wine*—that in its totality formed a serial *Picture of Dorian Gray* in which Philippe Giroux, timelessly jaunty in person, aged from his mid-fifties to his late seventies.

Philippe moved to stand beside me.

"That's Alain and Philip, when they were still in middle school. The fall of eighty-seven, I believe."

The photo to which he'd pointed showed one gangly teen in the seat of a John Deere tractor while the other stood upright in the trailing wagon, both of them facing the camera. Both wore cuffed dungarees and plain white T-shirts splattered with the purple gore of harvest. In their matching crew cuts and say-cheese smiles, the brothers looked like serial killers posing to memorialize their first offense.

"Anything more recent of Alain?" I asked Philippe, who turned an appraising circle.

"Over here. From Philip's wedding."

He led me to a family portrait in which siblings Claudia and Alain bracketed the smiling bride and groom. The latter, earnest and already balding, held hands with a sloe-eyed beauty who appeared at risk of drowning in a frothy sea of white lace and chiffon. To the bride's immediate left, darkly handsome in his mourning coat and striped cravat, stood a grown-up version of the boy on the tractor. Alain had obviously drawn inside post in the male division of the Giroux genetic derby, but even he ran distant second to the distaff side of the family.

Claudia, who had moved to stand beside us, rested a hand on my arm.

"God, look at my dress," she said in reference to her bridesmaid's gown of radioactive-pink satin. "I look like a Christo art project."

A door slammed and voices burbled in the front part of the house. Footfalls sounded in the hallway.

"*Dieu ait pitié,*" said Philippe, downing the last of his drink.

At present and in person, Phil and Lourdes Giroux resembled not so much the shining young couple in their wedding photo as a pair of shaggy teaching assistants on summer break from the People's Republic of Berkeley. Phil, whose hairline had long receded into memory, sported a rumpled seersucker jacket over jeans and socks and Birkenstock sandals, while the diminutive Lourdes, her hair in braids, looked unnervingly like a self-portrait by Frida Kahlo—right down to the faint unibrow and the embroidered peasant dress.

"Sorry we're late. I wanted to get those new barrels into storage." Phil limped to the canapé tray and had two in his mouth before turning to offer his hand.

"You must be our guest," he said, sucking a finger. "Welcome to Château Giroux. Have we met before?"

To the sound of a clearing throat, Phil turned to his wife, who stood with a hand on her hip.

"Oh, and this is Lourdes. Sorry, honey, I don't know what came over me."

Lourdes held up a paw, as though offering me the Papal ring, and I reached out and gave it a shake.

"Jack MacTaggart," I told her, raising my other hand in a fist. "*Sí se puede.*"

"It's always a treat to have visitors," said Phil, who was chewing again, "especially from L.A. We really don't get many opportunities to host around here, unless it's some charity event. The wine business might seem glamorous, what with all the magazines and our new Visitor Center and everything, but when you get right down to it, viniculture is farming and winemaking is chemistry, and both are hard, dirty work. Sorry to shatter the illusion."

"Blasphemy!" Philippe wheeled on his son. "The *vigneron* is a poet! The grapes are his muse, and the wine is his verse! Take this wine, for example." He lifted his glass to the light. "Dom Pérignon is bottled only in those special years when the harvest is deemed to be worthy. Did you know there have been fewer than fifty vintages produced since nineteen twenty-one? And that a bottle of the nineteen fifty-nine, the first rosé vintage, sold at auction in New York for over eighty thousand dollars? One bottle of wine, made from a humble handful of grapes. You can call that chemistry, but I call it alchemy. I call it magic."

"I'd call it a scandalous waste of money," said Lourdes, accepting a glass from her husband. "Imagine how many children we could feed with money like that, or how many school books we could buy."

"Folderol!" Philippe shook his silver mane. "You should thank your lucky stars there are people out there willing to support artisanal wine-making. Cultured people, who appreciate the finer things in life."

"So that you can charge outlandish prices, while paying poverty wages to your seasonal workers."

"My dear Lourdes, if we weren't turning a profit, we couldn't afford to hire those seasonal workers in the first place, and then where would their children be? Living in squalor in Mexico, that's where. It's called capitalism, my dear, and it's what makes this country great. It's the reason, in fact, that migrant workers flock here in the first place. You should think about that the next time you advocate for your so-called living wage that will serve no earthly purpose but to shrink our profit margins and force us—"

"Now, Father—"

"What about you, Mr. MacTaggart?" Lourdes spun to face me. "Do you regard wine as something to drink or as something one puts on an altar and worships?"

"Take it from a Catholic," I told her, "they're not mutually exclusive."

She lifted her eyebrow—*the* eyebrow—at Claudia.

"My. It appears we have a diplomat in the house."

"It's true that exclusivity is part of what we sell," Claudia said, moving to stand beside me. "As do the magazines, and the *négociants*, and all of the resorts. It's a grand conspiracy, and as Father says, we of all families should be grateful for it."

"Doggone it, you look so familiar to me," said Phil, stepping back again and giving me the once-over. "Haven't I seen you on television or something?"

Claudia looked to her father then, who arched an eyebrow in my direction. I took that as my cue to pinch my nose and fumble for the love seat behind me.

"Mr. MacTaggart? What is it?" Claudia rushed to my side. "Are you all right?"

The others crowded behind her, a triptych of mortal concern.

"It's . . . nothing too serious," I said, moving a hand to my temple, "but I get these occasional migraines. First a visual aura, then a splitting headache. I have some medication back at the hotel."

"I'll drive you," Claudia said. "My car's around back."

Philippe scowled. "Larry can certainly—"

"No, this is an emergency. Come on."

I let her take my arm and pull me, first to my feet and then across the carpeted room, her hundred-watt grin lighting our path down the hallway.

"I'm terribly sorry!" I called over my shoulder. "It was nice to meet you! And please thank Mrs. LaBoutin!"

Her car was the cherry-red Porsche I'd seen in the visitor's parking lot. It went very fast. Claudia drove it with one hand on the steering wheel and the other hand holding her strappy black heels.

Self-preservation dictated that I take the shoes.

"Thanks. How's that headache?"

"Better, thank you. Chalk it up to amazement. Does she always goad him like that, or was that for my benefit?"

"Let's just say she enjoys pushing his buttons. Lourdes isn't a bad person, mind you, she's just conflicted. And you don't have to thank me, you just have to buy me dinner."

We made the turn from the Château Giroux driveway onto the empty county road on what felt like two wheels, with both of them squealing in terror.

"Saturday night dinner in Napa Valley without a reservation might be a challenge."

"Good point," she said. "Thank goodness for room service."

She goosed the car into third, which sent it rising and dipping, banking through the hillside curves like a bobsled. Then she downshifted hard, the engine suddenly revving, the drag of the transmission slinging us, tires shrieking, southbound onto Silverado Trail.

"Wait, can we go back? I think I left something."

"What's that?"

"My stomach."

Up ahead, the sight of a familiar white billboard gave voice to that little man in my head who tries, with shocking futility, to keep me out of trouble. Sometimes he speaks in the sardonic baritone of my late uncle Louis, a backstretch philosopher who, before he could smoke and drink himself to an early grave, had been killed in a drug deal gone sideways. Tonight, however, he spoke in the measured tones of Russell Dinsmoor, my late friend and law firm mentor, who'd taught me that "coincidence" is the word people use when they can't see the puppeteer's strings.

"I had a few hours to kill this afternoon," I told Claudia's profile, "so I stopped by the Napa Springs Spa."

"I know. Andy told me."

"Ah."

"Look, we haven't had much of a chance to talk, so let me give you the lay of the land. Andy's an old family friend. He's also one of our biggest accounts here in the Valley, and like all of our good customers, I try to meet with him on a regular basis. Although in Andy's case, Father would blow a gasket if he ever found out, so please don't tell him. Which brings us to my role in all of this family melodrama."

The route back to the hotel took us eastbound off of Silverado and onto Rutherford Hill, another narrow, twisting mountain road. I tested the latch on my seatbelt.

"I like to think of myself as a buffer," Claudia continued, wrestling the car into second, "or at least a shock absorber. When Father bristles at Lourdes, I smooth his feathers. When he carries on about Andy Clarkson, I try to calm the waters. It's a role I've played all my life, even before Mother died. First between Phil and Alain, then between Alain and Father. Even between Father and Mother, who was a saint."

"Your father's convinced that Phil plans to sell part of the vineyard to Clarkson. Do you believe that?"

She gave a little shrug. "He can't, if Alain is still alive. But even if he could, it wouldn't be the end of the world. There'd still be a hundred acres left. Our grandfather built an empire on less acreage than that."

"Clarkson struck me as a pretty decent guy. I liked him."

"You frightened him. Now that he's met you, he wants Phil to bring in a big city lawyer. He's even offering to pay for it."

We rounded a final curve, the G forces shifting my internal organs, then came to a screeching halt behind one of the silver Mercedes convert- ibles that served as the hotel's courtesy cars. Claudia killed the engine, leaving the key in the ignition. I licked my lip, checking for a nosebleed.

"What about you?" I asked her. "Do you really believe your brother's alive?"

When she opened the door, the Porsche's warning system chimed *ding ding ding* in the cooling night air. She turned in her seat to face me.

"Of course I believe it. Why wouldn't I?"

A valet attendant had trotted out to greet us. He was a college kid, clean-cut and uniformed, who tried not to stare as Claudia swung her long, bare legs to the pavement and bent to replace her shoes. I climbed out of the passenger side and waited while Claudia tucked the valet ticket into her purse. She took my arm and led me, as the sighted lead the blind, through the bustling entry lobby and down the side hallway to the door of the luxury suite that, it suddenly occurred to me, she'd probably booked herself.

Housekeeping had turned down the bed, and they'd replenished the fruit bowl and flowers. Gas jets blazed in the fireplace. The room lights were dimmed, and the scarlet wash of sunset had turned the morning's blue panorama of vineyards and mountains to a deep and darkening purple.

I crossed to the balcony and slid the glass partition. There was music playing somewhere, and the low tinkle and murmur of diners. Claudia joined me after a minute, with two crystal tumblers and two mini-bottles from the bar.

"Scotch or bourbon?"

"Surprise me."

She poured the drinks, and we touched glasses. Mine was the Scotch.

"Your father tells me you're a lawyer."

"Not quite." She tasted her drink. "I did my undergraduate studies at the Sorbonne, in Paris. That was Mother's idea. Then I went to the law school at Boalt as part of my joint graduate degree program at Berkeley, but I've never taken the bar exam. Too confrontational, the whole legal paradigm. My passion has always been business."

"Where you can sneak up and stab your opponent in the back?"

She laughed. "Maybe that's the attraction."

We stood shoulder to shoulder gazing out over the valley, the lights from the swimming pool shimmering, animating the graceful oak trees below us.

"Tell me something. If Alain is still alive, then why hasn't he contacted anyone? Why would he go into hiding like that?"

She studied her glass, swirling the amber liquid. After a while she said, "Did Father tell you anything about his relationship with Grandfather?"

"A little. I take it they weren't close."

"Did he tell you about his high school graduation gift?"

"No."

"When Father turned eighteen, Grandfather booked him a steamship passage to France, to spend the summer with relatives. When Father arrived, he discovered that Grandfather had also contracted him to work at a winery there, in Bordeaux. Which would have been fine, except that it was a one-way ticket, and a three-year contract."

I turned to take in her profile.

"Father was furious, of course, but he stayed and honored the contract. I think his pride wouldn't allow him to quit. Or his stubbornness. That was in 1951. It turned out for the best, because Father learned the wine business, and he also met Mother, with whom he returned to California in 1954. He and Grandfather barely spoke after that. You would think they simply hated each other, but it was much more complicated than that. Each, I think, felt he could never measure up to the other's expectations, and each perhaps feared that the other's low opinion was justified."

She finished the last of her drink.

"It was only after Grandfather had died that Father, in going through his papers, found the induction notice that had come from the draft board on Father's eighteenth birthday. They'd have shipped him straight to Korea if Grandfather hadn't intervened as he did."

Now she turned to face me.

"I guess what I'm trying to say is that relations among the men of the Giroux family have always been complicated. Take Alain and Father.

Alain doesn't hate Father, and I truly believe that Father loves Alain. But he could never show it. He could never hug his son, or say the words out loud. Instead he rode him, and ridiculed him, and pushed him to be what he thought a son of Philippe Giroux should be. Just like Grandfather had done to him."

She set her glass on the railing and brushed past me, her hand lingering on the small of my back. I downed my drink and followed.

I found her by the foot of the bed, staring into the fire. A leather-bound guest folio rested on a side table, and I carried it to where she stood.

"Menu?"

She took it from me and tossed it onto the bed.

"I don't need a menu," she said, her arms encircling my neck, her body pressing into mine. Her lips just inches from my own.

"I already know what I want."

5

It wasn't often that Sam made a guest appearance at MacTaggart & Suarez, but Monday morning found him bounding back and forth outside my office door while our secretary Bernadette, grateful for any excuse to delay the work week, engaged him in a hallway game of Nerf-ball fetch. Sam is half golden retriever and half camp counselor, and he likes to keep the humans in his charge occupied.

"I hope he wasn't a burden," I said to Regan Fife, the former police officer, current office investigator, and future wife—or is it partner?—of my law partner Marta "Mayday" Suarez.

Is the life partner of my law partner my partner-in-law?

"He was no trouble at all," she assured me from where she sat in the client chair opposite my desk. "We took him to the zoo yesterday. His favorite animals were the pigeons in the parking lot."

The door opened and Mayday returned, sorting a stack of photocopies as she walked. A galloping orange blur streaked down the hallway as the door swung shut behind her.

"She's going to give that dog a heart attack," Mayday said, setting the copies on my desk and squaring them into stacks.

"Trust me, Bernie's arm will wear out long before Sam does. Any luck with finding a photo?"

"I think so." She removed her iPad from the other client chair and settled into its place. Regan leaned closer, and the women put their heads together—a contrasting apposition of Mayday's dark curls and Regan's blond spikes. After a few pokes and swipes at the screen, Mayday turned her tablet to face me.

"This is the best one. It was taken at a charity event in Yountville last year. The caption just refers to the Giroux family table."

I leaned forward to examine the faces—four smiling and one not—that encircled a wine bottle the size of an artillery shell from an Iowa-class battleship. Phil and Lourdes—the lone frowner—were seated to Alain's right, while Philippe and Claudia occupied the folding chairs to his left. Philippe wore his omnipresent ascot—burgundy on this occasion—while Claudia sported a tilted hubcap on her head that suggested either a royal wedding or the sixth race at Churchill Downs.

"That's Alain in the center," I told them. "The one with the full head of hair."

Regan leaned closer to examine the screen. "The blonde on the end is Claudia? The girl you told Marta was a hunchback?"

"With a clubfoot?"

"She looks like Catherine Deneuve."

"Ladies? Let's stay focused on the germane Giroux, shall we?"

Mayday rotated the tablet. "I can print a screen-grab, but it might be a little bit blurry."

"We work with the tools we have. Now what about the receipts?"

Regan reached for a stack of the photocopies. After a moment of sorting, she found the relevant pages.

"Okay, the seven credit card charges were spread up and down the coast. One is from a hotel restaurant in Lake Tahoe, and one's from a gas station in Mill Valley. Two are from the Paso Robles area, another restaurant and another gas station. One's from a café in Los Olivos, in the Santa Ynez Valley, and two are from L.A. One of those is a pizzeria in Santa

Monica, while the other's a wine bar on Melrose Avenue. Each of the food charges is for a single-serving meal, and in three cases the meal was breakfast."

"What's the chronology?"

Regan reexamined the receipts. "Tahoe and Mill Valley in April. Paso Robles, Los Olivos, Santa Monica, and West Hollywood were all in May."

"Paso Robles and Los Olivos are wine-growing regions," Mayday informed me. "That's significant."

"What did he order at the wine bar?"

"Wait a minute . . ." Regan looked up from the page. "Holy crap. A glass of Château Giroux Cabernet."

The thundering in the hallway had quieted, so I rose and crossed to the door. Sam, his tongue lolling, padded into the office and flopped down next to my desk.

"Consider this," I said, returning to my chair. "There are no rental car charges on any of the statements, so why are there gas station charges?"

"Maybe he was hitchhiking," Regan said, "and had to spring for gas now and again."

"Maybe."

"Or else someone rented a car for him. Or maybe he stole one."

"I suppose."

"You're skeptical," Mayday said.

"Hell, yes, I'm skeptical. If Alain wanted to go underground, the last thing he'd do is use his own credit card, knowing that the bills would go straight to Château Giroux. Which means one of two things. Either Alain is alive and he wants people to know it, or Alain is dead and somebody wants us to think otherwise."

Regan said, "A thief could have found the card."

I shook my head. "I thought the same thing. But if a thief had the card, he'd have racked up charges in a hurry, before the account could be closed. No, the visits to wine country, and especially that glass of Château Giroux Cabernet, those are messages."

Regan checked her watch and stood. "If I'm driving to Santa Monica, I'd better get started. What do you guys want on your pizza?"

"Wait," Mayday said, following her to the door, "let me print you that picture."

Alone at last with my dog, I put my feet up on the desk and closed my eyes, allowing the events of the last forty-eight hours to macerate in my brainpan.

Did I believe that Alain Giroux was alive? Maybe. Philippe certainly did, and so did Claudia, but their judgment was clouded by familial loss and longing. In Philippe's case, maybe by guilt. They were a grossly dysfunctional family—a milieu in which I'd had some personal experience—and that alone might account for Alain's disappearing act. On the other hand, both the nature of the credit card charges and the neat little trail they made from Lake Tahoe southward seemed entirely too perfect by half.

Did it matter whether Alain Giroux was alive? That was the better question, and the answer, I decided, was no. MacTaggart & Suarez had been handed evidence that might, if properly presented, defeat Phil's action and delay for another year the ownership transition at Château Giroux. If Regan could scare up additional evidence, then so much the better. We were professionals, Mayday and I, and that was our assignment.

Did I care whether Alain Giroux was alive? Another interesting question. I'd never met him, of course, and I wasn't about to get misty-eyed over a guy who'd flown off to college—albeit not his college of choice—in the family jet. But Claudia obviously cared, and I cared about her, and what matters to people who matter to me, well, it matters to me, too. I think George W. Bush might have said that.

All of which conjured, yet again, a diaphanous vision of Claudia, pale and naked, her slender figure backlit by firelight.

Sleeping with a client is a disciplinary offense in the prying eyes of the State Bar of California, but in this case it was Philippe who was our client, not his daughter. Not that sleeping with a client's daughter is ever a wonderful idea. Then again, it seemed pretty wonderful at the time.

A knock sounded, and Bernie entered with an armful of mail. Sam perked his ears as I lowered my feet to the floor.

"Mostly bills," she said, depositing the pile on my desk. She lingered to watch as I sorted.

"Something on your mind, Bernadette?"

"Oh, I don't know." She traced a figure on my desk with a hot pink fingernail. "What do you know about screenplays?"

"Screenplays?"

"You know, like movie scripts. Lance has a friend from high school who just sold a screenplay for half a million bucks, and the guy is, like, dumber than a box of Bisquick. I was thinking about taking a class, you know? Like maybe through UCLA Extension. There's one that starts next month in Westwood."

Lance, Bernie's sometimes boyfriend, aspired to heavy metal stardom, but had shaken a screw loose standing too close to the amps. Theirs was a match made in rock and roll heaven.

"Let me guess. You'll need to leave early to get there."

"Just Mondays and Wednesdays. If I skip lunch, I can leave here at four and still work a full day. It's only an eight-week class."

I handed her the bills to be processed.

"I think adult education is a wonderful thing, Bernadette. Just promise that when you win the Academy Award, you'll remember to thank me in your acceptance speech."

She brightened. "We'll see about that." She did a waltz step toward the door, and then a full pirouette. "Do you think I should wear Dior or Armani?" Then she snapped her head and tangoed, one arm fully extended, past Mayday in the open doorway.

"What was *that* all about?"

"Don't even ask."

In lawyer-speak, the American Express credit card statements and vendor receipts given to us by Claudia are what is called "hearsay evidence," meaning statements of fact made outside of court that are being offered to prove the truth of the matters asserted. "Claudia Giroux has a small mole on her ass," for example, is a statement of fact. But if you've never seen Claudia Giroux's ass, and are basing your assertion solely on what was told to you by others, then the statement is hearsay. And you're missing out on a really great ass.

The same concept can be applied to documents. In this case, the truth asserted by the AmEx statements and vendor receipts is that certain charges were made to Alain Giroux's credit card at the indicated times and locations. Since no testifying witness was there to observe those charges, that makes the documents hearsay and, as we already know, hearsay evidence is not generally admissible in court.

The rules of evidence, however, recognize the trustworthiness of certain out-of-court statements, and allow a judge to receive them in evidence as long as they fall under a recognized exception to the hearsay rule. Happily for Philippe, such an exception exists for records—like the AmEx documents—that have been maintained in the ordinary course of a trade or business.

There are two ways to introduce these so-called business records into evidence. The first is to have a witness, usually the custodian of the records, appear in person and describe for the court certain foundational facts about the documents, such as the sources of the information they contain, as well as their time and manner of preparation. More commonly, however, the records custodian will prepare a written declaration to that effect, which is then sealed in an envelope along with the records and delivered to the court, there to be opened by the judge at the time of the hearing.

If the admission of business records into evidence is important to your case, then you don't want to entrust to others, like the company's in-house counsel, the task of preparing and delivering the custodian's declaration. That's because nine times out of ten, that assignment will be given to some low-level pencil-pusher who's never seen the inside of a courtroom since the day he was sworn in to practice.

All of which explains why Mayday and I spent the next several days on the phone to New York, speaking with the American Express legal department and drafting the custodian's declaration ourselves. We also prepared the corroborating eyewitness declarations of Philippe and

Claudia Giroux. The former we'd overnighted to AmEx's corporate offices in Manhattan, while the latter we'd scanned and e-mailed to Claudia's office in Napa Valley along with instructions that the signed originals
be returned by air courier.

When those tasks were completed, we next turned our attention to
preparing written opposition to Phil's petition. Our central argument
would be that, given the credit card evidence described in the accompany-
ing declarations, Phil had failed to prove by a preponderance of the evidence that Alain Giroux was dead, notwithstanding the very compelling
eyewitness declarations of Phil and Brent Vroman, the Nordic search-
and-rescue guy, and notwithstanding the fact that Alain had not been
seen by friends or family for over four months.

Like I said, it wasn't going to be easy.

In a typical court case, in which time was not such a limiting factor,
we'd also have taken depositions—meaning pretrial testimony under
oath—from both Phil Giroux and Brent Vroman. But because of our short-
ened briefing schedule, and because our opposition strategy did not require
us to actually dispute their eyewitness testimony, we felt comfortable fore-
going this testimonial evidence.

Another casualty of time was our desire to fully investigate each of
the seven businesses at which Alain had used—or so we'd alleged—his
company credit card. Regan had drawn a blank at both of the L.A. locations, meaning there'd been no security cameras and no employees who'd
recognized Alain from Mayday's screen-grab photo. Finding such evidence, which Regan had likened to the hunt for Sasquatch, would have
cemented the case for Philippe. As it was, we'd barely finished our opposition paperwork in time for the Thursday filing deadline, when we sent
the whole package via messenger to the probate division of the Napa
County Superior Court, along with a service copy to Mark Rubenstein,
Phil Giroux's soon-to-be-busy lawyer.

And on the seventh day, we rested.

With the ball now squarely in our opponent's court, life regained a
semblance of normalcy at MacTaggart & Suarez, if you can call the con-
trolled chaos of a small-firm law practice normal. I had a new bad-faith

insurance client to meet with, and was scheduled to provide grand jury testimony in the prosecution of one Anthony "Tony Gags" Gagliano for murder, racketeering, and associated misbehavior. Mayday had an administrative appeal hearing in connection with Regan Fife's dismissal from the Sierra Madre Police Department—an event directly related to my grand jury testimony—while Bernie had taken to carrying film scripts with her at all times, reading them at the reception desk through a new, bookish pair of nonprescription eyeglasses.

It was on the following Wednesday—six days after our opposition had been filed in the Giroux matter—that the telephone rang in my office. The caller was a damsel, and she sounded distressed.

"A man was just here," Claudia said, more than a little breathless. "He served me with a fat roll of papers."

"That was me," I reminded her. "And those weren't papers."

"I'm serious, Jack. He served Father, too. He just barged in on a production meeting and dropped them in Father's lap."

"You're right, that wasn't me. Describe the papers."

"Wait a minute." She was shuffling pages, the telephone pressed to her shoulder. Her creamy-white shoulder, I imagined, soft and lightly redolent of perfume.

"There are four separate documents. The first is called a Reply Memorandum of Points and Authorities. The second is a Request for Hearing on Petition. Then there's a Notice to Appear and to Produce Documents. That's addressed to Father. And lastly there's something called a Civil Subpoena for Personal Appearance that's addressed to me. What's it all mean, Jack?"

"It means that our friend Mr. Rubenstein is more than a little concerned. Having read our opposition papers, he's asking the probate judge to hold an evidentiary hearing and take live testimony."

"Is that good or bad?"

"Indifferent. Just a little inconvenient, for you and your father."

"You mean we'll both have to testify?"

"Yes, if the court grants their request. But it's simply a matter of telling the same story to the judge that you've already told in your declaration."

There was a pause.

"I've never testified in court before."

"Nothing to it. Go watch Jack Nicholson in *A Few Good Men.*"

"I saw that movie. Didn't they haul him away to jail?"

"Okay, bad example. But remember, he was distracted by Demi Moore's legs. Plus he didn't have Jack MacTaggart there to protect him. And lest we forget, Mr. Rubenstein is, and I'm quoting your father now, no Clarence Darrow."

"Oh," she said, "that's the other thing. Phil has a new lawyer. I guess because of the hearing."

"What's his name?"

"Not a him, a her. Wait a minute."

More shuffling pages.

"Here it is. She's from Beverly Hills. Her name is Maxine Cameron."

6

The civil branch of the Superior Court of California for the County of Napa sits in a historic and appropriately imposing Italian Renaissance edifice with the word JUSTICE emblazoned in huge capital letters some two stories above its double entry doors. It was through this ominous portal that Philippe, Claudia, Mayday, and I passed at precisely 8:45 on the morning of July 6, having spent the previous hour in Claudia's office at the Château Giroux Visitor Center preparing for what lay ahead.

After subjecting ourselves and our belongings to the courthouse metal detectors, Mayday and I waited while Philippe and Claudia collected one leather belt, one key ring, two cell phones, and one stylish black handbag off the X-ray conveyor belt, whereupon we both flinched as Claudia's iPhone skittered to the floor in an awkward fumble that belied her outward calm.

"Darn it," she said, examining the phone and scrolling through its functions.

"Are you okay?"

She glanced around, watching as her father and my partner melted into the crowd ahead of us, making their way to the second-floor staircase.

Claudia took my arm and steered me into a corner, where she kissed me softly on the lips.

"That's a thank-you," she said. "I really mean it. In case I forget to say it later."

We made our way up to the second floor, where a clutch of local reporters had gathered by the door to the probate division courtroom. A photographer stepped from among them to capture our arrival.

"Miss Giroux, is your brother still alive?"

"Where is he now?"

"Why haven't you heard from him?"

We pushed through their midst, my guiding hand on Claudia's waist, and we joined Philippe and Mayday in a small but ornate chamber that predated the utilitarian ethos of modern municipal architecture.

Courtrooms are like airports, or maybe ballparks, in that the more of them you see, the more they look the same. This one, however, boasted a twenty-foot ceiling, dark wood paneling, and an imperious-looking bench overhung by the woodcut seal of the County of Napa. It was a genuine classic; more Wrigley or Fenway than Big A or Dodger Stadium.

Phil Giroux stood as we entered, leaving Lourdes and Andy Clarkson seated in the front row beside him. He limped forward to greet his father in the courtroom's central aisle, his demeanor sheepish, his hands thrust into the pockets of a familiar seersucker jacket.

"Hello, Dad. Hey, Claudia."

Philippe was glaring at Clarkson. "What's *he* doing here?"

Phil glanced over his shoulder. "He said he just came to watch. Look, I'm really sorry about all of this, and I want you to know that whatever else happens—"

"Step away from my client!"

The blast came from behind us, where an elfin woman of middle years stood akimbo in the doorway, her fists clenched, her raven hair coifed into a tightly-lacquered facsimile of Darth Vader's helmet.

Maxine Cameron was shorter than she appeared on television, and slighter than either her voice or her reputation presaged. She wore an impeccably tailored suit the color of arterial blood, along with matching heels on which she strode angrily forward trailed by a tall, bespectacled man hauling two heavy briefcases.

"I've never seen such *despicable* conduct in my life! You may *not* speak with my client outside of my presence, counsel. Even a lawyer from Sierra Madre ought to know that. And as for your earlier attempt to pose as a *journalist,* I'll have you know that I've already prepared an ethics complaint for the State Bar!"

This last pronouncement she'd made with her head turned toward the reporters who'd begun filing into the courtroom. They all stopped and scrawled hasty notes as she gripped Phil by the arm and frog-marched him past us to the front-row seats where Lourdes and Clarkson rose to greet her. Phil threw a chagrinned look over his shoulder.

"Maxine Cameron," I told Claudia, who seemed unnerved by the encounter. "The Pit Bull in Prada."

"I suppose that's a nice way of calling her a bitch."

We took our seats and waited for the judge, whose nameplate read MERCER, to ascend the bench. Ours was, it appeared, the only matter on the morning's probate calendar. The reporters found seats in the peanut gallery behind us, while across the center aisle, the enemy quintet sat huddled with lowered heads.

At precisely nine o'clock, the clerk, the court reporter, and the bailiff all materialized from a door behind the bench. The reporter took the empty chair behind her stenotype machine, while the clerk moved to her desk beside the bench. The uniformed bailiff remained standing, and now he faced the half-empty courtroom.

"All rise! The Superior Court of the State of California for the County of Napa is now in session, the Honorable Timothy Mercer presiding!"

We all stood while a beefy man with florid features appeared through the open door, paused to survey the courtroom, then clambered onto the bench, gathering the sleeves of his black judicial robes as he sat. He donned reading glasses and moved a microphone into position.

"*In re Estate of Alain P. Giroux.* Counsel will please come forward and state your appearances."

While the rest of the courtroom sat, Mayday and I followed Cameron and the bespectacled guy, whom I assumed to be Mark Rubenstein—no Clarence Darrow—through the low swinging gate. As counsel for the petitioning party, Cameron and Rubenstein took the table nearest the empty jury box.

"Maxine Cameron and Mark Rubenstein for Petitioner Philip Giroux, Your Honor."

"Good morning, Your Honor. Jack MacTaggart and Marta Suarez for Respondent Philippe Giroux."

The judge centered the thick stack of pleadings and declarations that his clerk had placed before him on the bench.

"Good morning, counsel, and welcome to Napa County. I can't recall the last time we've had so many distinguished attorneys visit us from out of town. Ms. Cameron, I take it you're requesting an evidentiary hearing this morning?"

"That is correct. The respondent and his daughter, both of whom have submitted declarations to this court, are present and under subpoena."

The judge, who I suspect had been hoping to make a quick ruling before squeezing in eighteen holes, looked to me for help.

"Any objection from you, Mr. MacTaggart?"

"Only to the extent that wasting judicial resources is always objectionable. As Your Honor knows, Probate Code section 204 expressly authorizes this court to act on the petition and supporting affidavits without having to take live test—"

"But this is a hotly contested matter, Your Honor, with a great deal at stake! The United States Constitution guarantees the right to confront and cross-examine witnesses!"

"To defendants in criminal proceedings," I said. "Not to civil petitioners."

"But this is literally a *matter of life or death*! To deny us an evidentiary hearing in this case would constitute a gross miscarriage of justice, would create immediate grounds for appeal, and would necessitate—"

"All right, all right." The judge eyeballed the clock on the wall. "Here's how we'll proceed. I'm accepting each of the five submitted declarations in lieu of live testimony, but I'll offer counsel a limited opportunity to cross-examine the declarants, three of whom appear to be present in court this morning. If you're ready, Ms. Cameron, go ahead and call your first witness."

While Rubenstein unloaded his briefcases onto the table before them, Maxine Cameron turned with a flourish, pointing a long, scarlet talon into the gallery.

"For his first witness, petitioner calls Respondent Philippe Giroux."

Pencils scratched as the old man rose from his seat. He'd worn a tie today, a blue silk number to match his pocket hankie, and he walked with ramrod dignity through the gate the bailiff held for him.

No sooner had the clerk administered the oath than Cameron strode forward toward the witness.

"You are the father of the petitioner, Philip Giroux, yes or no?"

"Yes, Philip is my eldest—"

"And also the father of Alain Giroux?"

"Yes, he—"

"And of Claudia Giroux, who is present in the courtroom?"

"Yes."

She returned to her table and collected some documents from Rubenstein, one of which she tossed onto our table on her way back to the witness.

"I hand you a document entitled Giroux Family Trust dated September the fourteenth, nineteen seventy-seven. Do you recognize it, Mr. Giroux?"

Mayday and I paged through the trust instrument, which, until that very moment, had only been described to us. I found the relevant language at paragraph twelve:

> *When the youngest living son of Philippe Giroux attains the age of forty (40) years, this Trust shall terminate and the corpus thereof shall be distributed to the living male issue of Philippe Giroux in equal shares. If all of the male issue of Philippe Giroux should die before attaining the age of forty (40) years, then this Trust shall terminate and the corpus thereof shall be distributed to the Roman Catholic Diocese of Santa Rosa, California.*

"Yes," Philippe said. "I recognize it."

"Is this the document whose terms govern ownership of a California corporation named Giroux Beverage, better known as the Château Giroux winery?"

"Yes, it is."

"Offer petitioner's exhibit A, Your Honor."

The judge looked to me for objection as Cameron handed two copies of the trust instrument to the clerk, who stamped them into the court file and passed one up to the bench.

"No objection," I said.

Cameron was already moving. "Directing your attention to paragraph twelve of exhibit A, is it your understanding that you hold the assets of Giroux Beverage only as trustee for your sons Philip and Alain, and that ownership of the Château Giroux winery will pass to your sons in equal shares when the youngest of them reaches the age of forty years?"

Philippe nodded. "Yes, that is my understanding."

"Your son Philip is how old, sir?"

"He'll turn forty next month, on August the thirtieth."

"And Alain?"

"Alain is thirty-eight years of age."

Behind me, I could sense a ruffle of excitement as the reporters exchanged whispered comments. The limited nature of Philippe's ownership had not, I presumed, ever been made public knowledge.

"So to summarize: If your son Alain is indeed dead, as the declarations of petitioner and Mr. Vroman clearly establish, then—"

"Argument," I objected, which the judge sustained.

"If your son Alain is dead, Mr. Giroux, then on August the thirtieth, this trust will terminate and ownership of Château Giroux will pass to your son Philip, leaving you with no further interest whatsoever. Is that your understanding, sir?"

"Yes, that is my understanding."

"You are currently the president of Giroux Beverage?"

"I am."

"And the chairman of its board of directors?"

"Yes."

"Elected as such because of your right as trustee to vote all of the capital stock of Giroux Beverage?"

"I suppose so."

"A right that you'll lose on August the thirtieth if Alain is adjudicated by this court to be deceased, is that correct?"

Philippe looked to me for assistance that was neither available nor, I hoped, necessary.

"Yes, were Alain declared dead, I would lose the right to vote as a shareholder on August the thirtieth."

Maxine Cameron moved to stand by the empty jury box, affording the reporters an unobstructed view of the witness.

"In your capacities as president and board chair, you received a salary last year from Giroux Beverage in the sum of eight hundred thousand dollars, is that correct?"

Philippe flushed. "I don't . . . I believe that's correct."

"Do you have any doubt about it? Because we can go through the payroll records if you'd like."

"No, I'm sure that's correct."

"And in addition to your salary, you also received a generous expense allowance, plus perquisites that included the use of a chauffeured limousine and a fractional private jet?"

"Yes."

"None of which is guaranteed to continue after ownership passes to your son Philip, is that correct?"

Philippe looked at his son.

"I suppose that's technically correct."

Now Cameron moved to stand, hands on hips, squarely before the witness.

"The market valuation of Château Giroux is how much, sir?"

Again Philippe looked to me, but Cameron sidestepped to her left, blocking his view.

"The total value? I wouldn't know, exactly."

"Come now, sir. Giroux Beverage prepares annual financial statements.

Your daughter Claudia, as chief financial officer, is in charge of doing so, is she not?"

"Yes."

"Shall I refresh your recollection by showing you a copy of a business appraisal the corporation commissioned earlier this year?"

She retreated to her table, where Rubenstein fumbled through another stack of documents.

"No," Philippe said. "That isn't necessary. I know the number."

Cameron turned to face him, her fists pressed onto the table.

"Please tell the court how much you stand to lose on August the thirtieth if your son Alain is adjudged to be deceased?"

Philippe's jaw tightened. "The winery is currently valued at approximately eighty-five million dollars."

Cameron eased into her seat. "No further questions."

7

The courtroom was buzzing now, and the judge gave his gavel a tap.

"Order," he said. "Enough of that."

I rose to redirect. Her theatrics notwithstanding, Maxine Cameron had actually accomplished little so far, other than to subject both the ownership and the financial condition of Château Giroux to public scrutiny. Mindful of the judge's tee time, I aimed to keep it short.

"How long have you known the terms of the Giroux Family Trust, Mr. Giroux?"

Philippe straightened in his seat, recovering his composure.

"Ever since my father's death in nineteen seventy-nine."

"So this change in ownership is something you've anticipated for over thirty years?"

"Correct."

"And is it your understanding that if Alain is adjudged *not* to be deceased, the ownership transition will occur anyway, only next year instead of this year?"

"Objection!" Cameron was on her feet. "The witness's understanding isn't relevant here. The trust instrument speaks for itself."

"The witness's understanding," I countered, "is precisely what's relevant. Counsel just spent twenty minutes trying to concoct some financial incentive to impugn my client's veracity, when all we're talking about is the difference between an ownership transfer that happens this year or next year."

"That's true," said the judge, turning to Philippe. "The witness may answer."

"Yes," Philippe said. "My understanding from the terms of the trust is that Alain's death will only accelerate the inevitable. However you look at it, I'll be retired soon enough."

"So if your motive isn't financial, Mr. Giroux, then why have you filed opposition to your son Phil's petition?"

As we'd rehearsed that morning in Claudia's office, Philippe turned in his chair and addressed the judge directly.

"Because Alain is my *son,* Your Honor, and I'm not going to sit by and let the government declare him to be dead when I know, both in my heart and from the evidence we've presented to the court, that he's still very much alive."

The two men held their gaze, until the judge gave an imperceptible nod.

I sat. "Thank you, Mr. Giroux. No further questions."

Mayday and I watched as Cameron and her co-counsel huddled in whispered debate. After a moment, Cameron again rose to her feet.

"Nothing further at this time, Your Honor, but we request that the witness remain available for rebuttal examination should the need arise."

The judge looked down at Philippe. "You may step down, Mr. Giroux, but please remain in the courtroom."

Philippe carried himself back to his seat with the same haughty bearing as had marked his arrival. I caught Cameron's eye as he passed between our tables. Her smile was enigmatic.

"Petitioner next calls Claudia Giroux."

Claudia had dressed for court in a snug gray suit with an above-the-knee skirt and a blouse of snow-white silk. Like her father before her, she approached the witness stand with an air of cool detachment, and as with her father, she was barely settled on the witness stand before the Pit Bull pounced.

"You are the chief financial officer of Giroux Beverage?"

"Yes."

"You hold a master's degree in business administration from U.C. Berkeley?"

"Yes."

"As well as a juris doctorate?"

"Yes."

"And you're the head of marketing for the Château Giroux winery?"

"I am."

Maxine Cameron half-turned toward the gallery.

"Will you please confirm to the court that my client, your brother Philip, is the corporate vice president of Giroux Beverage?"

"Yes, that is correct."

Rubenstein handed Cameron another set of documents, one of which she again tossed onto our table.

"Miss Giroux, I hand you what I believe to be a copy of your appointment calendar for the months of March through May of this year, and I would ask you to please identify it as such for the court."

The document she'd given us was a QuickBooks printout listing, in a weekly grid format, a dense amalgamation of meetings, telephone conferences, promotional events, and other business appointments. I flipped to the relevant dates. As I passed it across to Mayday, my stomach felt as it had in the passenger seat of Claudia's Porsche, the last time she'd taken me for a ride.

"Where did you get this?" Claudia demanded to Cameron's back as the Pit Bull did her business with the clerk.

"My client, whom you just acknowledged to be the corporate vice president of Giroux Beverage, printed a copy from the company's computer system, as was his lawful right. I believe this particular version he rescued from the deleted files."

Claudia's look in my direction was imploring.

"I repeat, Miss Cameron, can you please identify the document I've placed before you, which we've now marked as petitioner's exhibit B?"

"This is . . . my appointment calendar, yes."

"Directing your attention to the entry for the eighteenth of April. That's the same date as the first of the seven credit card charges that your father has submitted to the court. What he claims is evidence that your brother Alain is still alive."

Beside me, I felt Mayday stiffen with realization.

"All right," Claudia said, color now flooding her face.

"I call your attention to the entry that reads 'Incline Village Wine Festival.' Is that a promotional event you attended on April the eighteenth?"

Claudia hesitated. "I don't recall. I think so."

"You think so." Cameron turned to Rubenstein, who once again shuffled papers. "Would it refresh your recollection to see a photo of yourself that appeared in the *North Lake Tahoe Bonanza* on April the nineteenth?"

"No," Claudia said. "No, I remember now. I was there, yes."

"Incline Village is on the north shore of Lake Tahoe?"

"Yes."

"Approximately forty miles from where the first credit card charge was made at the Marriott Hotel in South Lake Tahoe on the morning of April eighteenth?"

"Yes." Claudia's voice was barely audible.

"Speak up, please."

"Yes, that's . . . that appears to be true."

The door to the courtroom opened behind us, and all heads turned. A bicycle messenger in shorts and a helmet paused in the doorway. Rubenstein waved him over.

Maxine Cameron looked on as Rubenstein signed for the package. He opened it and withdrew a sealed envelope from inside. He nodded once in Cameron's direction.

There was nothing enigmatic about the smile the Pit Bull now turned on Claudia Giroux.

"Next directing your attention to the calendar entry that appears on April twenty-sixth."

Claudia and Mayday flipped the same page in unison. "Shit," Mayday whispered. It was a word she rarely used.

"I have it."

"What is the Sausalito Cook-Off, Miss Giroux?"

"It's a charity food and wine event. To benefit a homeless shelter, I believe."

"You attended the Sausalito Cook-Off on April twenty-sixth?"

"Yes."

"And Sausalito adjoins the city of Mill Valley?"

"They're very close, yes."

"To drive from Napa to Sausalito, you pass through the city of Mill Valley?"

"Yes."

"And you drove through the city of Mill Valley on April twenty-sixth, did you not?"

"I . . . Yes."

"The same day that the second of the receipts in question, a service station charge from Mill Valley, appears on Alain Giroux's corporate credit card?"

Claudia didn't answer. Instead she lowered her head to the desk as her shoulders began to shake. Behind me, the reporters were chattering like blackbirds, and the judge again used his gavel.

Maxine Cameron turned around to face me.

"Why don't we do this? Let's cut to the chase, and try to save some of those judicial resources that are such a great concern to Mr. MacTaggart."

Rubenstein handed her the messenger's envelope, and Cameron carried it to the clerk.

"Let the record reflect that I am tendering to the clerk of court a sealed envelope that was just delivered to the courtroom by messenger. Inside is a declaration from the custodian of records of the American Express Company in New York. The same records custodian whose earlier declaration was filed with the court by Mr. MacTaggart."

While the clerk passed the envelope up to the judge, I twisted in my seat to look at Philippe. His face was a blank.

The judge sliced the envelope with a letter opener and thumbed through the pages inside. He appeared to visibly redden.

"I'll see counsel in chambers," he growled as he stood. "The court will stand in recess."

Like a quartet of ducklings, we trailed single-file in the judge's wake, past the witness stand where Claudia remained seated, her expression inscrutable, her cobalt eyes tracking me all the way to the door.

Inside the judge's chambers, Mercer slammed the envelope onto his desk as he sat.

"I've seen my share of stunts," he sputtered, "but this one takes the cake. MacTaggart, you've got some explaining to do."

"It might help to know what I'm being asked to explain."

Mercer flung the envelope across his desk, where it skipped once before smacking me square in the chest. Inside was the declaration Cameron had described. It was dated three days earlier, on July the third. Attached was a photocopy of an internal Lost Credit Card Order form dated in March. The March document referenced a telephonic request AmEx had received from Claudia Giroux, the chief financial officer of Giroux Beverage.

I passed the envelope to Mayday. "I don't have an explanation, Your Honor. This is all news to me."

"By God, we'll get to the bottom of it." He jabbed a button on his telephone. "Don't think we won't. John, bring in the witness and her father. Now."

We waited in silence, Cameron picking lint from her jacket, restraining herself from humming, until the bailiff opened the door to Philippe and Claudia. They entered the room together like sheep to a public shearing. I rose from my chair, but neither made a move to take it.

"What in God's name is going on here?" the judge demanded, brandishing the custodian's declaration. "Miss Giroux, do you have any idea of the trouble you're in right now?"

Claudia looked at her shoes. She nodded once, and then turned to her father.

"I told you it wouldn't work."

"*What?*"

She looked again to the judge, her right hand covering her heart.

"It was all Father's idea, Your Honor. He said that if we could make it look as though Alain were still alive—"

"I said no such thing! What are you—?"

I hooked two fingers into my mouth and blew a shrill blast that shocked the room into silence.

"Philippe," I said, "don't say another word, and that's an order. Claudia, you need to retain a lawyer. Perjury is a criminal offense, and you have the right to remain silent. That includes the right to refuse to answer Judge Mercer's questions."

Behind his desk, Mercer was turning the color of steak tartare. Claudia stepped forward to face him.

"First there's one thing I need to make clear," Claudia said. "Mr. MacTaggart didn't know anything about the replacement card or . . . or any of it. None of this is his fault."

Over Claudia's shoulder I could see Maxine Cameron examining her nails. Meanwhile, in an apoplexy contest between Philippe and the judge, I'd have had to call it a draw.

Mercer finally stood and jabbed the button on his phone.

"Very well, we'll have it your way. John? Get a holding cell ready, because we're coming back out!"

At the end of the day, nobody was sanctioned, jailed, or disbarred. Instead, Mercer completed the hearing with terse efficiency, giving Maxine Cameron the run of the courtroom before promptly and emphatically ruling for her client, thereby making official Alain Giroux's untimely demise.

At the conclusion of the hearing, Claudia and Philippe were called to stand before the judge, were informed that a transcript of the hearing would be referred to the district attorney for evaluation, and were further advised that the case would remain open until the D.A. acted on the court's referral. Father and daughter left the courtroom separately, neither meeting my eye, each to be ambushed by the reporters waiting outside in the hallway.

Cameron and Rubenstein, like the cats who'd shared the canary, had stayed to watch the denouement from their front-row seats alongside Clarkson, Lourdes, and Phil. As they all stood to leave, I overheard talk of a celebratory lunch. Ever the lady, Cameron acknowledged my presence only in passing, when she felt an irresistible urge to scratch the side of her nose with her long middle finger.

Mayday and I, still shell-shocked, were the last to emerge into the bright Napa sunshine, only to find no limousine at the curb, no messages back at our hotel, and no pilot awaiting us at the Napa County Airport. Instead we took a taxi to the public airport in Santa Rosa, adding another hefty line item to what was already a new firm record for monthly client expenses.

It was a long flight home. Mayday and I debriefed, then commiserated, then second-guessed ourselves until, exhausted by the effort, she drifted off to sleep. But not me. I ordered a second drink, and a third, and continued to brood over signals missed, and clues gone unheeded, and warning bells blithely ignored.

When my uncle Louis died over twenty years ago, a week shy of my seventeenth birthday, I remembered telling my mother how I'd always pictured myself as a minor character, a kind of pimply teenage sidekick in the rambling, shambling story of Uncle Louis's life. Only there, at his memorial service, did it dawn on me that it was my movie now and that in fact, it always had been.

The converse could be said of Claudia Giroux. Here I'd thought I was playing the lead in a romance, or at least a romantic comedy, when all along I was just the fall guy in a caper flick, the hapless sap to Claudia's scheming femme fatale. I'd been led by the nose—or by my own Sorbonne—down a primrose path, my radar jammed by fleeting whiffs of limousine leather and vintage wines and pale, perfumed shoulders.

I was the one who'd been blind to the puppeteer's strings. I was the one who'd been reading from the wrong script.

By the time we'd touched down at LAX, I was ready to forget all about the Giroux family and their Machiavellian intrigues and their intergenerational angst. I didn't care which of them was prosecuted for perjury, or what would become of their precious winery. I was finished with Napa Valley, and with the gilded asylum known as Château Giroux, and with each and every one of its ruthless, scheming inmates.

Or so I'd thought. But as it turned out, I was even wrong about that.

8

Night baseball.

Dodger Dogs sizzle on the upper concourse as the outfield palms fade with the last rays of sunset, and the green—the impossible, luminous green—of the infield grass glows under the high stadium lights. A cold beer in your hand, and peanut shells crunching underfoot. Bankers and bangers, lawyers and laborers all rubbing shoulders in the hard plastic seats, their immense and intractable differences in age, ethnicity, income, culture, language, and politics all eclipsed for one hot August night by a shared and incandescent yearning.

Root, root, root for the Dodgers. If they don't win it's a shame.

While I missed Helen Dell on the Dodger Stadium organ, and the stentorian echoes of Jerry Doggett and Ross Porter on a thousand transistor radios, we still had Vin Scully up in the booth, and Roger the Peanut Man down in the aisles. We still had kids with gloves and parents with scorecards. Usherettes in straw boaters were still booed for confiscating beach balls. Three strikes were an out, and six outs were an inning, and after six and a half innings, those who hadn't already left to beat the parking lot traffic still stood up to stretch.

And so did I.

"Want another beer?" I asked Gabe Montoya, whose seats we shared in the loge level behind home plate.

"No thanks. Long drive home, and I start a trial tomorrow."

Home for Gabe was Venice, some forty minutes due west on the Santa Monica Freeway, and work was as the head deputy D.A. in Compton, where Gabe had been exiled for the crime of competence by Tom Slewzyski, L.A.'s current and, one can only hope, soon-to-be-former district attorney. Gabe and I had first done battle years ago, back when he was a newly minted prosecutor and I was an idealistic young deputy public defender, and while I doubt either of us would still describe himself as an idealist, we'd managed to maintain an easy friendship over the years.

"What kind of trial?" I asked him as Nancy Bea Hefley milked the final chord of "Take Me Out to the Ball Game" and forty thousand proud Angelinos broke into applause.

"Felony drive-by attempted murder."

"Gang-related?"

"No, just a small misunderstanding over ballet tickets. Of course it was gang-related."

Gabe's banishment to South Central had made him a walking anthology of war stories from the 'hood. One of my favorites was the time the county decided to relandscape the Compton courthouse, a public works project that included resodding the ravaged grounds around the building. The workers finished the month-long job on a Friday afternoon. When the courthouse reopened on Monday, the grounds were back to bare dirt. But police helicopters reported emerald lawns stretching for blocks in every direction.

As for the Dodgers, they opened their half of the seventh with back-to-back base hits, putting runners on first and third with nobody out and the score tied at two.

My cell phone vibrated just as the Padres' manager stepped from the dugout and waddled out to the mound. The caller ID read A. CLARKSON. I put the phone back in my jacket.

"Screening your calls?"

"Wrong number."

"You should turn that fucking thing off."

"Spoken like a public employee."

Lusty boos followed the manager's slow progress back to the dugout.

The next Dodger batter, the number-eight hitter, chopped a first-pitch, seeing-eye grounder up the middle, driving in the go-ahead run and leaving runners on first and second with nobody out as the crowd roared its approval.

Again my phone buzzed. This time the ID read CLAUDIA GIROUX.

"What is it?" Gabe asked, reading my face.

"Nothing. Just an old client."

"I thought all your old clients were in jail."

"None of the ones you ever met."

There was action now in the Padres' bullpen as the Dodgers' pitcher snugged his helmet and stepped into the batters' box. Anticipating a sacrifice, the infield put on the shift.

"Christ, I'd have pinch hit."

"Sacrifice bunt," I told him. "Hit and run."

The batter squared, and the runners went. He laid a textbook bunt down the third-base line, where the Padres' pitcher and third baseman nearly collided, neither making the play. The crowd was on its feet, with the guy behind me spilling beer onto my shoes.

Bases loaded, nobody out. My phone vibrated again. It was Clarkson, and this time I cupped a hand to my ear.

"MacTaggart," I answered, trying for peeved.

"Jack, thank God. This is Andy Clarkson. I know I'm the last person you want to talk to, but please don't hang up. I just . . . Claudia asked me to call you."

"What is it? What's going on?"

He took a moment to gather himself. "It's Phil Giroux, Claudia's brother. He's dead."

"What?"

"They found him in the winery earlier this evening, in a fermentation tank. He'd drowned, apparently."

I stood and raised a finger to Gabe, then sidestepped down the row before turning up the stairs toward the concourse.

"Have the police been called?"

"They're over there now, with the medical examiner. I don't know all the details, but they're treating it as a crime scene."

I'd paused to stand near a souvenir booth, its riotous display of pennants and caps, jerseys and bobble-head dolls suddenly inappropriate—almost obscene—in this new and altered context.

"A crime scene? Why?"

"I don't know. I'm as much in the dark as you are."

"Claudia tried to call me a few minutes ago. Is she all right?"

"No, she's not all right. That's why I'm calling. The police have just arrested her for her brother's murder."

Bernie arrived *chez* MacTaggart at four in the morning, dragging a wheeled suitcase behind her. She wore a white cotton nightdress with her hair up in rollers, and with her weekend nightclubbing makeup still in place, looked exactly like Elsa Lanchester in *The Bride of Frankenstein*.

"Thank you for doing this," I told her, opening the door and lifting her bag over the stoop. I normally relied on Mayday or Regan to dog-sit Sam, but this morning, both would be coming with me.

"Don't worry, it's not like I kicked Bradley Cooper out of bed or anything." Sam greeted her with a stuffed toy and a hopeful expression, and she squatted to shake his orange ruff. "Hello, handsome. Is that for me?"

"I put clean sheets on the guest bed, and the fridge is pretty well stocked. Just make yourself at home."

She straightened, dangling the toy just out of Sam's reach. "How long do you think you guys'll be gone?"

"I don't know," I told her, stacking my briefcase atop my own roller bag. I was courtroom ready, shaved and showered, in a blue suit and tie.

"I packed for a week. Between the arraignment and a bail hearing and God knows what else, it could actually be longer."

"You realize of course that this is the first plot point," she said, tossing the toy and sending Sam skittering down the hallway.

"The first what?"

"Plot point. You know, the end of the first act. It's when something unexpected happens that takes the story and sends it off in another direction. Like in *Casablanca,* when Ugarte gets killed and Victor Laszlo shows up at Rick's with Ilsa Lund on his arm."

On the other hand, maybe the kennel was still an option.

"What are you even talking about?"

"Screenwriting. You don't have to thank me, or even pay me, but you do have to promise me one thing. You have to tell me all the gory details as they happen, so I can work them into my story."

"What story?"

"The one I'm writing for class. About the lawyer and the winery owner and his missing son. Antonio says it has great promise."

Antonio was Bernie's screenwriting instructor from UCLA Extension. I think he'd once written a Taco Bell commercial.

"You can't write about our cases. I already told you that."

"Don't worry, in my story the lawyer's an orphan who was adopted by a rock star and his beautiful girlfriend, but whose real father might be the winery owner whose missing son might be his brother. Also, the lawyer's a nice guy who treats his employees well and doesn't call them up at one o'clock in the morning."

A horn sounded at the curb out front.

"That's Marta. I left instructions on the counter. Sam gets his breakfast at seven and his dinner at six. Make sure there's water in his bowl. And just be aware that sometimes when I'm gone, he'll get diarrhea."

She frowned at her new charge, whose tongue was flopping and whose tail was dusting the hardwood.

"Diarrhea?"

"Not always, but sometimes. If it should happen this time," I told her, patting her on the shoulder, "just think of it as your first plot point."

. . .

We flew commercial this time, catching the first plane out of LAX to Santa Rosa, where we rented two cars for maximum flexibility. I drove with the luggage, while Regan and Mayday followed in their matching blue Ford Fusion. We arrived at the Napa Springs Spa and Golf Resort at 7:50 A.M., just in time for what looked like the shotgun start of a tournament. Two dozen golf carts were arrayed in martial formation in the lot by the Pro Shop entrance where Marco, the rumpled security guy, spied us walking from our cars. He hustled over to meet us.

"Mr. MacTaggart? Follow me, please. Mr. Clarkson's been waiting for you."

Marco spoke into his walkie-talkie as we trailed him through the central courtyard and then down a short concrete staircase to the Clubhouse whose lobby teemed this morning with ruddy men in ball caps sipping coffees or Bloody Marys and haggling over strokes. Regan and Mayday had also traveled in courtroom attire, and a dozen bushy eyebrows followed their skirted progress down an open hallway to a white paneled side door, where Marco knocked.

Clarkson rose from behind a desk as the door closed behind us, silencing the manly hubbub in the lobby.

"Jack. Thank God you're here."

The general manager's office had a tartan-plaid carpet and clubby furniture that included heavy wingchairs and dark mahogany tables. A series of framed lithographs illustrating *The Rules of Golf* were arrayed on the hunter-green walls like so many Stations of the Cross. The curtained windows overlooked the actual course where, two stories below us, a trio of groundskeepers in pith helmets and rubber boots appeared to be servicing a sprinkler head. The muffled hum of a lawnmower droned somewhere in the distance.

I made the introductions, and we moved chairs to form a semicircle in front of Clarkson's desk.

"I'm afraid I haven't anything new to report," Clarkson began, running a hand through his thick, black hair as he returned to his swivel chair. "It's been almost impossible to get information from the sheriff's department, since I'm not a family member. Best I can tell, they initially took her to the station for questioning, then booked her into the jail in Napa. That was close to midnight. That's the last I've been able to find out."

Clarkson looked exhausted, his blue eyes raw and haunted. His face was unshaven, and my guess was that if he'd slept at all, it had been right here on the couch in his office, in the same clothes he was wearing now, and had been wearing since yesterday morning.

"Have you tried calling Philippe?"

"Philippe? Are you kidding? He wouldn't talk to me *before* that hearing last month. Since then, well . . ."

"What?"

"Haven't you heard? The old man's become a hermit. No travel, no meetings, no public appearances. Rumor has it he sits around all day and drinks. The house staff's all quit, or been fired. He hasn't spoken a word to Claudia since the hearing. When they communicate at all, it's been by e-mail or by little Post-it notes he leaves on her desk in the Visitor Center. The only person he'll talk to is Phil. Was Phil."

Mayday asked him, "Why would the police think Phil's death was anything but accidental?"

"That's the thing, I don't know."

Clarkson pushed up from his chair and crossed to the windows, where again he did the raking thing with his hair.

"Claudia called around nine-thirty, obviously upset. All she said was that Phil was dead—that one of the winery guys doing rounds after dinner had found his body floating in a fermentation tank. She asked me to call Jack. Pleaded, actually. I thought she was being an alarmist, so I called but I didn't leave a message. Then she called me again around ten minutes later to say that she couldn't talk, but that she was going to be arrested."

He turned to face us.

"Why would they arrest Claudia? If it wasn't an accident—if it really was murder—then the old man's the natural suspect, isn't he? What with Phil's birthday this week?"

Mayday and I shared a look as Clarkson circled behind the desk and flopped back into his chair.

"Look," I told him, "you called me to come help Claudia, and that's why we're here. But first we need to get something straight between the two of us. I don't work for people I don't trust, and I don't normally trust people who've lied to me."

He held my gaze for the briefest of moments and then looked away. He nodded.

"All right."

"So why don't we start with the truth about you and Claudia."

He lifted a paperweight off his desk—a gold-plated golf ball on a square marble base—and he turned it in his hands.

"I've known Claudia since we were kids. I suppose it's an old story, your best friend's pesky kid sister—the gawky duckling that grows up to be a swan. We didn't start dating until after she'd moved home from Berkeley. That was around eight years ago. It was casual at first, but then . . ." He shrugged. "We're planning to get married. We've kept it on the QT because of her father."

"Good," I told him. "See how easy that was? Now let's talk about that Marlene Dietrich stunt she pulled in the courtroom."

"What do you mean?"

"I mean have you ever seen a film called *Witness for the Prosecution*?"

"I . . . I think so. You mean with Tyrone Power?"

I nodded.

"But what has that got to do with—"

"Okay, never mind." I pushed up from my chair and started for the door. "Have it your way. Come on, ladies, let's go."

"Wait!"

His voice stopped me. I turned to watch him put down the paperweight and slide open a drawer in his desk. He removed an ashtray and a lighter, and he set them on the desktop. He shook a cigarette loose from a hard pack of Marlboros.

I returned to my chair.

"It all started with the old man," Clarkson said, his eyes avoiding mine as he tapped his cigarette on the blotter. "After the accident, he told Claudia they needed to make it look like Alain was still alive, to prevent Phil from selling off the vineyard. He told her to order the replacement credit card and then charge a few items each month whenever she traveled."

"Which she did."

He nodded.

"And then she double-crossed him."

He lit the smoke with an unsteady hand and returned his lighter to the drawer. He blew a stream to the ceiling.

"She knew how much I wanted that second golf course, so she told me about her father's plan. Me and Phil both. She said it was the perfect opportunity. She said that if Phil filed suit to declare Alain dead, and if she and her father were exposed in court as liars, then the judge would have no choice but to rule in Phil's favor. I was against it at first, because of the risk to her, but she insisted. She can be headstrong that way, just like her old man."

The story itself was no surprise—I'd figured as much by now—but Claudia's willingness to take a perjury rap for Clarkson, and to do so at my expense, still stung me more than it should have, leaving a bright red welt on my ego.

"What?" Clarkson asked.

"You're telling me Claudia was willing to risk estrangement from her own father just to help you buy some land?"

"Estrangement? From Philippe? Don't make me laugh." He leaned forward and tapped his ash with a finger.

"Why is that funny?"

"It's a long story. Let's just say that he treats her like shit, and that he always has. Just like he treated Alain."

Mayday asked, "Whatever happened with that perjury referral to the D.A.'s office?"

"Nothing, as far as I know." He leaned back in his chair. "You need to understand something about Philippe and the district attorney. The old man's a big supporter. Supposedly gave him a bunch of money to get elected. Which way that cuts, I don't know."

I chewed on that for a minute, rolling it around on my tongue as Clarkson watched me, mistaking my silence for reticence.

"Look, I know what we did was wrong, and probably stupid, but for whatever it's worth, Claudia felt really bad about lying to you. She told me so herself."

Now it was my turn to stand and cross to the windows. Down on the golf course, the groundskeepers had all moved off. A lone cart glided silently down the fairway.

"They say confession is good for the soul, Andy. How do you feel right now?"

"Worried, Jack. Worried about Claudia."

"And now you want me to help her. The guy you both played for a patsy."

"She wants it. She said you're the only lawyer she trusts."

"And what about you?"

"Yes, damn it. If you're willing to forgive what we did."

I turned around to face him. From my angle, with the sunlight catching the rising smoke as it wreathed his head and shoulders, he had the appearance of a cipher, or a kind of avatar—a man whose body was present, but who wasn't really there.

"All right, Andy, today is your lucky day. I'm running a special on absolution. Now get out your checkbook."

9

I'd promised Clarkson that I'd go to the jail in Napa, and while that was true enough, it wasn't our first destination. If Claudia had been booked around midnight, then she'd probably been up into the wee hours and could use the extra sleep. Plus I was sure that, as the jail's star prisoner, she was getting the kid-glove treatment.

She'd hold for the time being. In fact, the experience might do her some good.

Instead we'd left Regan to oversee our accommodations—a two-bedroom apartment above the Spa building—while Mayday and I set out to visit the real seat of power, in this or any other county in the State of California.

"How did you know?" Mayday asked me as we hit Silverado Trail and followed it southbound toward Napa.

"When you're being arrested, you don't call a customer for help."

"Not about Clarkson. About the probate hearing."

We had the windows up and the AC blasting, with the digital thermometer on the dashboard already registering an outside temperature of ninety-one degrees. It was going to be a scorcher.

"I guess I've been dwelling on it more than you have. The fact that Phil was able to hire Maxine Cameron, and then find Claudia's calendar, and then obtain a declaration from AmEx in New York, all within a space of three or four days. Something about that just never felt kosher."

Mayday nodded, her sunglasses turned toward the dusty vineyards that scrolled past her passenger window. I recognized that stony silence.

"What?"

"You know what."

"Listen, Diogenes. If we only represented saints, we'd be out of business in a year."

She turned from the window to face me.

"There's a world of difference between representing a saint and representing a woman who's already used us once to perpetrate a fraud on the court. What happened to 'I don't normally trust people who've lied to me'?"

"That was a statement of general principles. Now we're making an exception."

"And why is that, exactly?"

"You heard her fiancé. I'm the only lawyer she trusts."

She turned back to the window, and we drove for a while without speaking.

"What did you think of Clarkson?"

She shrugged. "I think he's worried about her, and that he cares for her very much. That's on the credit side of the ledger."

"That and his check for fifty grand."

She didn't smile. "On the debit side. I thought there was more going on than concern for his girlfriend's welfare. I thought he was nervous. Maybe even frightened."

"Worried, nervous, frightened. That's semantics."

"Maybe. Like I said, it's just a feeling. What about you?"

It was an excellent question. I too felt that we weren't getting the whole story. It was like we'd witnessed a performance in Clarkson's office—a man in the spotlight, hitting the marks he'd choreographed and delivering the lines he'd already rehearsed. Then again, he'd been waiting hours for our arrival, and he'd almost certainly known he'd be asked to explain what had happened in Judge Mercer's courtroom. Under those circumstances, spontaneity might have been asking a lot.

"I guess I was struck not so much by the emotions he showed," I told Mayday, "but by the emotions he didn't."

Again she turned from the window. "What do you mean?"

"I mean anger, frustration, disappointment. Here the guy'd been plotting for months to acquire fifty acres of Giroux's vineyard, and he'd gone so far as to suborn perjured testimony to get it. And now that he's days away from seeing his goal realized, the one person he needs to make it all happen takes a swan dive. Worried or not, if I were Clarkson, I'd be pissed."

"Maybe he cares deeply enough for his girlfriend that worldly concerns fall by the wayside. She's quite attractive, if you hadn't noticed."

"I noticed. But I'd still be pissed."

"That's because you're not a romantic."

"What are you talking about? I'm a romantic. How am I not a romantic?"

"When's the last time you did anything even remotely romantic?"

"Let me think. I bought flowers for a girl."

"What girl?"

"A girl. A girl who kept the flowers, and left me by the wayside."

We phoned ahead to the D.A.'s office to tell them we were coming, and then we sat back and enjoyed the scenery. The drive took less than thirty minutes. As the top of the hour approached, Mayday fiddled with the car radio, looking for an all-news station. She found KQED at 88.5, an NPR affiliate from San Francisco. The death of Phil Giroux was, not surprisingly, their lead local story.

Napa County Sheriff's officials confirmed this morning that the suspect held in connection with the death yesterday of Napa Valley winemaker Phil Giroux, the thirty-nine-year-old son of legendary vintner Philippe Giroux, is in fact the dead man's sister. Claudia Giroux, age thirty-four, is the director of marketing for the Château Giroux winery empire, and served as honorary cochair of this year's Auction Napa Valley, which raised over eight million dollars for local charities. Police are not releasing any information on the circumstances surrounding either the winemaker's death or his sister's arrest, stating only that their investigation is ongoing.

"No media leak," I said, poking the power button. "That's refreshing."

"But not very illuminating."

"I like it. It tells me they're reluctant to stick their necks out. That maybe their case isn't as strong as they'd like."

The directions Mayday read from her iPad delivered us to a modest brick storefront one block north of the county courthouse. We parked around back, on the second level of a municipal structure whose shade, we hoped, would shield the car's paint job from solar blistering.

"Mr. MacTaggart and Ms. Suarez. We're here in the Giroux matter," I told the girl behind the glass partition inside. "We called ahead."

She picked up a phone. While we waited for admission, I surveyed the framed photos on the wall behind us—a somber parade of district attorneys stretching back, I presumed, to the formation of Napa County.

A woman finally appeared through the security door. She led us inside, through an open bullpen area and then to a small conference room where not one but three people rose from their chairs as the door swung inward. One of them I recognized, from the last photograph outside in the lobby.

"Mr. MacTaggart? Ms. Suarez? I'm Ronaldo Herrera, the district attorney here in Napa County. These are our lead investigators assigned to the case, Yolanda Walker and Carlos Garza."

We exchanged handshakes, and then business cards. Herrera was short and thick, with an olive complexion and dark, close-cropped hair. His brown eyes behind rimless spectacles, if not exactly warm, were definitely intelligent. He wore a gray suit with a baby-blue shirt and a solid blue tie, as though maybe when he'd dressed for work this morning, he'd recognized the likelihood of being photographed.

"Please make yourselves comfortable," Herrera said. "Can I offer you something to drink?"

"Too early for me," I said. Mayday requested coffee.

Herrera nodded to the escort woman as she withdrew, then took his seat at the head of the table. We moved to the empty chairs opposite the investigators, both of whom wore shields on their belts and both of whom had that unnerving cop habit of watching you as though sizing you up for handcuffs.

Walker, who I made as the lead, had Whoopi Goldberg dreadlocks on the cusp of going gray. She'd dressed for work today in jeans and a white cotton blouse, the jeans too tight in the seat for the extra padding she carried on her five-foot, four-inch frame. She too wore cheaters, but low on the nose, as though she'd just been reading from one of the two manila folders that rested on the table before her.

Garza was the hard case. He was young and fit, with fine features that included dark, probing eyes and a thin mouth fixed into a permanent sneer. He sported gray slacks and a white dress shirt open at the neck. He wore his hair high and tight in accordance with the Army Grooming Standards Manual, which had me thinking Iraq or Afghanistan—a local kid who'd gone to war and come home with skills that would keep him out of the vineyards at harvest time.

While Walker used me to practice her perp stare, Garza couldn't help himself from making doe eyes at Mayday, which called into question his powers of detection.

"Have you been over to the jail yet?" Herrera asked me, already knowing the answer.

"No. Since we're unfamiliar with your local procedures, we thought it best to start here. I've always found it wise to begin where the discretionary authority lies."

Herrera's smile held all the warmth of a steel chisel.

"I'm afraid you'll find discretion in short supply today. We're compelled to oppose bail in all violent felonies as a matter of office policy."

"Violent felonies?" I looked at Mayday. "I thought we were here on an OSHA violation."

The escort woman reentered the room without knocking, setting a Styrofoam cup on the table. She left again without speaking. Herrera pushed the cup in Mayday's direction.

"Yolanda? Perhaps you could bring our big-city friends up to speed on your investigation."

Whoopi arranged the two file folders side-by-side before her.

"All right, Mr. MacTaggart. Would you like to start with perjury this morning, or with murder?"

"Eenie, meenie, miney, mo," I said, pointing to the newer, thinner file. She opened it and adjusted her glasses. She read from the first page of what I presumed was the medical examiner's report.

"Philip Jean Giroux, age thirty-nine. Male Caucasian, five feet nine inches tall, one hundred sixty-three pounds. No tattoos, piercings, or distinguishing birthmarks. First through third toes surgically excised from his left foot."

She licked a finger and flipped to the next page.

"Preliminary time of death is seventeen-thirty hours, Pacific Daylight Time. Preliminary cause of death is asphyxia secondary to pulmonary edema. The victim also suffered a nondisplaced cranial fracture to the temporal skull, apparently from blunt-force trauma."

I turned to Mayday, the doctor's daughter, who translated.

"He got hit on the back of the head and drowned."

"Goodness." I turned a concerned look toward Herrera. "Bathtub? Swimming pool?"

"Wine," Walker said, clapping the file closed and sliding it across the table. "He drowned in a tank of wine. Pinot noir, to be exact."

"That file is yours to keep," Herrera said. "Consider it our discovery to date. We're filing our complaint this morning as soon as the clerk's window opens. You'll find a copy inside."

"All of this is tragic," I told them, opening the file and spreading its contents on the table, "and possibly ironic, but it doesn't explain why you think a crime was committed, let alone why our client is in custody."

Both investigators looked to Herrera, who nodded his assent. Walker reached across the table and teased two color photos from the fan of documents.

They were eight-by-ten glossies. The first showed a large metal tank, photographed from ground level. The second was taken from above rim-level, looking down into the tank. Phil Giroux's body, fully clothed, lay on what looked like a carpet of crimson shag, his head and shoulders submerged below the surface.

He looked like a hiker lost in some volcanic hellscape that had lain down to drink from a pool.

Walker asked me, "How much do you know about winemaking?"

"Nothing," I said, sliding the photos to Mayday. "Less than nothing."

"The tank in question is stainless steel, twelve feet tall and fifteen feet in diameter. It had a rolling staircase parked beside it, as you can see in the first photo, and an aluminum catwalk across the top, which you can just make out in the second photo, there in the lower right foreground. That catwalk is where the winemaker stands to punch down the cap—the floating layer of skins and stems and whatnot from the crushing. To do that he uses a tool called a punch-down. Picture a long-handled rake, but with a giant potato masher on the end."

"Okay."

"During maceration, when the must from the crush is still in the tank, the winemaker will punch down the cap at least twice a day. Château Giroux doesn't ordinarily bottle pinot noir, so this particular batch was some kind of special project, and the victim insisted on doing the punch-downs himself. Two of the winery employees left the building at exactly seventeen hundred hours, which they both corroborate. As they were leaving, they greeted your client, Miss Giroux, entering the building. That left the victim and your client alone together in the winery building between five o'clock and the estimated time of death a half hour later."

I looked at Herrera. "You're joking, I hope."

"There were two punch-down tools," Walker continued, "in the area of the tank. One ended up in the tank with the victim's body. That's the one he was using. You can just see the handle there, at the top of the picture. The other tool had been dropped to the floor beside the rolling staircase, after the handle had been deformed by an impact. That's the weapon the assailant used to strike the victim on the head from behind. Probably while standing on the little landing there at the top of the stairs."

"Or else he just slipped and hit his head."

Walker's head shake was emphatic. "The handle of the punch-down tool was dented by a blow to the victim's head. That's been conclusively established by laboratory analysis. You'll find the report in there."

"Fingerprints?"

"There were five sets of identifiable prints, both on the pole and on the staircase railing. Exemplars were taken on-scene from all the winery workers. Voluntarily, I might add. One set belonged to the victim. Three belonged to other winery employees, and all of those appear to be older. The most recent prints, the ones that were atop the others on both the staircase railing and the handle of the punch-down, belong to your client, Claudia Giroux."

She left the accusation hanging while I looked again at the photos, arranging them side-by-side before me.

"Why is the body lying like that atop the cap, or whatever you call it? Surely a full-grown man would have been fully submerged from a fall. His clothes don't even look wet."

The Garza kid spoke up.

"The cap is very firm," he said, from what sounded like experience. "If it hadn't been punched down since the morning, then it would have been like an air mattress, thick and buoyant. A body falling from the low height of the catwalk wouldn't necessarily break the surface."

"But break the surface it did." I pointed. "His head and shoulders are submerged."

"We have a theory about that," Walker said, her gaze steady. "We think that after she knocked the victim unconscious, your client then used the punch-down tool to hold his head under the surface."

10

Herrera personally escorted us to the jail, a two-block schlep from his office, most of it shaded by buildings and street trees and the tall, fragrant pines that lined the courthouse mall. Even so, I could feel my shirt clinging to the small of my back as we walked.

"I hope you won't think me boorish if I point out a few flaws in your case."

Herrera gave me a side-glance. "I'd be disappointed if you didn't."

"For starters, my client is no dummy. She's an educated and accomplished businesswoman, a community leader, and not the sort who'd be prone to homicidal impulses. Which is why you'll have a hard time selling either of your scenarios to a jury."

"Either of my scenarios?"

"Sure. Either she planned to kill her brother, or she killed him on impulse. Which one do you like better?"

"I'm sure you're about to tell me."

"Okay, let's say she planned it. If so, then she'd never have allowed herself to be seen by the departing winery workers. Nor could she have counted on her brother putting himself in such a vulnerable position, on the catwalk above the tank. Nor would she have left her fingerprints on something as obvious as the handle of the murder weapon. The whole picture is wrong, from start to finish."

Herrera couldn't resist. "Maybe she had other plans, but took advantage of the situation that presented itself."

"That doesn't address the departing workers. If she'd come to the winery intent on murder by whatever means, she'd have called it off right then and there."

Herrera was silent for a while. "Go on, I'm listening."

"All right, second scenario. She came for some other reason, they argued, and she swung for the fences. That one's even worse. First of all, she'd have to be a psychopath, which we both know that she isn't. Secondly, all she needed to do to obliterate her fingerprints was to shove the potato-masher into the soup. That would have been a no-brainer, and remember, she's no dummy. Instead she whacks him on the skull, then uses the punch-down tool to hold his head under the surface, then she drops the thing on the floor? And then she strolls back to her house, where she waits for the body to be discovered? Is that really your theory?"

We'd reached the criminal courts building; a modern temple of glass and limestone directly across from the old civil courthouse. Herrera led us around to a side door, to what looked like an airport security checkpoint. The uniformed guards who manned the metal detectors and X-ray machines all rose to acknowledge the district attorney, who removed his belt, keys, and cell phone and placed them in a plastic tub on the conveyor belt. Mayday and I followed suit.

"All of which," I told him as we reoutfitted ourselves on the other side, "brings us to your biggest problem, and that's motive. Specifically, you don't have one. Why would Claudia Giroux want her brother dead?"

Herrera paused to consider how much he should be telling me.

"When Judge Mercer referred the perjury matter to my office," he said, "I handled the investigation myself. The Giroux family is very prominent in this community, probably more so than you realize. So I know all about the ownership succession, and the significance of Phil Giroux's fortieth birthday. But if you'll excuse my saying so, I also wonder about the propriety of having this discussion with a lawyer who's representing both Philippe and his daughter."

"Then let's be clear about that. I represented Philippe in the probate matter, which is concluded. I represent neither father nor daughter in connection with your perjury investigation. As for the murder charge, I've provisionally agreed to represent Claudia, subject to the attorney-client meeting we're about to have."

Herrera grunted. He was walking again.

"When I heard that Phil had been killed only a few days before his fortieth birthday, my first thought was Philippe, naturally. But under the terms of the grandfather's trust, if neither of Philippe's boys reaches age forty, then the winery goes to the Catholic Church. If we're analyzing motives, that pretty much eliminates Philippe as a suspect, doesn't it?"

"Yeah, and it also eliminates his daughter who, unless she's planning to join a convent, had nothing to gain from her brother's death."

The D.A. didn't answer. We followed him around a corner and down a short hallway, through a door that opened onto a kind of lobby. Another door on the opposite wall bore a sign reading NO WEAPONS BEYOND THIS POINT. Beside it was a double-thick window into which a metal speaker had been fitted. Herrera waved to the guy behind the glass, then turned to face us as a buzz sounded and the jailhouse door clicked open.

"I'll leave you two to your client meeting. You have my number. Felony arraignments are heard upstairs in Courtroom D."

"I'll be asking for bail," I told him.

"Of course you will. Have you seen our bail schedule?"

I nodded.

"In that case," he said, turning to leave, "I'll be seeing you on Wednesday as well."

He'd only gone a few steps before he stopped again and turned.

"This isn't some fishing expedition. We have a suspect in custody who had both means and opportunity, and there's solid physical evidence linking her to the crime. Up here in the boondocks, we call that a case. And as far as motive is concerned, our investigation is ongoing. But whatever it was, I can assure you that we'll find it. There's always a motive."

. . .

We'd been waiting in the attorney interview room for nearly twenty minutes when the door on the other side of the Plexiglas finally opened and a uniformed matron entered leading Claudia Giroux by the arm. The prisoner wore blue surgical scrubs, orange rubber Crocs, and the haunted look of a woman who'd spent the last nine hours of her life staring into the void.

"Just wave when you're done," the matron said, pointing to the uniformed officer seated behind a glass partition on Claudia's side of the Plexiglas. She closed the door behind her, leaving us alone with our client.

No sooner had Claudia dropped into her chair than she'd begun to sob, her face tipped forward over the narrow counter, her shoulders quietly shaking.

"Sorry," she said into the speaker, straightening and wiping her nose with her wrist. "I told myself I wouldn't do that."

"I'd say you're entitled," I told her. "Are they treating you all right?"

She managed a weak smile. "It's not Ritz Carlton, but I do have a private cell. And they brought me my breakfast this morning."

I checked my watch. "We need to ask you some questions, Claudia, and I'm afraid we haven't much time. Not if we hope to get you into a courtroom before noon."

She took a deep breath and shifted in her chair. She nodded. "All right, go ahead."

"First of all, what have you told the police?"

"Nothing. At least, not since they read me my rights. I remembered what you said that time in the judge's office. I told them I needed to talk to my lawyer before I answered any more questions."

"Good. Don't talk to anybody about what happened, and that includes the guards or any of the inmates, understand? Especially the inmates."

She nodded.

"Okay. Now I'm about to ask you to tell us everything you can remember, starting with why you were in the winery building last night around five o'clock. But first, there's something you need to understand. I don't care whether you're guilty or innocent, because both the guilty and the innocent are entitled to representation. What I do care about is that you not lie to me. Because if you tell me one version of the facts today, but offer a different version at the time of trial, I'll have to recuse myself as your lawyer."

"Because you can't elicit false testimony."

"That's right. So either tell us the truth now, or simply say that you'd rather not discuss it. Either is perfectly fine with me."

She nodded. "I understand."

We waited as she squared her shoulders and composed her hands on the counter.

"I went to visit Phil in the winery building. There was no special reason—I just knew that he had Alain's pinot in the vat, and I hadn't talked to him all day, so—"

"What do you mean Alain's pinot?"

"I'm sorry. Phil had the idea to do a special bottling. We don't ordinarily make sparkling wine at Château Giroux, but Phil had a source for some really good coastal pinot noir, which is an early ripening grape. He thought he could process a batch before things got crazy with our fall harvest. It was a pet project of his, a kind of tribute to Alain. I think he got the idea from that night we all met for cocktails, when Father talked about that bottle of Dom Pérignon Rosé. Phil was going to use one of Alain's old paintings on the label."

"Tell me what happened when you got to the winery building."

"The day shift was just knocking off, and Phil and I were alone. He was getting ready to punch the cap. That's the floating layer—"

"I know. Skins and stems and whatnot."

She nodded again. "Phil was moving a ladder to the maceration tank. I helped him push it into place. We were just talking, about Father mostly, his health, how he was getting along without Frederique. You may not know it, but—"

"You and your father weren't talking, and the household staff had all left. Andy already told us."

"You met with Andy?" Claudia straightened again, her eyes darting from Mayday to me. "What did he tell you?"

"For one thing, the truth about the probate hearing. Also, that you're planning to get married. Congratulations."

"Andy told you that?"

Mayday leaned toward the speaker. "He wanted you to know that he loves you very much, and that he's counting the hours until he sees you again."

"He's hired us to represent you," I told her. "Assuming that's what you still want."

"Yes." She nodded once. "Yes, that's what I want."

Again I checked my watch. "We were at the part where you'd just helped Phil move the ladder."

"Yes, I'm sorry. We were standing and talking, and then Phil climbed onto the catwalk. I grabbed another punch-down and started up after him, but he forbade me to step onto the catwalk, since I was wearing heels. He said it was too dangerous. So I climbed down and left. I told him I'd see him tomorrow."

"What time was that?"

"I'm not sure. Five-fifteen or thereabouts. Maybe five-twenty. Not much later than that."

"And the last time you saw Phil alive, he was up on the catwalk still holding the other punch-down tool?"

She nodded. "I remember the last thing he told me. He said that dinners at Father's house weren't the same anymore without me."

She was sobbing again, her head lowered and her shoulders shaking. Mayday and I shared a glance. We gave her a moment to compose herself.

"Tell us what you were wearing."

Again she wiped at her nose. "Heels and a skirt. And a silk blouse. Short-sleeved. It was hot yesterday, over ninety, but the winery was cold. Freezing, actually, which is why I didn't stay very long."

"When you left the winery building, where was the punch-down tool that you'd just been holding?"

"I set it on the floor, leaning against the tank. At the base of the ladder."

"Was the handle straight or was it dented?"

"What?"

"The handle of the tool you'd been holding. Was it straight or dented?"

"I don't remember it being dented. Why?"

"Never mind. Tell us what happened after you left the winery."

"I walked back to the office, checked my phone messages, and then went home. My house is just behind the château. It's what we call the Petit Trianon. You know, like at Versailles. It's a family joke. I went home, changed my clothes, poured myself some wine, and turned on the television. I watched part of the news, and then I started cooking dinner. At around seven-fifteen, Sandy McAfee, one of the winery workers, banged on my door. He said there'd been an accident, and I should come right away. When we got to the winery, Father was already there, and so were Tom Harding and Jean Gagne. They said I shouldn't look, but I had to. It was horrible. His head was . . ."

"I know, we saw the photos. Who are Harding and Gagne?"

"They work in the winery. They're the ones who were leaving when I first arrived."

Mayday was typing notes on her iPad.

"What about Lourdes, was she there?"

"No. At least, I don't remember seeing her."

"At all?"

"Not last night. I don't know where she was."

Again I shared a look with Mayday.

"Did anyone see you go back to your office after you'd met with Phil?"

She shook her head. "I went in the back, to avoid the tasting room. It was Sunday, and tastings had ended at five. The staff would have been out front cleaning. They usually mop the back bar on Sunday evening."

"What about when you walked from the Visitor Center to your house?"

She shook her head again as Mayday chimed in.

"Did you log into your computer, either at the office or when you got home?"

Claudia thought about that for a moment. "No, I don't think so."

"When you arrived back at the winery with McAfee," I asked her, "where was the punch-down tool you'd been holding earlier?"

"I . . . I don't know. I might have been standing on it for all I cared. Somebody—maybe it was Father—had called the police. They arrived soon after I did, maybe ten minutes later. They asked me some questions, then one of them escorted me back to my house. He sat with me until the others came and took my fingerprints. By then it was nine o'clock or so. The way they were acting, the tone of their questions, it frightened me. I called Andy then, and I asked him to call you. When I didn't hear back from him, I tried to call you myself, but I didn't leave a message. After that, they told me I was under arrest. I asked if I could make one more call, and I phoned Andy again."

Claudia's story fit the facts to a T, but with a couple of holes in the sleeves. First, she'd gone from the winery to the Visitor Center to her home, all without a single eyewitness to corroborate her whereabouts. Second, having publicly perjured herself only a month or so earlier, there was nobody in the D.A.'s office, the local judiciary, or the media who was likely to believe another word that she said.

"Can you get me out of here? I don't know if I can stand it another night."

"I'm afraid it's not that simple. Because the charge is murder, we'll need to give the prosecution two days' formal notice that we're requesting bail. We'll do that this morning, at your arraignment. We'll ask the court to set a bail hearing for Wednesday morning. That's the earliest possible date under the law."

She sagged a little, but still managed a nod. "All right, I understand."

"Think you can choke down a few jailhouse meals?"

"I'd been meaning to start a new diet."

"Good girl. Okay, now comes the big question."

"What's that?"

"Who do you think would have wanted to kill your brother?"

She leaned forward into the speaker, a fire entering her eyes.

"Nobody, Jack. That's the thing. I've been up all night asking myself the same question. Phil was a sweetheart. He didn't have an enemy in the world. If it really was murder . . ." She shook her head. "It doesn't make any sense."

"Your brother was three days away from inheriting a fortune."

"I know that, but think about it. Lourdes would be better off if Phil were alive, and so would Father. None of the winery workers even knew about the trust. Even if they did, they all worshiped Phil and they wouldn't have risked their jobs on a change in ownership. It seems like the only person I can think of with a motive to see Phil dead can't possibly have killed him."

"Who's that?" Mayday asked.

Claudia turned to her and blinked.

"Why, Alain, naturally."

II

The term "bail" refers to a surety bond posted with the court in order to secure a criminal defendant's appearance upon her release from custody. In most cases, the availability of bail is a Constitutional right. In capital cases, however, meaning those punishable by death, the court has discretion to deny bail if the evidence adduced at the bail hearing indicates the defendant's guilt.

For a charge of murder to become a capital case in the State of California, a so-called "special circumstance" must be proved. Examples of special circumstances include multiple murders, or the murder of a police officer, or murder to prevent a witness from testifying. There's also a catchall special circumstance involving murder committed "for financial gain," which is why Herrera's ongoing search for motive had implications beyond the simple question of Claudia's guilt or innocence. If his investigators could uncover credible proof of a financial motive on Claudia's part, then Herrera could not only seek the death penalty, he could also ask a judge to hold her in custody until trial.

In a noncapital murder case, which is what the D.A.'s complaint presently described, the court enjoys broad discretion to consider a number of different factors in determining whether to grant bail. These include the defendant's prior criminal record, the likelihood that the defendant will appear for trial, and any possible threat to public safety should the defendant be released from custody.

As far as the amount of bail is concerned, the Constitution prohibits "excessive" bail, meaning a bail amount that is intended to punish the defendant or that is otherwise disproportionate to the crime alleged. For this reason, each county in the State of California publishes a bail schedule from which, in the case of murder and other violent felonies, the court may deviate only after holding a noticed hearing.

Unfortunately for Claudia, the bail schedule in Napa County provides for "No Bail" even in a case of noncapital murder—a fact that, in my role as paid pessimist, I'd made a point of researching before we'd left Los Angeles. This meant that before we could even address the issue of bail, we first had to give the prosecution two days' formal notice of our request for a deviation from the schedule, making that—more so than the entry of our not-guilty plea—the main purpose of this morning's arraignment hearing.

"All rise!"

Claudia and I stood as a judge named Walter Saxby took the bench. Saxby was tall and gaunt and mostly bald, his face radiating all the warmth and compassion of a no-knock search warrant. He bore in his appearance and demeanor all the hallmarks of a former prosecutor—a law-and-order, God-and-country, Rotary Club Republican. After ten years of practice, I'd learned to recognize the type.

At the table opposite ours, Herrera and Walker rose in tandem. Walker had changed from her tight-ass jeans into a navy skirt and jacket, and she wore her dreads now banded into a thick ponytail.

In the public gallery behind us, over two dozen spectators had gathered. Most appeared to be reporters, but the assemblage also included Mayday and Regan, and, across the center aisle, an anxious Andy Clarkson, straining to make eye contact with his fiancée. Seated next to Clarkson, a thin arm locked onto his, was the grieving widow herself. Lourdes Giroux wore a simple black dress and a black pillbox hat, her face obscured by a Jackie Kennedy veil under which she dabbed at her nose with a tissue. A thin gold crucifix glinted in the pale hollow of her throat.

"*People versus Giroux,*" read the judge from the open file on his bench as Herrera and I remained standing to announce our appearances. The judge swung his scowling maw first to the defense table.

"The defendant will rise and state her true name."

I nodded to Claudia, who stood in her blue surgical scrubs.

"Claudia Marie Giroux, Your Honor."

He studied her for a moment, this pale and delicate flower whose photo graced the front page of every morning newspaper. He then turned his gaze to the prosecution table.

"Have the people provided defense counsel with the complaint and the people's discovery materials?"

"We have, Your Honor."

Like a scavenging vulture, the judge swung his beak back to me.

"Does the defense waive reading of the complaint?"

"We do, Your Honor, as well as a reading of the defendant's rights. But we would at this time request that a bail hearing be scheduled at the earliest possible date, and hereby notify the people of our intention to seek a deviation from the local schedule. Wednesday morning would be preferable to the defense, Your Honor."

The beak swung again, and Herrera said, "Wednesday would be fine for the people."

The judge was making a calendar note when his head jerked up at the sound of the hallway door. We all turned to witness Larry the Driver guiding an unsteady Philippe Giroux by the arm. The old man shuffled forward and paused in the center aisle, looking momentarily confused by his surroundings. Larry eased him into a seat near the door as a dozen pens scratched on a dozen reporters' notepads.

Philippe, I noted, had chosen a black ascot for the occasion and, in the best tradition of his forebears, a wide black armband. He appeared to have aged a decade in the month since I'd last seen him, silent and angry, exiting a different Napa courtroom.

The judge cleared his throat. "Mr. MacTaggart, how does your client plead to the charges filed against her?"

"Not guilty, Your Honor."

No sooner had I spoken those magic words than Lourdes sprang to her feet, and an accusatory finger swung toward the rear of the courtroom.

"She's not the one who's guilty! *He's* the guilty one! *He's* the one who murdered my husband!"

The courtroom erupted. The judge, banging his gavel for quiet, half-rose from his seat as his bailiff burst through the gate. Lourdes, meanwhile, her hand now splayed at her breast, pulled a vintage Victorian swoon, fainting right into the arms of Andy Clarkson. This sent the reporters into renewed frenzy, surging forward to where Clarkson stood blinking while a dozen cell phone cameras flashed.

Amid the noise and general pandemonium, I turned toward Herrera, who stood with his hands in his pockets.

Our eyes met. We both shrugged.

Russ Dinsmoor, my late friend and mentor, once told me about a case he'd handled as a young lawyer. His client was the newly widowed wife of one of Pasadena's most solid citizens; a pillar of the business community who'd served on all the right boards and belonged to all the right clubs. He was the president of a bank, as I recall it, or the CEO of a major company. He and his wife had five adult children, a quintet of handsome and care-free trust-funders who volunteered with the Junior League, or swam at the Valley Hunt Club, or posted low handicap at the Annandale Golf Club.

They were the kind of golden, fizzy family that others around town envied, or emulated, and her children were the brightly polished apples of their mother's doting eye.

Her husband however, had a secret. As he lay on his hospital death-bed, he confided to his wife that the family was broke. Flat broke, in fact, borrowing from Peter to pay Paul, all because the husband had lost everything they'd owned, not to mention all he could borrow, in the poker rooms and blackjack tables of a dozen Vegas casinos.

Following the funeral, the widow called a family conclave. How did her children react to the news of their septuagenarian mother's penury? Of her imminent eviction from her home of forty years? They sued her, of course. They sued her because she—a former debutante whose arithmetic capabilities ended at the calculation of a twenty-percent restaurant tip— was alleged to have been "grossly negligent" in allowing her CEO husband to raid their children's trust funds.

"Blood may be thicker than water," Russ had told me, his head wagging at the memory, "but money is a powerful anticoagulant."

I thought of Russ's maxim that afternoon, sitting as we were in the kitchen of Phil and Lourdes Giroux's modest bungalow home on the grounds of the Château Giroux wine estate, where a window air conditioner hummed somewhere in a back bedroom and where two days' worth of dishes sat moldering in the kitchen sink.

Lourdes had changed from her black widow's weeds into jeans and a scarlet T-shirt with the word HUELGA! emblazoned above the image of a clenched fist. She ate her lunch—a cold-cut tray we'd purchased at the Oakville Grocery on our way back from the courthouse—in delicate little bites interspersed with a rambling commentary on her father-in-law's moral and parental shortcomings.

"The *nerve* of him showing his face like that," she continued. "He ought to be in jail, not swanning around town in his chauffeured limousine."

"I was surprised to see Larry with him," I said, pushing away my half-eaten sandwich. "I thought the staff had all been fired."

"Quit, not fired. But just Henri and Frederique. At least they had the sense to realize they'd been working for an ogre. I'd been telling them as much for years."

"Who's Henri?"

"Frederique's husband," Clarkson explained. "Henri LaBoutin. He was Philippe's gardener."

"So why did they quit?"

Lourdes shook her head. "I don't know. All I know is they weren't in church yesterday, or the Sunday before that."

"Church?"

"St. Apollinaris. It's in Napa. I usually saw them at the eight o'clock Mass, and so I asked Larry, and he told me they'd up and quit without giving notice."

Mayday stood and began clearing plates. Of Lourdes, she asked, "How long do you think Philippe will let you stay on here at the estate?"

"I'd leave tomorrow, if I had any money. There was no life insurance, and we had no savings to speak of. The winery was going to be our nest egg."

Her lip began to tremble, and she laid her sandwich aside.

"We had *plans,* Phil and I. Plans for the future. We were going to build a barracks for the workers, with a playground and a communal garden. Offer daycare, and a preschool. Maybe a health clinic. We were going to remake Château Giroux into a model of responsible ownership. Now look at me. I'm broke and I'm bawling, and the only thing I'm planning is a fucking *funeral.*"

As she dabbed at her mascara, I said, "I know this is small consolation, but whoever killed Phil would theoretically be liable to you in a civil lawsuit for wrongful death. Assuming the killer has any assets, of course."

"Really?" Her chin came up. "You mean I could actually sue Phil's father?"

"I said you could sue Phil's killer. What I still don't understand is why you think it was Philippe."

"Think? I don't think, Mr. MacTaggart, I know. Philippe hates me, in case you haven't noticed, and ever since Alain was killed, it's only gotten worse. God knows I tried to get along with him, if only for Phil's sake, but he made it totally impossible. Men like to talk about their mothers-in-law, but believe me, they've got nothing on Philippe. And then he was so afraid we'd sell some of his precious vineyard acreage to Andy. As if we don't make enough wine already. The fact is, it's almost cheaper to buy the grapes than to grow them. Even Phil used to say so."

My cell phone vibrated. The caller I.D. read MACTAGGART & SUAREZ. I excused myself to step outside.

From the bungalow's front porch I could make out the upper turrets of the stone château, their tiled nose cones poking above the canopy of oaks. This part of the property sloped into a shallow ravine, and the surrounding oak trees trailed Spanish moss like riven spiders' webs.

"Bernie?"

"You guys are all over the news! I turned on the TV in the conference room and CNN had pictures of the widow fainting in the courtroom. They said she'd just accused your client of killing his own son."

"Our former client."

"Whatever. Talk about a McGuffin."

"A what?"

"McGuffin. You know, a plot device to move the story forward while distracting the audience's attention away from the real killer. You need to get out to the movies once in a while."

"Bernie—"

"But that's not why I called. Are you ready for this? Are you sitting down? Because right after the story ran, Antonio called. Did I tell you he worked with Ethan Scott on *Abattoir, Part Three*? Anyway, he told Ethan about my screenplay, and Ethan is totally psyched to meet you guys and get all method and shit. And get this—maybe even option the film rights!"

"Who?"

"Ethan Scott! He's, like, the hottest young actor in Hollywood right now, with the emphasis on hot."

"And what film rights are we talking about?"

"To my screenplay! *Sour Grapes,* or maybe *Grape Expectations*. I'm not sure yet, but that doesn't matter. The point is, Ethan freaking Scott is flying up to Napa tomorrow to talk to you and maybe follow you around for a few days to get what he calls 'the zeitgeist.' How cool is that? Antonio gave him your private number, so you can expect a phone call. Aren't you excited? Antonio says it's a *Wag the Dog* moment."

"You can't just—"

"Oh, my God, I forgot the best part! The beautiful girlfriend of the aging rock star? The one who adopts the homeless street urchin who grows up to become the idealistic young lawyer? Are you ready for this? Are you ready? Cher!"

"Can I just say one thing?'

"Of course."

"Whoever this is that I'm talking to, please ask Bernadette to finish the month-end timesheets and then take Sam for a walk when I hang up. Which is now."

12

Lourdes had washed down her tofu sandwich with a beer-and-sleeping-pill chaser before retiring to the bedroom, leaving the four of us to kitchen detail. It was around three o'clock by the time we'd finished, at which point—according to the thermometer on the front porch post—the outside temperature had risen to ninety-five in the shade.

"I need to shower and change," Clarkson announced as he stood by his shimmering car, his jacket slung over a shoulder, "then I have to check on my golf tournament. Are you guys free for dinner tonight?"

"That would be great."

"How about Pilate's Trattoria at seven?"

"Think you can get us a table?"

He tossed his jacket onto the passenger seat. "Quality, not quantity."

We watched as his silver BMW roared up the driveway, leaving a cone of trailing dust.

Regan stretched as she yawned. "God, I'm asleep on my feet."

Mayday moved behind her, laying both hands on her shoulders. "Nothing a poolside nap won't cure. And maybe a piña colada."

I rode in the backseat as the women refined their plans, which expanded to include a couple's massage and seaweed facials. Our rental car followed the driveway out of the ravine and through a wooded copse that opened onto acres upon acres of trellised vine rows. We passed the Petit Trianon, and the big stone château, and as we approached the rear of the winery building I noticed a pair of beeping forklifts working with ant-like industry, moving pallets of cardboard boxes from a loading dock onto a waiting truck. Around front, a gaggle of tourists were exiting the adjoining Visitor Center and following a tour guide toward the winery entrance.

"Drop me right up here," I told Mayday, stripping off my necktie.

"What for?"

"Wine tasting. I'll catch you later at poolside."

I was out of the car before it had stopped, loping across the Visitor Center parking lot where a trio of news vans was bivouacked. I bypassed the front entrance and caught up to the rear of the tour group just as the door to the winery building was closing behind them.

"Once the grapes have been harvested by hand, they're brought here to our state-of-the-art winery for processing," the tour guide continued, stopping and waiting for her charges to cluster. She struck a Vanna White pose next to a hulking piece of industrial machinery with a sloping con-veyor belt. "Their first stop on the road to your local wine shop is right here, at our crusher-destemmer."

The group was a mixture of young and old, fit and flabby, all of whom crowded the huge machine, oohing and ogling its stainless steel contours. Somebody snapped a cell phone photo.

"From the crusher-destemmer, the juice of the grapes, along with the pulp and skins, is pumped into tanks like these behind me to begin the process we call primary fermentation."

Vanna turned and led the group to a pair of towering steel tanks, each around twice the size of the one I'd seen in the crime-scene photos.

I hung back a little, surveying the room. It was an industrial-looking space, cold and sterile, with corrugated steel walls framing a smooth concrete floor. A vaguely chemical odor of bleach and old wine perme-ated the air-conditioned chill. Along the far wall, a double row of oak wood barrels rested on elevated racks. Fire hoses lay in coils alongside slumbering hulks of machinery while rooftop air conditioners hummed.

The group was asking questions—how big, how long, how much?—while I turned a circle, my eyes uplifted to the steel-raftered ceiling as I drifted farther and farther from the droning voices. Then, as the group shuffled on to the next attraction, I moved in the opposite direction.

An unmarked door on the back wall opened into a room the size of a squash court. Winemaking is chemistry, Phil had told me, and here were the sinks and refrigerators, the beakers and test tubes to prove it. At the room's opposite end was another door, this one standing alongside a picture window that looked onto a larger version of the room I'd just exited.

I moved like a burglar, or maybe a peeping Tom, with my back to the side wall, alert for signs of activity. Seeing none, I tried the handle and stepped through the door by the window.

A dozen steel tanks, like the paired pistons of an enormous engine block, stretched before me in two ordered rows. Beyond these, a sea of racked wooden barrels lay slumbering, dumbly quiescent, beneath dim overhead lighting.

I stopped to listen, but the only sounds I could discern above the incessant hum of the air-conditioning were the faint *beep beep beeps* of the distant forklifts.

I moved forward quietly

Beyond the pistons, an area opened across from the barrels in which three smaller tanks stood orphaned and alone along the room's western wall. Two of these were huge oak vats that seemed of another age, like square-rigged schooners docked amid a fleet of steel battleships. The third vat I would have recognized from the D.A.'s photos, even without the yellow crime-scene tape encircling it like a halo.

There were no punch-down tools anywhere to be seen, but the stairway ladder, like an airport jet bridge, still stood inside the taped-off perimeter. I paced for a moment, back and forth, contemplating both the geometry and the ethics of the situation before ducking under the tape.

The locking mechanism on the stairway's wheels disengaged with a kick, and without using my hands, I rolled it forward until it docked with the tank, the boom of metal on metal reverberating into the room's high rafters. I held my breath and listened. In the distance, the muted *beep beep* continued as I stamped the wheel-lock into place.

A dense cloud of insects—fruit flies—hung above me as I climbed. Atop the small rectangular landing, I fanned at the bugs as I leaned over a moldering swamp of crushed and rotting grapes, the stink of its oily putrescence bringing a reflexive hand to my face.

The punch-down tool whose handle I'd seen in the crime-scene photo had been removed, and the cap itself had healed like human skin, leaving no visible evidence of the wound left by Phil Giroux's head.

The catwalk—an aluminum plank, really, maybe three feet in width—was still in place, forming a diagonal bridge across the tank's fifteen-foot expanse. I advanced a tentative step, testing it under my weight.

"A waste of perfectly good pinot," said a voice behind me, sending my arms flailing until I'd regained by balance and turned.

Between two rows of barrels, Philippe Giroux was seated on a folding chair. His legs were crossed, and he wore the same clothes from this morning's appearance in the courtroom—the black ascot, and the navy blazer with the black armband.

He'd been watching me the entire time.

"The police wouldn't let us near it, and now it's ruined, I'm afraid. I should have ignored them. If only I'd had your mettle, Mr. MacTaggart."

The old man stood and stepped into the light.

"I believe this is the part where I'm supposed to thank you for so gallantly representing my daughter, even after what she did to you. What she did to both of us." He advanced to the edge of the crime-scene tape, where he halted with his hands joined behind him, his body tipping forward into the forbidden space. "But I'm sure you'll understand if I don't."

"And why is that?"

He looked up to where I stood.

"Why? Because she murdered my son, of course."

. . .

The door swung inward as Philippe Giroux backed into the sitting room
with a tray in both hands. He bent and placed it on the coffee table, then
took the chair opposite mine.

"I'm fending for myself these days," he said by way of apology for the
Spartan fare: a wedge of runny Brie, some green table grapes, and a fan of
Ritz crackers.

"I heard Frederique had left."

He nodded. "Her husband, I'm sorry to say, accepted a job out of state.
Damn foolish of her to go with him, but who am I to judge the human
heart? I can't bear the thought of training a new chef, but I suppose I'll
have to face it."

The wine he'd already procured, and now he took up the bottle and
trimmed its foil cap with a small blade on his corkscrew. I noticed several
empties on a table by the door to the dining room.

"You must have quite a wine collection. Where do you keep it all?"

He paused to regard the bottle. "I have a cellar downstairs. A cellar
with far too many bottles that, like their owner, are well past their prime.
I'm like that boy with a barrel of apples who, every time he's hungry,
chooses the one that's about to go rotten. By the time he's reached the
bottom, he's eaten a barrelful of bad apples."

Philippe sunk the screw and twisted like a veteran sommelier, lever-
ing the cork from the bottle. He gave it a sniff and nodded. He poured our
glasses full.

"Rumor has it you've been living a monastic existence. No interviews,
no public appearances. Holed up like a hermit."

He snorted. "Rumor. The fact is that it's always a quiet time, just before harvest. But then I suppose the news stories that followed our last
courtroom debacle have given me pause. One doesn't relish being a laugh-
ingstock. Not at my stage in life."

He gave his glass a swirl, eyeballing the wine, appraising its color.

"Which brings us, I suppose, to your presence here at Château Giroux."
He leveled his gaze. "I could have had you arrested, you know. Instead I'll

merely observe that your capacity for forgiveness far exceeds mine. Clearly, you're a man who believes in second chances. For that, at least, I salute you."

He raised his glass and drank, eschewing, I noticed, the old sucking and bubbling routine.

"Claudia rang me last night," I told him. "From the winery. I was out, and I didn't take the call. Later, when I heard she'd been arrested, I guess I felt a little guilty."

All of which was true, if not exactly complete. There was no sense mentioning Clarkson and spoiling the moment.

"Curious that she'd telephone you, don't you think? With all those law school classmates of hers to choose from?"

"I must have made an impression."

"And will you continue to represent her?"

"Any reason I shouldn't?"

He set down his glass. "Reason? My God, man. First she lied to me about Alain, and to you. Then, when she was caught red-handed in her lie, she tried to feed me, her own father, to the wolves. If that doesn't convince you that she's some sort of . . . sociopath, I don't know what will."

His face had flushed, and now he took up the little cheese knife and gouged a chunk of Brie.

"So you're telling me you had no idea that the credit card charges were faked?"

The cracker halted halfway to his mouth. He set it down carefully.

"Oh, dear. She's gotten to you, hasn't she? What was it, her fluttering eyelashes? Her girlish charms? Or is there something more going on between you?"

Now it was my turn to blush.

"Let me tell you something about my daughter, Mr. MacTaggart—something you'll do well to remember. Claudia is a manipulator. Ever since she was a little girl, we saw it, Marie and I. First in school, then later with boys. Later still in business. She possesses a unique talent for persuasion unbounded by conventional notions of ethics or propriety. Useful, I'll concede, in certain business contexts, but damned infuriating for a parent.

And when she fails to get her way, well, let's just say that the consequences can be daunting. You're aware, are you not, of her hospitalization?"

"No."

He grunted. "While in graduate school, she attempted suicide. With sleeping pills, apparently. All because she'd failed to achieve—what do you call it—the law review?"

I nodded. "It's an academic honor, offered to the top students in the class."

"She couldn't accept the fact that her many hours of hard work had gone unrewarded. That the system had failed to recognize her budding genius. Don't get me wrong, Mr. MacTaggart. I admire ambition as much as the next man, as much as the next father. But not to that extreme. Claudia is the kind of girl—the kind of woman—who will not hesitate to use every advantage she can gain in order to get what she feels she deserves. And what she feels she deserves is *everything.*"

He chomped the cracker and washed it down with another mouthful of wine. I took care in framing my next question.

"What do you think she stood to gain by making you believe Alain was alive?"

He shook his head. "That's a question I've been asking myself for over a month now, and I'm afraid I haven't an answer. Perhaps you'll be perspicacious enough to discover one."

"What did she say when you asked her?"

He smiled thinly and wagged a finger. "Tut-tut, that's an old lawyer's trick. The fact is, I haven't spoken to my daughter since she accused me of masterminding her little . . . whatever it was."

"And now you think she's murdered her brother?"

His smile faded.

"The police apparently think so, as does the district attorney. They were together, Philip and Claudia, at the time of the murder. Her fingerprints, I'm told, are on the murder weapon."

"That can all be explained," I said, mindful of the attorney-client privilege. "She could have been visiting Phil, then left the winery before it happened."

"Is that her story?"

I didn't answer. Which was, I suppose, an answer.

Philippe shook his head again. "Claudia had no business being in the winery, Mr. MacTaggart, and the fact is, she rarely goes there. But go there she did, according to Tom and Jean both."

"Which brings us back to motive. What could Claudia possibly gain from causing Phil's death?"

He swirled his glass and drained it, then refilled it again from the bottle.

"That's another answer I can't give you, but I can assure you of one thing. If there was something of value to be gained by Philip's murder, however inconsequential it might seem to you or me, then Claudia was fully capable—"

The doorbell rang, and Philippe grunted. He excused himself, and with some effort pushed himself upright from his chair.

I finally tasted the wine. A ninety-seven, I ventured, before checking the label. It was a seventy-six.

From down the hallway, I heard the front door open and voices raised in what sounded like an argument. A moment later, Philippe appeared in the doorway to the sitting room.

"It's the police," he announced. "They say they're executing a search warrant."

13

Regan lay in full sun reading a magazine, while Mayday's chaise longue had been pulled back into the shade. Both women wore small bikinis, and both were sipping piña coladas garnished with little red cherries.

I tossed Herrera's discovery file and my *New York Times Sunday Magazine* onto the chaise between them.

"I see you've started without me."

Regan lifted her sunglasses. "Where have you been? It's almost time to get ready for dinner."

"Investigating," I told them, just as the cute little brunette I remembered from last month's visit—the one from the fitness center service bar—approached us with a tray. Today she wore khaki short-shorts, a Napa Springs Spa golf shirt, and the burnt-umber complexion of Jersey Shore Barbie.

"Hi. Do you remember that green health-shake concoction that Clarkson had me drinking here last month?"

"Sure, I remember you."

"Good. Whatever you do, do *not* bring me one of those. I'll have a cold Budweiser, hold the lime, hold the glass."

It was nearly six o'clock, and the sun was preparing to nest itself high in the treetops. I dragged my chaise to face it, peeled off my Loyola Law T-shirt, and resumed the crossword I'd started on the airplane.

"Investigating?" Regan was sitting up now. "I thought that was my job. And please don't tell me you entered the crime scene, because that's a major no-no."

"I know. Philippe's already scolded me."

Mayday glanced over her iPad. "Philippe Giroux?"

"The same. He invited me into his man cave. We pulled a cork and discussed bad apples."

I filled them in, up to the part when six sheriff's deputies arrived with a search warrant and began emptying the contents of Philippe's home office into cardboard boxes marked EVIDENCE.

Mayday had set her tablet aside. "You think they're looking for a financial motive?"

"That would be my guess."

The clue for nineteen-across was *Muddle,* nine letters, starting with *o* and ending in *e.* I took a flyer on *obfuscate.*

"But why are they targeting Philippe?"

"They're not. They also had warrants for the Visitor Center, for Claudia's house, and for Lourdes and Phil's house. I didn't hang around to watch."

The bar girl, whose name tag read RACHEL, returned with a frosty-cold Bud and a bowl of cocktail peanuts. I could have kissed her. In fact, I put it on my to-do list.

Regan swung the foot of her chaise to face me. "Wait, so her father claims that Claudia fabricated the credit card evidence without telling him, but he has no idea why?"

I nodded. "I'm guessing he still doesn't know about Clarkson."

"I'm not following."

"Think about it. If Claudia's telling the truth, and if her father's the one who put her up to the credit card stunt, then we know why she double-crossed him."

"To help Clarkson, by assuring a favorable court ruling."

"Right. So what if Philippe is telling the truth?"

She considered it. "I suppose the same reasoning applies. Claudia feared there wasn't enough evidence of Alain's death, so she figured if she fabricated contrary evidence, and then got caught doing it, the judge would have no choice but to rule in Phil's favor, which still would have benefited Clarkson."

"Okay," I told her, "so even if Philippe is lying, he could still be in the dark as to why his daughter double-crossed him."

"Because he doesn't know about the relationship between Claudia and Clarkson."

"Exactly. And if Philippe *is* telling the truth, then he'd be even further in the dark, wondering why his daughter cooked up the whole Alain-is-alive canard in the first place."

I needed thirteen-down, *Dogged,* eleven letters, starting with *u* and including an *r* and an *m.*

"So," Regan said, "you think Philippe is telling the truth, and that it was all Claudia's idea?"

"I don't know. When Philippe told me that, I believed him. But when Clarkson told us otherwise, I believed him, too."

"And why do we even care about the credit card scam? Isn't that water under the bridge?"

"Because," Mayday told her, "whoever's lying about the credit card might also be lying about Phil's murder. A witness who's willfully false in one part of her testimony should be distrusted in the rest."

Mayday was paraphrasing a California jury instruction. The actual language was:

> *A witness, who is willfully false in one material part of his or her testimony, is to be distrusted in others. You may reject the whole testimony of a witness who willfully has testified falsely as to a material point, unless, from all the evidence, you believe the probability of truth favors his or her testimony in other particulars.*

I've always said it was one of the few jury instructions with general application beyond the four walls of the courtroom.

Regan was frowning. "I hope you're not suggesting we go back to investigating the credit card fraud."

"No," I told her. "At the end of the day, it's Philippe's word against Claudia's."

"And Clarkson's."

"Not necessarily. Claudia could have lied to Clarkson as well. Set the whole thing up herself, all while attributing it to Philippe."

"But why would she lie to Clarkson? In fact, wouldn't she have wanted to take the credit? You know, look at all the trouble I went through on your behalf, honey? Look how much I love you?"

Mayday was nodding. "Regan's right. Why would Claudia, if she'd planned the whole thing herself, have told Clarkson otherwise?"

"I can think of one reason," I said. "She would have anticipated the perjury rap. By telling Clarkson it was Philippe's idea, then later blaming Philippe, she made Clarkson a corroborating witness."

"I don't know," Regan said. "You're talking about a lot of forethought, a lot of advance planning."

I returned to the puzzle, and inked in *unremitting*.

"I know. It would almost take a sociopath to have carried it out."

Like Generalissimo Francisco Franco, Pilate's Trattoria was still dead, with only three of its inside tables occupied for dinner. We dined al fresco, and but for the marble woman in the flowing robes, we had the patio all to ourselves.

Dusk had settled on the eastern flank of the valley, painting the fairway below us in shades of blue and gray. Even the fountain in the lake had called it quits, leaving a glassy black surface that reflected the rising quarter moon.

"I wonder what they're feeding her in jail?"

Clarkson posed the question to his poached sea bass, which he prodded listlessly with a fork. Despite a shower, a shave, and probably a nap, our host still looked like a kid who'd broken the string on his birthday balloon.

"I'm sure she's fine," I assured him. "With all the press she's been getting, she's probably having dinner with the warden."

My cell phone vibrated. The caller ID read TERINA WEBB. I showed it to Mayday before sending the call to voice mail.

Mayday told him, "We caught some of the news coverage on television. It's becoming quite the national story."

"Great. That's just what she needs."

"So Andy," I said, instinctively lowering my voice, "this may be a little bit delicate, but Philippe mentioned something I wasn't aware of, involving Claudia's time at Berkeley. . . ."

"You mean her so-called overdose?"

I glanced at Mayday. "So-called?"

"Look, there's nothing to it. Claudia was in a bad place, that's all, what with her mother's death and then the pressures of school and everything. Apparently, she took a few pills and went to the hospital. She told me it wasn't really a suicide attempt. That if she'd wanted to kill herself, she knew how to do it. My theory is it was more like a cry for help, or attention, or whatever. From her father. Christ, she was only twenty-two or twenty-three. They let her back into school, and she went on to graduate with honors. It's not like she's nuts or anything. Far from it. She's about the most focused person I've ever met in my life."

"Who else knew about this?"

"Nobody. Well, Philippe, obviously, and maybe Phil and Alain, but I'm not even sure about that. Trust me, that's a family that knows how to keep secrets."

"Can they use the suicide attempt against her?" Regan asked me.

"It's complicated, but probably not. First they'd have to find out about it. Then Claudia would have to testify. Then she'd have to put her mental condition in evidence somehow. The laws protecting your medical and mental health privacy are pretty strict."

Mayday said, "I have a question. How did Lourdes become so involved with the United Farm Workers?"

Clarkson shrugged. "If you want my opinion, it's a case of ethnic guilt. Lourdes grew up on Long Island, for Christ sake, and she barely speaks

Spanish. But she got into social work after college, and from there into the labor movement. Union organizing. That's how she first met Phil. She was picketing Château Giroux with the UFW. That was around twelve years ago."

"Talk about meeting cute."

"I'm not a shrink, but I think that once she married into the family, she's had to make a point of proving that she hasn't sold out her principles. According to Claudia, the union's been threatening Philippe with another strike. Overtime wages, I think, or maybe heat regulations. Anyway, Philippe blames Lourdes for pushing the strike, for using it as an opportunity to burnish her antimanagement credentials."

Regan asked me, "Where was Lourdes when Phil was killed?"

"According to the sheriff's investigation report, she was at a UFW meeting at that church she attends in Napa. There are a dozen corroborating witnesses, including a priest."

"And where was Philippe?"

"At home in the château. Alone, apparently. The guy who found the body, McAfee, went to the château first, and then to Claudia's place."

Clarkson looked up from his plate. "Can I ask you a question about this search warrant business? Like, do we even know what they were looking for? Or what they might have taken from Claudia's office? Isn't there like a receipt or something they have to give you?"

"There is, and they probably left it with Philippe. We're surmising they were after financial records. Checkbooks, bank statements, computer files. Anything that might evidence a financial motive on Claudia's part for wanting to kill her brother."

"Financial motive?"

I explained to him the significance of motive, both as it relates to evidence of guilt and, in this case, to the availability of bail.

"Are you saying they could ask for the *death penalty*?" Clarkson laid down his fork. "Is this some kind of a joke?"

"Relax, Andy. Searching the home of a murder defendant is standard procedure. Don't read too much into it."

"Christ," he said, slamming his napkin and shoving away from the table. He stood and walked to the balustrade, his hand caressing the statue's marble robes. Like me, Clarkson was a pacer. After a brisk back-and-forth, he turned on his heel. We watched in silence as he pushed through the glass doorway into the restaurant.

"That went well," Regan said.

Mayday said nothing, her gaze still on the statue.

"What?"

"Pilate's Trattoria," Mayday said, inclining her head. "The wife of Pontius Pilate was named Claudia. It's a Roman name, the feminine of Claudius."

Now we all looked at the statue.

"What are you suggesting?"

"I don't know. The Romanesque architecture, the statue, the restaurant name. It's like this whole resort is some kind of a temple, with Claudia at its center like a sacred icon."

Again our eyes moved to the statue.

"That's either very romantic," Regan said, "or else it's really, really creepy."

The glass doors opened again, and Clarkson strode to the table, tucking his cell phone away.

"I'm sorry," he said, arranging the napkin in his lap. "I don't normally lose it like that. It's just that it's all very frustrating, this legal mumbo jumbo. So tell me the truth—what are the chances she'll make bail on Wednesday? It would kill her to miss her brother's funeral."

I'd wanted Clarkson to have a few glasses of Chianti under his belt before we got to this part of the conversation.

"Here's the thing about bail, Andy. Even if she's eligible, which means even if we win on Wednesday morning, we're still looking at a million dollars minimum for a charge of murder. That means putting up security in that amount, plus a ten-percent premium in cash. It's a cinch her father's not going to help us, so it's probably up to you."

"Sure." He didn't even blink. "That's not a problem."

I turned to Mayday, who lifted her eyebrows.

"All right, we'll make the arrangements. We'll also turn Regan loose on the witnesses we know about so far—McAfee, Gagne, and Harding. Plus she'll try to find someone who might have seen Claudia leaving the winery."

"Won't the police have plowed that ground already?"

"Yes, so don't get your hopes up. But maybe we'll get lucky. Stranger things have happened."

Clarkson's phone rang, and he checked the caller ID.

"Excuse me," he said, standing again. "I have to take this."

We watched again as he retreated inside. This time he stood in the corner of the restaurant farthest from the other diners. He spoke into the phone with his head down. He made a chopping gesture with his hand.

Regan asked, "Do you really want me to reinterview all the witnesses the D.A.'s already talked to?"

"No," I told her, still watching our host through the glass. "I said that for his benefit. What I really want you to do is put a tail on Andy Clarkson."

14

In June of 1958, in the pine woods of rural Maryland, John Brady and
Donald Boblit made plans to rob a bank. In need of a getaway car,
they decided to steal one from a mutual acquaintance, one William
Brooks. Late in the evening of June 27, Brady and Boblit placed a log
across the dirt road leading to Brooks's house and then waited for him to
come home. When Brooks alighted from his car to move the log, the two
would-be Dillingers knocked him on the head with a shotgun and placed
him in the backseat of his car. They then drove to a secluded field, walked
their groggy prisoner to the edge of the woods, and strangled him to
death with a shirt.

Boy Scouts they were not.

After both were arrested for Brooks's murder, Brady and Boblit each
gave a series of conflicting statements to the police. Brady consistently
accused Boblit of being the killer, whereas Boblit, after initially blaming
Brady, finally confessed on July 9, 1958, that it was he who'd done the actual deed.

They received separate trials. Prior to Brady's trial—the first to be
held—the defendant's lawyers asked the prosecution for copies of any
confessions made by Boblit, to which the prosecution responded by

turning over all of Boblit's statements to the police. All, that is, except for the one given by Boblit on July 9.

Brady was tried, convicted of first-degree murder, and sentenced to death. Some months after the conviction, Brady's new lawyers read the transcript of Boblit's trial, in which the July 9 confession had been introduced into evidence by the prosecution in order to convict Boblit. They cried foul. Specifically, they filed a post-conviction motion seeking a new trial for Brady based on newly discovered evidence. That motion was denied by the trial court, and a series of appeals ensued, eventually landing the case on the docket of the United States Supreme Court.

In *Brady v. Maryland,* the court ruled on May 13, 1963, that state prosecutorial agencies have an affirmative duty to disclose to criminal defendants any and all exculpatory evidence material to the issues of guilt or punishment, and that the failure to make such disclosure violates the Due Process Clause of the United States Constitution. Later, in 1976, the Supreme Court extended *Brady* by holding, in *United States v. Agurs,* that a state prosecutor's *Brady* obligation applies even in the absence of a formal discovery request by the defense.

All of which goes to explain the telephone call that preempted my breakfast on Tuesday, our second day in Napa Valley and the morning after our dinner at Pilate's Trattoria.

I'd woken at seven to the smell of fresh coffee, and stumbled from my bedroom to find Mayday in the kitchenette of our little guest suite, her iPad propped upright before her, a hollowed-out grapefruit still reposing on her plate.

"You're up early," I said, pouring myself a cup.

"I saw Regan off at six. Fortunately, she'd packed a thermos."

"Cop habits die hard." I kicked back a chair and sat at the table and regarded the back of her tablet.

"SpongeBob?"

She looked up from her reading and turned the iPad to face me. The screen bore a red "CNN/Justice" banner above the headline "Plea Entered in Winery Slaying: Widow Fingers Giroux Family Patriarch in Dramatic Courtroom Showdown."

Below the headline was a color photo of a veiled Lourdes Giroux doing a back bend into the startled arms of Andy Clarkson. It looked like that famous photo from V-J Day, or maybe a promo still from *Dancing with the Stars.*

"Do you think they'd have phrased it that way if the sexes were reversed?"

Mayday ignoring me, resumed her reading.

"This says Lourdes is holding a press conference today at the Château Giroux Visitor Center at two o'clock, and that she's expected to announce a reward for information leading to the arrest of her husband's killer."

"Wonderful."

She looked up again. "We don't welcome the public's help?"

"We don't welcome every loose nut in the coffee can rolling up here on some kind of a treasure hunt. Plus, where's Lourdes getting the money for a reward? Last I heard, she couldn't afford to move."

Mayday swiped at her screen. "I've been reading up on Lourdes Martinez-Giroux. Did you know that she sits on several charity boards, and that one of them is the Rural Food Project of the Roman Catholic Diocese of Santa Rosa, California?"

She gave me a meaningful look.

"Not so fast," I told her. "With Phil dead, then the Church gets Château Giroux, but with Phil alive—"

"I know, I know. I just thought it was interesting, that's all. Another piece of a jigsaw puzzle in which no two pieces quite fit together."

"Brought to you by a family that knows how to keep its secrets."

"What?"

"I'm quoting Clarkson, remember? About Claudia's suicide attempt that wasn't."

Mayday powered off her tablet and closed the case. "I also found a bail bondsman who checks out. Do you want me to call him?"

"No, I want you to visit him and make the arrangements in person and see if you can negotiate down the premium. Then, depending on what Regan comes up with—"

And that's when my cell phone vibrated, skittering in a little half-circle on the Formica tabletop. The caller ID read HERRERA.

I showed the readout to Mayday before swiping the screen.

"MacTaggart."

"Jack? It's Ron Herrera. Sorry to call you so early, but we need to have a little talk. How's about I buy you breakfast? I think you'll be glad that I did."

Mayday dropped me at the Starbucks nearest the Napa County courthouse, where I entered to find Herrera and Yolanda Walker huddled at a corner table already littered with the remains of their breakfasts. I ordered an orange juice and a bran muffin from the tattooed barista, and I nabbed a copy of the *Chronicle* on my way over to join them. Herrera stood at my approach, sinking a hand into his pocket.

"Here, let me pay for that."

"Uh-uh, no you don't." I waved him off. "I can't be bought at any price. At least not without eggs Benedict."

They moved some papers, clearing a space for me to sit. I laid out my breakfast, using the torn muffin bag as a placemat.

"Hell of a photo," Walker said, nodding to the front-page, above-the-fold image of Lourdes's infamous back bend. "You ask me, I think she was hoping he'd kiss her. Not that I blame her. That is one good-looking man."

Herrera cleared his throat.

"As you already know," he said, "the sheriff's department executed a series of search warrants yesterday at Château Giroux. Which begs the question of why you were there with Philippe. I thought he was no longer your client."

"He isn't. I was asking his advice about wine. I was thinking of investing in a nineteen fifty-nine Dom Pérignon Rosé. Did you know that since nineteen twenty-one there have been fewer than fifty vintages—"

"All right, never mind. The results of the search warrants are being analyzed as we speak, and I'm sure we'll be issuing follow-up subpoenas, but with the bail hearing set for tomorrow, we thought it prudent to make a *Brady* disclosure today, which is why we've asked you to join us."

He handed me a single sheet of paper. It was a page from a Merrill Lynch brokerage statement, for the personal account of Philippe Giroux.

"This is your disclosure?"

"Read it."

It was a check register, showing deposits made and checks issued during the month of July, with one of the entries highlighted in yellow.

"Henri LaBoutin," I read aloud. "A hundred thousand dollars."

"Philippe Giroux's gardener," Herrera said. "The check was issued on July thirty-first, two weeks before LaBoutin moved off the Château Giroux property. Almost a month before Phil Giroux was murdered."

"Allegedly murdered. What is it, some kind of a severance payment?"

"We think that's what he'll call it," Walker said, "but the gardener was only earning eight hundred a week. Plus you'll note it's a cashier's check."

"LaBoutin's wife was Giroux's chef," I told them.

"So we've heard," Herrera said. "But that's not all."

Walker reached down to the floor and hefted an oversized leather bag into her lap. From it she extracted another, multi-page document.

"The payment to LaBoutin caught our eye, of course, so we checked him out. Turns out he's got quite the little record over in France. Assault, assault with a deadly weapon, mayhem. When he moved to the United States, he was still on probation. Had to get a special visa from the State Department. Giroux sponsored him, claiming he had special skills and guaranteeing his job at the winery."

She showed me LaBoutin's immigration documents. They referenced eight criminal priors, all for acts of physical violence. The guy'd broken more bones than a black-diamond ski run.

"Maybe it's nothing," Herrera said. "But still."

"Where's LaBoutin now?"

"That we don't know."

I handed the documents back to Walker.

"All right, so let's recap. We have a violent felon who's paid a hundred

grand in cash, essentially, by the father of the victim, and who then disappears two weeks before the murder? I'd call that more than nothing. In
fact, I think you've cracked the case. Congratulations. I assume you'll be
dropping the charges against my client?"

Herrera smiled. "Save it for the jury, counsel. Claudia's still our prime
suspect, and her prints are still on the murder weapon. But given this . . .
development, we wanted to extend an invitation."

"We have an appointment with Philippe Giroux in less than an hour,"
Walker said, checking her watch. "He's lawyered up, apparently. And
since the meeting is likely to generate further *Brady* material, we thought
it would be simpler just to have you come along and sit in."

"With only one proviso," Herrera added, draining his coffee and gathering up his trash. "We do all the talking."

Like mushrooms after a warm spring rain, the trio of news vans outside the Château Giroux Visitor Center had grown to over a dozen, and
the arrival of Herrera's official county vehicle set off a mini-stampede. The
car was mobbed before it had stopped, and the camera lenses pressed like
so many suction cups to the windows triggered a childhood memory of
Captain Nemo's submarine in the grip of a giant squid.

"Lord have mercy," Walker said.

"Happens wherever I go," I told her, unbuckling my seat belt. "Whatever you do, don't look them in the eye."

We forced our way out of the car and across the parking lot to the
Visitor Center, where a uniformed guard—a new addition to the tasting
menu—stood watch at the door. Once inside the lobby, the cameras still
flashing through the plate glass behind us, we were escorted through the
tasting room and then down the back hallway to what I'd come to regard
as Claudia's office.

Philippe stood to greet us, as did an older, bearded gentleman in a
khaki summer suit that he'd paired with a green bow tie and yellow silk
hankie. Together with Philippe's purple ascot, they looked like the Mor-
timer brothers, Duke and Randolph, from the film *Trading Places*.

"Hello, Ron," the graybeard said as he offered a liver-spotted hand to Herrera. "As I said on the telephone, you have our full cooperation in this matter."

Herrera introduced us. I recognized the name, Thaddeus Melchior, from my very first meeting with Philippe over a month earlier. He was the guy who'd been corporate counsel to Giroux Beverage, but who'd recused himself from the dispute between Philippe and Phil on conflict-of-interest grounds.

I was somewhat conflicted myself—torn between thanking him and kicking him in the shin.

"You know I only do contracts," Melchior said to Herrera, but with his eyes still focused on me. "So you'll pardon my ignorance in asking if this is technically proper?"

He was referring, I believe, to my presence at his client's interview.

"We can exclude him," Herrera said. "That's certainly your right. But in all likelihood, I'll have to disclose to Mr. MacTaggart everything we discuss, so I was just hoping to save myself some paperwork."

"Well then, by all means." Melchior chuckled, giving me a pat on the shoulder. "We lawyers know all about paperwork, don't we, Jack? Come sit, come sit."

We took our places around the coffee table, and before we could even start with the small talk, Walker withdrew a file from her bag and passed it to her boss. Herrera removed a page from the file and handed it to Melchior.

"Among the documents we obtained with our search warrant," Herrera told him, "was a brokerage statement evidencing a payment made by your client to an Henri LaBoutin on July thirty-first. Given the size of that payment, we wanted to ask its purpose."

Melchior showed the page to Philippe, who donned reading glasses from an inside pocket of his blazer.

"Henri LaBoutin worked for me," Philippe said. "He was my gardener, responsible for upkeep around the château and the other family residences. He'd worked for me for over ten years, as had his wife. Mr. MacTaggart has met Frederique, who was my personal chef."

"And the payment?"

Philippe leaned back in his chair.

"Henri and Frederique were leaving my employment." Philippe removed the glasses and returned them to his pocket. "This payment represents severance—a reward for ten years of loyal and dedicated service."

"It's rather unusual," Herrera said, taking the words from my mouth, "to pay severance with a cashier's check."

"Yes, I suppose it is. But Henri had closed his bank account, and they needed immediate funds for their moving and other expenses. Furniture, things of that nature. A new car. Having lived at Château Giroux ever since their arrival from France, they didn't have any of those things."

"They could have charged them on a credit card while a regular check cleared the bank."

Philippe shook his head. "As far as I know, the only credit card they ever had was the one issued to them by Giroux Beverage. They surrendered that, of course, when they left our employment."

"Where did they go?" Walker asked, causing Philippe to shift in his chair.

"Dashed if I know. Henri said something about a job opportunity out of state. I tried to inquire, but he didn't seem to want to talk about it. Wouldn't even accept a ride to the airport. Frankly, I didn't care about Henri leaving, or where he went. Frederique, on the other hand, was a great loss. Good private chefs, as Thad will tell you, are difficult to find."

My cell phone vibrated as Philippe and his lawyer debated the vagaries of domestic employment. It was Regan, and I reluctantly sent it to voice mail.

Walker said, "You must have some way to contact Mr. LaBoutin. A phone number?"

"Henri was issued a company cell phone, which he also returned. The same with Frederique."

"A hundred thousand dollars is quite a generous severance for a cook and a gardener," Herrera said, again echoing my thoughts. "I would think two or three months' wages is more the norm."

The old man nodded. "You're probably right, but I calculated five thousand dollars for every year of service. Times two, of course. I believe my math is correct."

His math was flawless, not to mention convenient. Walker, meanwhile, had removed what I recognized as the immigration documents from her bag.

"Mr. LaBoutin appears to have had some problems with the law over in France," she said to Philippe, who shook his head with a knowing sadness.

"Frederique graduated Le Cordon Bleu, and she came with excellent references, but also, I'm afraid, with certain baggage. Henri was a football hooligan. A crude man, to say the least. What Frederique saw in him, I'll never really know." He turned to Melchior. "L'amour est aveugle."

"You can understand our curiosity," Herrera pressed. "A man with a record of violent crime who's paid a large sum of money and then disappears without a trace two weeks before your son is killed . . ."

Melchior, straightening in his chair, had finally caught the drift.

"Hold on a minute. You're not suggesting Philippe had anything to do with his own boy's murder, are you? Because that's a hell of an accusation to make, and I needn't remind you that to do so in public would be slanderous per se and would cause irreparable damage both to—"

"It's all right, Thad." Philippe patted his lawyer's knee. "The district attorney is under a great deal of pressure, what with the press camped on his doorstep and Mr. MacTaggart clinging to his tail. I'm sure he meant no offense."

"Still," Melchior huffed. "The temerity."

"But you'll concede it's a fair summary?"

"What I'll concede is this," Philippe told Herrera, leaning forward and brushing aside a restraining hand from his lawyer. "Both my sons are dead, and my daughter is in jail, and all of the records I need to conduct my business have been carted off by your jack-booted storm troopers! God only knows what I've done to deserve any of this, but I can assure you of one thing. No matter what fairy tales my daughter has been telling you, I can assure you that neither I nor Henri LaBoutin had anything whatsoever to do with Philip's murder."

"You already have the murder weapon with the killer's fingerprints on it," Melchior added, rising to his client's defense. "For God's sake, Ron, what more do you need?"

Walker shot me a glance before shifting again to face Philippe.

"Why would your daughter want to kill her own brother, Mr. Giroux?"

"Why don't you ask her?" Melchior interjected. "Perhaps she was jealous, what with her brother about to inherit the business. Or maybe she just snapped. There's nothing *rational* about murder, Miss Walker. By definition, it requires an irrational state of mind. And on that subject, I trust you're aware of Claudia's mental health history?"

"Her what?"

"Now, Thad—"

"Objection," I said, lifting from my seat and earning eye-daggers from both sides of the coffee table. "My client's medical history is neither relevant nor public, and any disclosure of same would violate her Constitutional right of privacy."

"Of course, Mr. MacTaggart, of course." Melchior's eyes were dancing now. "We'll leave that small detail for the district attorney to decide. Or better yet, for the court."

15

What mental health history?" Walker demanded, turning to face me.

We stood in the tasting room, drawing looks from the crowd at the bar. I moved to the farthest corner of the boutique, where the D.A. and his sidekick followed.

"Never mind that. What about the gardener?"

Walker had left her scowl in place. "Giroux admits that the severance payment was overly generous, but he explained it to my satisfaction." She glanced at her boss. At the end of the day, there's no physical evidence linking LaBoutin to the crime scene, so even if we could find him, what's he going to say? I'd call it a dead end."

"The severance story is bullshit, and you know it. A hundred grand? A cashier's check? And now the guy's vanished into thin air?"

"Keep your voice down," Herrera said, looking toward the bar. "For the sake of argument, let's say I was to pull resources away from the investigation in order to find this LaBoutin character and interview him. He'll say he was paid severance. Okay, so then what? You want us to waterboard him? Without a link to the crime scene, it's a total waste of time."

"I don't believe this!"

"Here's a piece of free advice, MacTaggart. Instead of chasing after shadows, maybe you should take a closer look at your own client. Don't forget, I read that hearing transcript. She lied to you once, my friend, and she hung you out to dry. What makes you so positive she isn't doing it again?"

"What makes you think you can just ignore evidence that doesn't fit your pet theory of the case?"

Walker put a hand on her hip. "You really think the old man's good for it? First he puts a hit on his son, and then he frames his own daughter, all so the Church can take his winery? Is that your brilliant theory?"

"First he was your client," Herrera reminded me, "and now he's some kind of homicidal maniac? Because without a financial motive, that's what he'd have to be."

"That's the missing link," I told them. "You said so yourself, there's always a motive. Right now we're playing blind man's bluff. We find the motive, and the blindfold falls away."

"When the blindfold falls away," Walker said, "you may not like what you see."

What I saw, over her shoulder, was a familiar face—Larry the Driver's—entering from the lobby. He paused under the archway to survey the tasting room.

Herrera checked his watch. "You want a ride somewhere? We need to get back to the office."

"I wouldn't want to take any resources away from your investigation."

"Suit yourself," Walker said, pulling her boss by the arm. "Come on, Ron. Mr. MacTaggart looks like he could use a walk to clear his head."

As they strode for the exit, they passed Larry under the archway where, I noted, there were no signs of recognition. When Larry continued across the room toward the hallway door, I grabbed a couple of T-shirts from a display rack.

"Excuse me, but do you like the crew neck better, or the tank?"

"Mr. MacTaggart!" He grinned and pumped my hand. "Great to see you again." Then, looking around, he added in a lower voice, "And thank you for everything you're doing."

"I was shoplifting."

"No, I mean defending Miss Giroux. I can't believe the cops would think she killed her own brother."

"Matter of fact, I was hoping you and I could talk about that. Plus I need a lift back to Napa Springs Spa. Any chance I could mooch a ride in the company car?"

"Sure." He looked to the hallway door. "But first I need to check in with the boss. If he doesn't need me, then I'm all yours."

While Larry popped in on Philippe, I checked my voice messages. There were two—Regan's call from this morning, and yesterday's call from Terina Webb about which I'd totally forgotten. The newswoman, as was her custom, got straight to the point:

"Jack? It's Terina Webb. I'm heading up to Napa tomorrow to get in on the Giroux action. I told my producer I had an inside track, so don't make a liar out of me. I'll call you when I get up there. I'm counting on you for my six o'clock broadcast."

Regan's message, left at 10:18 this morning, was more subdued in tone. From the traffic sounds in the background, I knew she was calling from her car:

"Hey, it's me, just checking in to report that Clarkson left his house at eight o'clock sharp. I followed him in traffic all the way to San Francisco, which was a heck of a good tail. Anyway, guess where he went? To the Wells Fargo Bank branch in Pacific Heights. He was inside for a half hour, and now he's out again, and we're headed back toward Napa. No traffic this direction, so we'll make good time. Give me a call when you get this and let me know how long you want me to stay with him."

It was now ten-fifty. I thumbed the CALL BACK button.

"Jack?"

"Yeah, I just got your message. What's going on?"

"I'm still in the car, but now I'm sitting outside the Bank of Napa branch at Highway twenty-nine and Redwood Road. Clarkson came straight here from the city. He's been inside for five minutes or so."

"Busy banking day."

"You can say that again. What do you want me to do?"

"See where he goes next. If it's home or to Napa Springs Spa, then break it off. I'm at the winery right now. Lourdes is holding some kind of a press event here at two o'clock. I'm heading to Napa Springs now, and then I'm coming back here. Have you heard from Marta?"

"No, not yet."

"Okay. I hope to see you at the apartment, but if not, then let's plan to meet here at the winery at two."

"What are you doing at the winery?"

"Long story. I'll fill you in later."

I looked to the hallway door, and then I punched up Mayday.

"Hello?"

"Hey, it's me. Can you talk?"

"I'm just heading back to the apartment. How'd it go with Herrera?"

"I'm heading there as well, and I'll tell you in person. Meanwhile, can you do me a favor?"

"Sure."

"Can you lay your hands on that retainer check we got from Clarkson without crashing into a drunk driver?"

"Sure, hold on, it's in my bag. Wait a minute. Okay, I've got it."

"On what bank was the check drawn?'

"Wait a sec. Bank of Napa. Redwood Road branch."

The hornets' nest in front of the Visitor Center hadn't gone quiet, exactly, but the drones were sufficiently busy that Larry and I were able to slip from the front doors to the limo without being swarmed or stung.

"Okay if I ride up front?"

We drove a half loop around the parking lot, with both of us watching the three-ring circus of news trucks and equipment and reporters preparing to cover the afternoon press conference. Near as I could tell, Terina Webb was not yet among the latter.

"What do you know about this thing at two o'clock?" I asked Larry.

"Only what I heard on the radio. I guess Phil's wife is offering some kind of a reward. I think that's what the boss and his lawyer are meeting about."

He steered the Town Car into the long driveway, the olive trees speeding past us as he quietly accelerated.

"Has anyone questioned you about Phil's death?"

He looked at me and smiled. "Not until now."

"Mind if I ask when you first heard about it?"

His demeanor became somber. "I clock out on Sundays at five, so I went to the movies that night, and then I had a few beers. So it wasn't until yesterday morning, when the boss wanted a ride to the courthouse. I couldn't believe it. Phil was a real decent guy. Near as I could tell, everybody liked him. It makes no sense that he was murdered, especially at the winery. I mean, who would do such a thing?"

He slowed to check for traffic, then signaled and made the turn onto the county road.

"How was Philippe handling it?"

"I'm not supposed to talk about stuff like that, what's said in the car. Like a priest and what do you call that? The confessional. But I'll tell you he looked pretty numb. Almost like he was in shock. I mean, the poor guy loses two of his kids in the space of a year?" He shook his head. "That ain't right."

"I was sorry to hear that Frederique had left," I said, taking care in how I approached the subject. "What was that all about?"

"Beats me. She kept to herself, that one. Mostly spoke in French, and almost never to me. No great loss, if you want my opinion."

"What do you mean?"

"Did you ever meet Henri, the husband? He was a real piece of work. Always hustling, always working some angle. Making book. Breeding pigeons. Plus he smacked her around a little, but don't quote me on that. I say good riddance to the both of 'em, even if it means I do the grocery shopping."

He signaled again as we descended to Silverado Trail.

"When, exactly, did they leave?"

He considered it. "Around two weeks ago, middle of August. If they gave any notice, I didn't hear about it."

"Any idea where they went?"

He shook his head. "We weren't exactly close. Tell you what, though, I was surprised to hear they'd left. They had a pretty sweet deal here—cushy work, a house on the property, a company car. At least I never heard any complaints. Then again, I don't speak French."

Up ahead, the sign for Napa Springs Spa rose into view.

"I won't ask you to betray any confidences," I told him, "but I'm curious to know whether you've heard of any changes in the works at Château Giroux."

"What do you mean changes?"

"I don't know. Talk of bringing in new management, or laying off employees. Anything major."

Again he shook his head. "There's been a lot going on, what with Phil and Miss Giroux and all, but . . . nothing like that. Why, do you know something I don't?"

"I doubt that very much," I told him, fishing a C-note from my pocket as we slowed by the front entrance to the club.

"I can't take that, Mr. MacTaggart."

"I know you can't," I told him, dropping the bill into the cup holder, "but try to find it a good home."

On the fairway below us, a lefty with Phil Mickelson's swing hit it straight and long, his divot flying and his ball seeming to hang suspended in the heavy summer air before disappearing over the low rise that guarded the distant green. I figured the hole for a par five, which he'd just reached in two. He clapped a high-five with his playing partner.

"Nice shot," Regan said as the waitress returned with our lunch orders and we drifted back to the table.

Looking up from her iPad, Mayday shook her head at our approach. "Nothing," she said.

The waitress made an adjustment to our umbrella before beating it back inside to the air conditioning. It was incrementally cooler today, with the mid-day mercury just under ninety and enough breeze to bend the conical spray of the fairway water fountain. Even the statue seemed refreshed somehow, as if the breeze were actually rippling her marble robes.

"We'll find him eventually," Mayday added, setting her tablet aside. "LaBoutin is an uncommon name, and if he's moved out of state, he'll be getting a driver's license and registering a car and signing up for utilities. Buying new cell phones. There should be plenty of tracks to follow."

"Eventually doesn't cut it," I said, sawing into my sausage-and-cheese calzone. "It could take months for him to resurface."

"Which is why we should focus on trying to track him from this end," Regan said. "What about the check? He had to cash it somewhere, right? Probably at Philippe's bank. We could start there."

I shook my head. "Even if we could get past the banking secrecy laws, that wouldn't tell us anything about where he's headed."

"Okay then, what about his plane ticket? You said he was heading to the airport, right?"

"That's what Philippe said, but we don't know that for sure. Or when. Or which airport, Santa Rosa or Oakland or SFO. And what airline?"

"It's almost too perfect," Mayday said, her fork poised over her Mediterranean salad. "No car, no cell phone, no bank account, no credit cards, no forwarding address."

Regan nodded. "I was thinking the same thing. Like someone who was planning to disappear."

"Like someone who had help."

"Wouldn't Giroux Beverage need a forwarding address? To mail him his W-2, for instance?"

"In theory," I told her. "Sometime before next April."

My telephone vibrated, and I checked the caller ID.

"MacTaggart."

"Are you coming to this circle-jerk or what? It starts in forty minutes."

I winked at Mayday. "Welcome to wine country, Terina. Yes, it is a lovely day."

"Lovely my ass. We've been on the road since sunrise, it's hotter than hell's kitchen, and there's something like twenty sound trucks already here. It's like a goddamn broadcasters' convention."

"You should feel right at home."

"And I wasn't kidding about going on-air tonight. I need something nobody else has."

"Let me think for a minute. Not hairspray, certainly. Wait, I know! How about a code of broadcast ethics?"

"Very funny. Track me down when you get here. We'll go out afterward and drink some wine."

She rang off, and I pocketed my phone.

"I just thought of something," Mayday said. "If Philippe wanted to make Henri LaBoutin disappear, he could have flown him on his private jet."

"Maybe. But even private flight plans are a matter of public record. There are Web sites you can check."

Regan said, "So let's check. Meanwhile, what do we make of Clarkson's trip to the city? Is he moving money?"

"Nothing wrong with that. He just wrote us a retainer check, plus we told him to expect a hefty bail premium."

"Yeah, but why would he bank in the city, so far from where he lives and works?"

The waitress popped her head out to check on us. I asked her for *l'addition, s'il vous plait.* Or was it *il conto, per favore*?

"Hey, wait a minute," Regan said, straightening in her chair. "Henri and his wife lived on the estate, right?"

"That's what Larry said. There must be some kind of a guest house or servants' quarters."

"So if the D.A. didn't even know about LaBoutin until after he saw the brokerage statement . . ."

I nodded, catching her drift. "And if they don't care enough to even try to look for him now . . ."

We both turned our faces to Mayday.

"What?"

"Then *ipso facto*," I told her, "nobody's conducted a search of the LaBoutins' house."

16

After driving yet another lap around the packed parking lot, we settled for a makeshift space on a shady strip of grass on the north side of the winery building. The crowd that had gathered by the entrance to the Visitor Center consisted mostly of media types, but with a surprising number of tourists jostling for position among the tripods, cables, and open equipment cases.

Many of them, I had to believe, had been drinking.

The object of their attention—a portable wooden podium bristling with microphones—stood empty as yet, looking almost forlorn in the high afternoon sun.

"Where do you suppose she got the lectern?" Mayday asked as we threaded our way through the cars.

"Beats me. I know it wasn't from Philippe."

We took up positions at the back of the crowd. I craned my neck, searching for familiar faces, and spotted Terina Webb's to the left of the podium. The L.A. anchorwoman was talking with another blow-dried blonde in a business suit, both women thumbing away on their BlackBerries.

"I wonder if Philippe is watching from somewhere," Mayday said, lifting her gaze to the glass façade of the Visitor Center.

"Maybe through a sniper scope on the roof."

When Lourdes finally made her appearance it was not, as the crowd had expected, from the glass doors of the lobby, but from around the south side of the building. She wore her black widow's dress, this time without the veil, but with a pair of oversized shades. Her progress—slow and unsteady—would later be attributed to reticence, but I credited the stiletto heels that seemed to catch and twist in the soft grass of the lawn. Fortunately for Lourdes, Andy Clarkson walked beside her, his guiding hand on her arm.

The reporters pocketed cell phones and stamped out cigarettes as they moved into position, and what cameras weren't already mounted on the spindly forest of tripods were hefted onto shoulders as the crowd inched forward to listen.

"Hey," said a voice behind me. "You must be Jack."

The speaker was a kid of around twenty-five. He wore baggy shorts and flip-flops and a patchy three-day beard.

"That's right."

"I'm Ethan Scott," he said, lifting his Ray-Bans and offering his hand. "Antonio told you I was coming, right?"

Around me, heads were turning toward the voice—first a few, then a few more, the effect like ripples spreading outward in a pond.

Good afternoon.

Lourdes's amplified voice echoed in a metallic reverb across the crowded parking lot as she unfolded a sheet of paper.

Thank you all for coming today.

By now Ethan Scott's ripple of recognition had reached the cameras up front, a couple of which turned from the podium and began shoving backward through the crowd. Meanwhile, a throaty revving of diesel engines—a low chorus of rumbling and growling—rose up from the direction of the winery.

Lourdes was reading now. *As you know,* she began, her voice rising against the noise, *my husband, Phil Giroux, lost his life on Sunday evening, in what police are calling a homicide . . .*

Three yellow forklifts appeared from the side of the Visitor Center, lurching and trundling on the sidewalk. The crowd backed and parted and a camera toppled sideways as the big machines roared and beeped into position, forming a triangle around the podium.

Lourdes, her hand now visibly shaking, continued to read from her script as the engines revved and smoke belched and a fog of sooty haze began to envelop her where she stood.

After a futile minute of this, the crowd began to splinter. The civilians drifted off to their next tasting appointment while the reporters, hands cupped to ears, pressed closer to the podium. Many, however, simply turned their backs on the spectacle, opting instead to surround us with their cell phone cameras, snapping photo after photo of an oblivious Ethan Scott.

"Dude," he finally called to me over the roar of the engines. "I can't hear a word this lady is saying."

Lourdes sat with her shoulders hunched, her face buried in her hands.

"Can he get away with that?" Clarkson fumed, pacing the floor behind us where we'd gathered around Lourdes' kitchen table.

I turned around to face him. "Did you really think he'd sit by and let you use his winery as a backdrop while you publicly accused him of murder?"

"I wasn't going to accuse him!" Lourdes wailed, hot tears streaking her face. "I just wanted to offer a reward!"

"You mean Andy's reward," Mayday said, to which Lourdes nodded, unfolding her script.

" 'Fifty thousand dollars for information leading to the arrest and conviction of whoever did this terrible thing to my husband.' " She crumpled the paper in her fist. "And double if it leads to that greedy old bastard we already know is behind it."

"Don't you worry," Terina Webb said, leaning forward and patting Lourdes's hand. "We'll go live on my six o'clock broadcast. If we don't pull a twenty share, I'll post that reward myself."

"Well, there you have it." I stood and clapped a hand to Clarkson's shoulder. "We'll leave you two in Miss Webb's capable hands."

"Wait a minute," Terina protested. "Aren't you coming on?"

"I'd love to, you know I would, but we have a big day in court tomorrow, and I need some time to prepare. So if you'll excuse us?"

"What about you, Ethan?" Terina was standing now, eyeballing the movie star like a housecat eyes a canary. "I'm sure my audience would love to hear about your interest in the case."

The kid had been standing with his back to the table, studying a poster on the wall. He turned at the sound of his name.

"Uh, no thanks. Big day in court tomorrow, and we need to prepare."

The servants' quarters were sided in white clapboard, the paint peeling over the empty trash cans and the weedy garden out back. The old house was two stories tall, with maybe fifteen-hundred square feet under roof. An empty pigeon coop, its doors open and rusted, completed the vaguely Appalachian tableau.

"All that's missing is a dead horse," said the kid, and Mayday shushed him.

I dropped to a knee and studied the layout. The house stood in a clearing surrounded by live oaks whose trailing moss wafted like Tibetan prayer flags in the light summer breeze. The lawn out back was dead, its brown expanse bisected by a sagging clothesline. The nearest house—the one where Lourdes continued her post-press conference lament—was nearly a quarter mile away.

Satisfied that the coast was clear, I stood.

"Okay, let's go."

We moved single-file, scuttling across the clearing like inmates on a jailbreak. Regan was the first to reach the house, and she held the screen door while I tried the knob, putting my shoulder to the windowed door within.

"Locked."

"I'll check around front," the kid said, disappearing before we could stop him. Then we all flinched as he stumbled into something, the clang and crash flushing a cloud of small birds from the trees.

"I wish he'd stayed in the car," I said, rubbing my shoulder.

"I can't believe he's actually here," Mayday said. "I loved him in *Chelsea's Farm.*"

"If he thinks he's tagging along with us all week, he's in for a rude surprise."

"Oh, come on. He seems sincere."

"Yeah," Regan said, "and he's cute besides. He followed us home, Daddy, can't we keep him for a while?"

We heard another sound from the front of the house, then a dull thump, and then the slap, slap of flip-flops on a hardwood floor. After a moment, the kid's grinning mug appeared on the other side of the door. He removed his shades and pressed his face to the inside glass.

"Jesus H. Christ."

The back door entered into a utility room—washer and dryer, plastic sink, cheap laminate cabinets. The cabinets were empty but for a few fluorescent lightbulbs still in their plastic clamshell packaging.

"Nothing here."

The kid asked, "What are we looking for, anyway?"

"Marta's better judgment."

Mayday slapped my hand. "Anything that might tell us where the tenants went. They moved out around two weeks ago. Or at least we think they did."

We moved through an open doorway and into a good-sized kitchen. Light from the single window above the sink revealed a scarred wooden table and chairs, spotless counters, and a hulking six-burner range that clearly wasn't native to the environment.

"Check it out," the kid said, running his hands along the gleaming stovetop. "I need to get me one of these."

While the others rummaged the cabinets and drawers, I checked the stainless steel Sub-Zero fridge. It was empty save for an open box of baking soda.

"Here's something," Regan said.

The Napa County Yellow Pages, its cover scuffed and curled, lay nested in a drawer by the dishwasher.

"Dude, aren't you worried about fingerprints?" the kid asked as I took the book and set it on the table.

"We already know who was using it. It's where they went that's the issue."

I riffled the pages, looking for bookmarks or dog-ears, notes or circled entries. I found nothing.

"Zip."

Regan had gone ahead, and we joined her in a small living room with threadbare furniture arranged on creaking hardwood floors. This room was brighter, with the afternoon sunlight streaming through a trio of curtained windows in front, one of which stood partially open.

"Check under the cushions," I said, moving to close the window. "We'll split the money four ways."

Regan and the kid set about disassembling the couch and love seat, while Mayday and I examined the bookshelves flanking the fireplace. They were built-ins stocked with an assortment of hardcovers and paperbacks, two-thirds in English and one-third in French. The books were mysteries, mostly—*M is for Malice, Explosive Eighteen*—interspersed with a few dusty classics and a long row of old *Wine Spectator* magazines.

"There's nothing here," Regan said, from behind us "Not even lint."

We split up then—girls to the bathroom and boys to what looked like an office just off the main living room. The office was home to a heavy desk and chair, another faded love seat, and a low coffee table.

"Dude," the kid said after a minute. "Looks to me like everything's cleaned out. One thing's for sure, they didn't leave in a hurry."

"Or else someone cleaned up after them."

The upstairs level consisted of two bedrooms, another small bathroom, a linen closet, and a television room, all accessible off a carpeted hallway. Like the downstairs, all had been vacuumed and dusted, swept and polished to a fare-thee-well.

"Nothing," Regan said as we regrouped at the head of the staircase. "Our condo should be so clean."

"You know what's strange?" I said, examining the floor plan in my head. "There are two bedrooms, an office, and a family room, but no nursery."

"What do you mean?"

"Henri's wife, Frederique, was pregnant when I met her. She'd be around seven or eight months by now. You'd think they'd have set up a nursery."

Below us came the crunching sound of tires on gravel.

"Shh."

We held our breaths, listening first to the slam of a car door, then to the click and scratch of a key in the front-door lock.

"In here, quick."

We backed into the upstairs bathroom just as the door below us opened. Footsteps thudded and paused on the living room hardwood.

"Who is it?" Regan breathed in my ear as I knelt and peered through the door crack.

"I can't see."

"Hello?" called a voice from downstairs. It was a man's voice.

I stood. The four of us all but filled a narrow space with a tub-shower along one wall and a toilet and vanity in back. A window on the end wall cast a milky backlight, rendering my coconspirators in gray silhouette.

Below us, the footsteps moved off, booming and creaking.

"We could make a run for the front door," Mayday whispered while, behind her, Ethan Scott threw a latch and raised the bathroom window.

"Shh."

"There's a roof out here," he said with his head outside in the breeze. "We could climb out and make our way toward the back, then shimmy down the drain spout. I did a scene like that with Manuela Arcuri in *Roman Wedding*. Of course, the spout broke and we ended up in a fountain."

"We'd sound like a herd of elephants," I told him.

"Shh," Regan repeated, and we all heard the tread of footfalls on the stairs.

I eased aside the shower curtain, its plastic O-rings whispering on the rod, and one by one we stepped into the tub.

Muffled by carpeting, the footsteps paused in the hallway before turning left toward the master bedroom. I slid the curtain closed.

We were standing bumper-to-bumper, all of us facing the same direction. I had Mayday's ass in my lap and her hair pressed under my nose. She in turn was hugging the kid, who rear-ended Regan where she stood with her ear pressed to the tiled end-well.

The kid whispered, "Like I told Megan Fox when we did that bathtub scene in *Abattoir, Part Three:* I hope you'll forgive me if I have an erection. And I hope you'll forgive me if I don't."

Regan covered her mouth to giggle just as the footsteps in the hallway returned and the bathroom door swung inward on its hinges.

Our visitor entered and stood for the briefest of moments, then turned and disappeared, leaving the door wide open behind him.

I twisted my neck to watch through the gap in the curtain, and through the crack in the doorjamb saw the figure of a man pause once more before heading down the hallway.

A man in a green bow tie.

17

In the front row of the courtroom, Terina Webb stood with her foot on a chair looking down at the kid who sat stiffly in his dark suit and tie, newly clean-shaven, studying my every move. Terina had her notepad out and was scribbling as she spoke, the reporters behind her leaning in for a listen. I wouldn't swear to it, but from the length of her skirt and the angle of her pose, I think she was trying to give Ethan Scott an exclusive.

"Nervous?" I asked Claudia, who appeared thin and pale in her blue surgical scrubs. Despite dark circles under eyes devoid of makeup, she was still the prettiest woman in the room.

"Should I be?"

"So far," I reminded her, "I'm oh-for-one at the hearings you've attended."

Mayday and Regan reentered the courtroom in the company of a slender, ponytailed gent in a sport coat and faded jeans, a battered briefcase at his side. The guy nodded once to the bailiff before taking a seat by the door. He wore a Western-style bolo tie and four turquoise rings, and in any other context I'd have made him for a drug dealer.

"Mr. Green is in the house," I said to Claudia, who turned to watch as

Andy Clarkson rose from his seat and crossed the aisle to sit beside the bail bondsman.

I took a moment to survey the rest of the courtroom. Philippe Giroux sat in a middle row on the prosecution side of the aisle—a nonverbal declaration common both to weddings and court proceedings—while Regan took a seat directly behind me, next to the kid. Lourdes was nowhere to be seen this morning, wisely choosing to avoid both her father-in-law and the assembled armies of the fourth estate. Or maybe she was busy planning her husband's funeral.

"Isn't that . . . ?" Claudia asked, still turned, her gaze falling on Ethan Scott.

"Unfortunately."

"What's he doing here?"

"It's a long story."

Mayday passed through the gate while nodding to Walker and Herrera, both of whom were seated at the table opposite. She slid into the seat beside me.

"What are they plotting, I wonder?"

I looked. The D.A. and his lead investigator were now huddled and whispering, and the intensity of their discussion gave me a moment's pause just as the door behind the bench opened and the courtroom chatter subsided.

"All rise!"

The Honorable Walter Saxby, robed and ready, settled on the bench like a vulture on a telephone wire. His shoulders were hunched and his pink head was scanning the courtroom, his nose moving side to side, waiting for absolute quiet.

"In the matter of *People versus Giroux*," the judge began, "we have a number of reporters and spectators in the courtroom this morning, and I want it understood by those in attendance that we will have no talking, no gum chewing, no telephones, no photography, and no interruptions or outbursts of any kind during these proceedings." He appeared to be searching the courtroom for Lourdes. "Consider that an order, ladies and gentlemen, the violation of which will compel me to close these proceedings to the public."

He turned to where we sat at the defense table.

"Mr. MacTaggart, I believe this is your motion."

"Thank you, Your Honor," I began, standing to face the judge. "As the people must concede, my client, Miss Giroux, has no criminal record and represents no credible threat to public safety. And while the charges against her are indeed serious, the evidence to support those charges is circum-stantial at best, and is easily explained. In fact, the only evidence linking my client to her brother's death is, first of all, that she was seen entering the winery building shortly before Philip Giroux is alleged to have been killed, and secondly, that her fingerprints are alleged to be on a tool present at the scene—a tool commonly used in the wine-making process."

I took the complaint I'd been holding and tossed it, with a theatrical flourish, onto the table.

"There's nothing nefarious, Your Honor, about one winery employee visiting another during the workday, particularly when it's her own sib-ling. A sibling she loved, I might add, and had no reason or motive to harm. Secondly, even the district attorney will concede that the tool in question had been used by many of the winery workers, including the decedent, and bore all of their fingerprints."

Here I paused to look at Herrera, whose attention remained focused on the judge.

"At the risk of stating the obvious, I would submit to the court that the strongest evidence of my client's *innocence* in this case is the very evi-dence on which the people rely for their charge. That's because only an idiot would contemplate murder scant moments after having been seen entering the winery building by two eyewitnesses, and only an idiot would neglect to wipe her fingerprints off a weapon she'd just used to commit that murder."

The judge grunted, scribbling a note. I waited for him to finish.

"Allow me to assure the court that my client is no idiot. To the contrary, she is a successful, well-educated, well-known, and well-respected member of this community, caught up in a nightmare of circumstance and conjecture. But more important for purposes of today's proceedings, Miss Giroux has family, friends, employment, and deep roots in this community, and cannot be said to represent a flight risk should bail be granted."

For the grand finale, I again half-turned to Herrera, this time ticking the points off on my fingers.

"So to summarize, Your Honor: A weak and circumstantial case. No criminal record. No motive whatsoever. No risk of flight. No threat to public safety. For all of these reasons, the defense requests that Miss Giroux be admitted to bail in a nominal sum, or that she be released from custody on her own recognizance."

Having run short of both arguments and fingers, I sat. Claudia patted my knee under the table, while Ethan Scott leaned over the rail and murmured, "Awesome, dude."

The judge, now frowning at the kid, said, "For the people?"

Herrera stood and adjusted his eyeglasses.

"The evidence of the defendant's guilt in this matter is anything but weak, Your Honor. First, we have eyewitness testimony placing Miss Giroux at the scene of the crime at exactly five o'clock in the evening. Second, we have forensic evidence establishing the time of death at approximately five-thirty P.M. Third, we can and will prove both that the weapon used to kill Philip Giroux bears the defendant's fingerprints, and that the defendant was the last person to handle that weapon. Lastly, and despite Mr. MacTaggart's efforts to paint his client as a model of stability, we will demonstrate a history of mental illness and suicidal—"

"Objection!" I said, jumping to my feet. "The district attorney knows better than to make an argument like that in open court."

"Quite right, Mr. Herrera. If you have evidence for the court to consider *in camera,* then by all means let's go off the record."

The judge studied the district attorney who, realizing he'd overplayed his hand, began fumbling with some files on his table.

"Mr. Herrera?"

"In light of Mr. MacTaggart's objection," the D.A. said, "we'll reserve that issue for another day. Suffice it to say, Your Honor, that the people will prove both means and opportunity beyond a reasonable doubt, and will place the murder weapon directly in Miss Giroux's hands. And that brings us at last to the question of motive."

Herrera found the file he'd been looking for, and now he strolled over and dropped it onto our table.

"On Monday afternoon, Your Honor, the Napa County Sheriff's Department executed a series of search warrants at the Château Giroux winery. Among the items seized were two computers used by the defendant, Claudia Giroux, in the course of her duties as chief financial officer of Giroux Beverage, the winery's holding company. These computers were of particular interest to the people, given this defendant's recent history of secreting electronic data prior to offering perjured testimony in court."

I kept a poker face as Herrera stepped to the clerk's desk with another copy of the records I was now paging through. They were electronic bank statements from various accounts in the name of Giroux Beverage.

"While the material recovered from the defendant's computers is still being analyzed as we speak," Herrera continued, "it very clearly demonstrates a massive and long-running scheme by Miss Giroux to embezzle millions of dollars from the business accounts of Giroux Beverage, all for her own personal benefit. This is a scheme that appears to have been in effect for over seven years, Your Honor, and to have involved hundreds of fraudulent transactions. Needless to say, a superseding indictment will be forthcoming once the full extent of the defendant's embezzlement is known."

The courtroom had started to hum and the kid, leaning forward again, whispered, "Dude, this is bogus." Farther back in the courtroom, Philippe made an odd strangling sound. I turned to watch as he rose from his seat and lurched for the hallway door.

The judge banged his gavel.

"Order, I warn you. Mr. Herrera?"

The D.A. cleared his throat.

"The import of this evidence, Your Honor, is twofold. First, of course, is that it provides us with the motive Mr. MacTaggart claims has been missing from the people's case. As to the precise motive, we can only speculate at this point, but several possibilities suggest themselves. Perhaps the victim discovered his sister's crime and threatened to report it. Or, the accused may have feared the scrutiny that a change in ownership would bring to the books and records of the family business if her brother lived to inherit. Whichever it was, it's now perfectly clear that Miss Giroux had ample reason for wanting her brother dead."

Claudia, seated beside me, was staring into the half distance. Her fingers were tightly laced, and the color was draining from her hands.

"The second reason this evidence is important, Your Honor, is that the Penal Code precludes a defendant's admission to bail where, as in this case, the bail premium or collateral is unlawfully gained. For that reason alone, bail should and must be denied to this defendant, and the people ask that the court so rule."

Herrera sat. Again the judge used his gavel to silence the courtroom.

"Mr. MacTaggart?"

Outwardly placid, and with a smile frozen on my face, I was actually reeling inside—my nose bloodied and my ass on the canvas, the referee counting me out. This was the second time in as many bouts that I'd been sucker-punched by Claudia Giroux, and now I was torn between standing up to fight and rolling over to spit out my mouthpiece.

"Mr. MacTaggart? Any rebuttal?"

"Yes, Your Honor," I said, regaining my feet.

"The District Attorney has me at a disadvantage with his new allegations, as I suspect was his intention. But I'd remind the court that we're not here today to litigate an embezzlement case that the people haven't seen fit to file as yet, and may never get around to filing once all the facts are known. We're here on a bail motion in a case of first-degree murder. That's the case with the half-baked theory of guilt, the easily explained circumstantial evidence, and the defendant who's neither a risk of flight nor a threat to public safety. Given those realities, it's no wonder Mr. Herrera feels the need to muddy the waters with new and equally wild accusations."

Frowning as he paged through the D.A.'s documents, the judge asked, "But what if the people are correct, Mr. MacTaggart, and the bail premium would be feloniously obtained?"

"Then the people have a clear statutory remedy, Your Honor. They can file a declaration of probable cause. Mr. Herrera hasn't bothered to do that. Moreover—"

"But this evidence only came to our attention this morning, Your Honor. If the court likes, we could take a recess—"

"Excuse me, I wasn't finished." I turned from Herrera back to the judge. "What I was going to say is that this is a nonissue in any event. The fact is that the bail premium in this case is being paid not by Miss Giroux, but by a friend, Mr. Andrew Clarkson, who's present in the courtroom this morning. So you see, we've been diverted yet again by one of Mr. Herrera's flights of speculative fancy."

If I'd learned anything in my decade before the bar, it's that being right is only half the battle, and the lesser half at that. Sometimes, all it takes is landing the last, clean punch.

"Very well," said the judge. "Is the matter submitted?"

"Submitted," I said, and after a moment, Herrera nodded.

"Submitted."

The courtroom fell silent as the judge made a steeple of his fingers, raising them to his lips. He looked at Claudia, frail and hauntingly beautiful, still lost in her thousand-yard stare.

"All right, gentlemen, I'm prepared to rule."

To my left, Mayday held her pen poised over a clean legal pad. Across the aisle, Herrera did likewise.

"In the matter of *People versus Giroux,* the court finds that while the charged offense is quite serious in nature, the defendant Claudia Giroux has no criminal record, does not pose a credible risk of bodily harm to others, and does not represent a significant risk of flight from this jurisdiction. For all of these reasons, it is the judgment of this court that the defendant be admitted to bail, but with the bail amount to be set at one million dollars."

Saxby turned to the D.A., who looked like a man watching his train pull away from the platform.

"Needless to say, Mr. Herrera, if the people wish to challenge the source of the bail premium, they can always file a declaration of probable cause. Furthermore, if new evidence comes to light that bears on any of the court's findings this morning, then the court will be happy to hear a motion to increase or revoke the defendant's bail. Fair enough?"

The D.A. looked down. He nodded. "Fair enough."

"Is time waived?"

I stood again. "It is, Your Honor."

The judge looked to his clerk, who said, "October tenth."

"Counsel?"

We each checked our calendars. I looked at Herrera, who again nodded his head.

"The tenth of October is fine."

Now the judge shifted in his chair and addressed himself directly to Claudia.

"Miss Giroux, you have a Constitutional right to a preliminary hearing within ten days from today's date. Do you knowingly and voluntarily waive that right so that the court can set a preliminary hearing on the date your lawyer and the district attorney have just agreed upon?"

Claudia's voice was barely audible. "Yes."

The judge stood.

"Then the matter is continued for a preliminary hearing in this courtroom on October the tenth at nine A.M."

He gave his gavel a ceremonial rap.

"The court will stand in recess."

Behind us, the reporters surged forward with their camera phones flashing, their shouted questions like hailstones pelting the seated figure of Claudia Giroux who, like the marble statue of her namesake, weathered them in stony silence.

I could hear Terina Webb hectoring Ethan Scott for his reaction to the court's ruling, while somewhere toward the back of the mob came the voice of Andy Clarkson, hoarsely shouting his girlfriend's name.

In the midst of it all, I leaned sideways toward my client and whispered in her ear.

"We need to have a little talk."

18

At the side door to the courthouse, video cameras were lifted onto shoulders as the television reporters—all of them women, all of whom had for the previous hour been amiably standing and chatting, smoking and texting—now jostled one another for position.

"It's like a wedding," the kid said, "when the bride gets ready to toss the bouquet."

"Or feeding time at the zoo."

"Or like right as your limo pulls up to the red carpet."

I glanced at him, both of us in our shirtsleeves, both slouched against the side of the rental car.

"I'll take your word on that one."

He lowered his head, scratching at the back of his neck.

"Did I just sound like a total dick?"

I didn't respond.

"Sorry, man. If it happens again, go ahead and slap me."

As much as I hated to say it, I was warming up to the kid, who, despite the hubbub that attended his every word and gesture, seemed to have both feet more or less firmly on the ground. Certainly more so than I would have had at his age, living the life he was leading.

"Tell me something. Do you like it?"

"What?"

"You know. The whole movie-star thing."

He thought about that for a minute. "It has its advantages, obviously."

"You mean the women."

"Yeah, but it's not just that. Somebody once said that the best part about being famous is that when you're at a party, and the conversation starts to get dull, the person you're talking to thinks it must be their fault."

We watched the reporters cluster, microphones at the ready, like picadors awaiting the bull.

"But what I do is bullshit compared to you," he said, turning to face me. "I mean, you make a difference in people's lives. Life or death, freedom or prison. That's the real deal, man. And that verbal jiujitsu—" he made a kung fu move with his hands—"that was some awesome shit. You took that guy's best arguments and turned them against him. That's exactly the kind of thing I was hoping to see by following you around."

"Tell me something. This screenplay of Bernadette's, is there any chance it'll actually be optioned for a film?"

"Who's Bernadette?"

"Bernadette Catalano, my secretary. Antonio's screenwriting student?"

The door finally opened. Claudia, with Clarkson's arm draped over her shoulder, stepped into the sunlight wearing the faded jeans and black T-shirt into which she must have changed on the night of her brother's murder. She walked with her head down as Clarkson cleared a path through the cameras with his free arm, like a lifeguard towing a drowning swimmer to shore.

Behind us, the doors to the other rental car opened.

"Look at the bright side," Mayday said, stretching and checking her watch. "At least now we know what we're dealing with."

"You're right about that," I told her. "For a while there I thought she might be innocent. Now I know she's innocent."

"What?"

Clarkson saw us at the curb and began paddling in our direction. The reporters, Terina Webb prominently among them, followed behind in a frothy wake.

I opened the rear door of the car.

"I'll explain later. Take Ethan with you. I'm guessing we're headed to the club, where there's security."

I drove, cabbie-style, with Clarkson and Claudia in the backseat, the former's arm still sheltering the latter like a Ming dynasty vase. I adjusted the mirror.

"I heard a good one yesterday. Larry, your father's driver, said that the inside of his car is like a confessional—that what's said in the limo stays in the limo. It's a nice concept, and today I'm expanding it to include rental cars."

Neither of them spoke.

"Oh, and just so you know, the D.A. wasn't kidding about a superseding indictment. For him it'll be like wearing a belt and suspenders. If he can't nail you for murder, then at least he has embezzlement to fall back on. And you can probably count on a civil lawsuit from your father."

Clarkson turned his face to the window. "Can we discuss this later?"

"Later? You mean after you've had a chance to collude on another fairy tale? I don't think so."

They didn't respond to that, so I checked the road behind us, where a phalanx of vehicles—Regan and Mayday, followed by a colorful caravan of cars and news vans—snaked for as far as the eye could see. My cell phone vibrated then, and I sent the call from Terina Webb to voice mail.

When Claudia finally spoke, her words were barely audible.

"If I'd spent another night in that place I'd have gone crazy."

"You're welcome. And maybe it's my fault for failing to explain the concept of attorney-client privilege, but whatever you tell me in confidence remains in confidence, just like a priest in confession. They can pull out my fingernails, and I won't tell them a thing. I'd lose my license if I did. So all of this secrecy between us is pointless, Claudia, and it's been very counterproductive."

Clarkson said, "But what about—?"

"You? That's an interesting question. If I'm right, and if you were in-volved in this from the get-go, then you'll need an attorney as well. Not me, because that would pose a conflict, but another criminal lawyer who'd work with me in mounting a joint defense. So I'm guessing we're okay to talk. Plus, don't forget, we're in a confessional."

"Andy had nothing to do with it."

"Bullshit, Claudia, and you're not listening to me. Andy has access to your bank account at the Wells Fargo branch in Pacific Heights, where I'm guessing all that family money is stashed, and he's been using it to hire me, and to offer a reward, and now to post your bail."

More silence. Again I glanced in the mirror.

"I lied for you back there, do you realize that? And at some point the D.A. is going to figure out that I lied, although I'll deny it, and he's going to try to revoke your bail because it came from the funds you embez-zled."

"Christ," Clarkson said.

"Yeah, I know, it sucks. And do you know what's worse, Andy? When he figures out you've been fronting this whole land-purchase deal for Claudia, he's gonna get the crazy idea that maybe both of you conspired to kill her brother."

They were quiet again, both of them thinking, both of them working the angles. It was Claudia who broke the silence.

"When did you figure it out?"

"About an hour ago, sitting in that courtroom with a stupid grin on my face. I figured Andy needs another golf course like I need a brassiere. I figured fifty acres represents one-third of the Château Giroux vineyard. I figured that's the third you would have inherited if you'd been born with outdoor plumbing. I figured you hatched a plan to buy it, using the money you've been stealing from your father. A sort of do-it-yourself in-heritance, using Andy as a front."

"Her *fair* share," Clarkson said, pulling her closer. "She's been manag-ing the business for years, and for what? So Alain and Phil could get rich, while she lives paycheck to paycheck? Just because she's a woman?

Where's the fairness in that? If it wasn't for Claudia, they'd have run that place into the ground years ago."

"So when Alain died," I said, "Claudia saw the chance not only to close the deal, but also to move up the timetable. She just had to make sure Phil inherited. Which means that the whole kabuki theater in probate court was for her benefit, not yours."

"I didn't kill Philip," Claudia said.

"I know that. I know it now more than ever. He was the last person you wanted dead. Unless."

Clarkson said, "Unless what?"

"Unless he found out what you were up to, and maybe threatened to expose you."

"Phil knew nothing," Claudia said. "He never set foot in the business office. I told him I'd planned the credit card scheme to help Andy buy the acreage."

"Did you?" I watched her in the mirror. "Plan it? Because that's what your father is claiming."

She disengaged from Clarkson and leaned forward, her shoulders hunched between the front seats.

"I know you won't believe this, but I was telling the truth when I said it was Father's idea. Around two weeks after Alain died, he came to my office and said that we had to do something to delay Phil from inheriting. He said that Phil would sell the acreage to Andy unless I helped him make it look as though Alain were still alive."

"Said the fly to the spider."

She settled back in her seat. "Not a fly, Jack. More like a wasp. Don't make the mistake of underestimating my father. He's a man who's accustomed to getting what he wants."

"I'm sorry to hear that, because from everything I've heard, he's got clout with the district attorney. Plus, he really believes you murdered your brother."

Even in the mirror, I could see that it rocked her. After a moment, she shook her head.

"All my life he's misunderstood me. He's underestimated me, patronized me, and patted me on the head. All while I turned his little cult winery into an international brand, tripling its value in the process. Do you remember that business appraisal we mentioned in court? I was fielding purchase offers from all over the globe. France, Argentina, New York. We could have gotten a hundred million for Château Giroux, but Father would never consider it. And do you know what? I didn't care. Not about the money. All I ever wanted was for Father to say to me, 'Nice job, Claudia. Look what you've accomplished. I'm so proud of you.'"

By now we were on Silverado Trail, maybe ten minutes out from Napa Springs Spa.

"It wasn't a coincidence," I told her, "Phil being killed that night, right after you'd left the winery. Someone is setting you up."

"Who?" Clarkson asked.

"That I don't know. Someone with a motive to stop Phil from inheriting. Or maybe to prevent Claudia from getting her share." I looked in the mirror. "Who else knew about your plan?"

"Nobody," she said. "I'm sure of it. Just Andy."

"Andy?"

He shook his head.

"That's too bad, because we're running short on suspects. Any chance your father cut some kind of a backroom deal with the Church?"

"No." Claudia's head-shake was emphatic. "That's impossible. Father thinks all religion is flim-flam. Plus the Santa Rosa diocese has always supported the UFW against the winery owners. Father despised the Church. He'd rather see Andy build condos on the property than let the diocese take it over. I'm certain of that."

"Well as of right now, the Santa Rosa diocese owns Château Giroux. The thing is, they probably don't know it yet. That would be your father's duty as trustee to inform them, and from what I've been able to tell, he's taken no steps to do that, or to arrange for a transition of ownership."

We drove for a while in silence, with Claudia sitting apart from Clarkson, her gaze out the opposite window, watching the vine rows scroll past in their hypnotic geometry. Clarkson pulled out his cell phone and dialed. He asked for security.

"Tell me about Thad Melchior."

"What about him?"

"He's representing your father now in connection with the D.A.'s investigation. I'm guessing your father ran straight to his office from the courthouse this morning."

"Thad's done corporate work for Giroux Beverage. Licensing and trademark, that sort of thing. Some collective bargaining. He and Father are old friends. But he's not a trial lawyer to my knowledge."

"Collective bargaining, like with the union?"

"He has a reputation as a hard-nosed negotiator. It's been a constant source of friction with Phil and Lourdes, who've urged Father to fire him, or at least to rein him in."

"How about immigration work?"

"I don't think so. Why do you ask?"

I filled her in on the LaBoutins, and the cashier's check, and our ménage à trois. She listened in silence and then turned again to the window.

"You're right to be suspicious. Father liked Frederique, but he'd never pay that kind of severance money to anyone. Charity isn't exactly his strong suit."

"Any idea where the LaBoutins might have gone?"

She shook her head. "I thought they'd quit. That's what Phil told me. Remember, Father and I haven't been talking."

We turned, at Clarkson's direction, into the driveway at Napa Springs Spa. He then leaned forward and said, "If what you're suggesting is true, that means Philippe is responsible for killing his own son. I know the guy's a bastard, but do you really think he could sink to that level?"

"I don't know, Andy, but the way I see it, this LaBoutin character is the only lead that we've got. Despite what you see in the movies, not everyone is capable of killing a man, especially by bashing his skull. That requires a certain temperament. But I'll tell you what, from the records I've seen? Henri LaBoutin is just the sort of guy who could do it."

19

I was sprawled on the sofa in our little apartment above the spa, my feet on the coffee table and the D.A.'s newest investigation file open in my lap. I had a cold Bud in my left hand and the television remote in my right. On the screen with the sound muted, two talking heads from ESPN were questioning a shaved-head behemoth in a gray T-shirt, three hundred pounds of mean and stupid, the interview punctuated by video clips of the Niners' training camp—sled drills and blocking drills and a no-contact scrimmage.

Forget the changing colors or the migrating birds—in North America, preseason football is the first true harbinger of fall.

I'd loaned my swim trunks to Ethan Scott who, despite renting a suite at the nearby Meadowood resort, seemed intent on hanging around wherever we did. He'd gone to poolside with Regan and Mayday, and was probably at that very moment whispering sweet nothings in Rachel the bar girl's ear.

Meanwhile, in some sub-basement war room at the district attorney's office, Herrera and his minions were plotting the downfall of Claudia Giroux—I pictured a whiteboard with flow charts and diagrams—while her father and Thad Melchior, similarly engaged, sat huddled in a plush Napa conference room.

Feeling like the tank guy in Tiananmen Square, I set down my beer and groped for my cell phone.

"MacTaggart and Suarez," Bernie chirped. "How may I direct your call?"

"Hey, it's me."

"Oh, my God! Is Ethan Scott with you?"

"Never mind that. How's Sam?"

"Sam is fine. In fact, we're picking out our china pattern. When are you guys coming home?"

"I'm not sure. We had our bail hearing this morning, and Phil Giroux's funeral is tomorrow, so maybe on Friday. It all depends."

"How did it go in court?"

"It wasn't pretty, but at least she's out of jail. You can catch the highlights on the evening news."

"Come on, what happened? Remember, you promised."

I sighed. "The D.A. seems to think that our client's been embezzling money from the family winery. Lots of money, in fact."

"Oh, my God, I knew it!"

"You knew what?"

"The midpoint reversal! That puts you somewhere near the middle of the second act."

"Bernie, please. Real life doesn't follow the structure of a screenplay."

"Oh, yeah? I'll bet there's a half-dozen suspects, any of whom could have done it, and a secret romance that's complicating things for the hero."

I stared at the phone.

"So what about Ethan? Is he there? Is he cute? Did he mention my name?"

A knock sounded at the door. I powered off the TV as I rose to answer it.

"Yes, maybe, and no. I have to run, but here's a free piece of advice. Be careful who you trust in the film business, starting with your friend Antonio."

Claudia stood barefoot on the threshold, her hair still wet from the shower and a bottle like a caveman's club slung over her shoulder. She wore her same faded jeans from this morning, but with an oversized Napa Springs Spa golf shirt in place of the tee.

"I hope I'm not interrupting."

I stepped aside. She strolled into the living room and gave the place the once-over.

"Is that to drink, or to beat me over the head?"

She held out the bottle. "It's a thank-you, and a peace offering. Inadequate for either purpose, I know, but I'm improvising. They didn't have any Dom Pérignon at the restaurant."

The wine was still cold, with condensation beading its bright orange label. I carried it to the kitchenette, where I'd noticed champagne flutes in one of the cabinets.

"This is cozy," Claudia said, pacing the living room, her hand trailing over the furniture. "Who sleeps where?"

"We play spin the bottle at night."

I peeled off the foil and gave six quick twists to the wire cage holding the cork. The cork surrendered with a *pop,* ricocheting off the backsplash as the wine overflowed into the sink.

"I'm jealous," Claudia said, her voice closer now, her hand on the small of my back. "Can I come over and play?"

I filled both glasses, turning and handing her one.

"You know what they say. Three's company, but four's a traffic jam."

We sipped, each of us eyeballing the other.

"You must think I'm an awful person, but there's one thing I want to be sure you understand."

She moved closer, our bodies almost touching.

"What happened between us wasn't part of any plan. It wasn't some tactic to worm my way into your confidence."

"Oh, yeah? What was it then?"

"It was this," she said, leaning against me and raising on tiptoes, her lips touching mine.

She stepped away.

"You don't believe me."

"I believe that if I'd known about you and Andy, you'd never have been in my hotel room in the first place."

"If you'd known *what* about me and Andy? Our business arrangement? Or our so-called engagement?"

"So-called?"

She turned away, looking out toward the living room.

"Andy is a friend, Jack, and that's all he is. We've grown close out of necessity, but—"

"Grown close? What does that mean, exactly?"

She turned again to face me. "I'm not in love with him, if that's what you want to know."

I set down my glass.

"How's your Roman history?"

"What do you mean?"

"I mean Andy Clarkson worships the ground you walk on, Claudia. He's lied for you, and he's stolen for you, and he might even go to jail for you. Most women I know would give a kidney for that kind of devotion."

"Devotion." She drained her glass and set it on the counter. "If I wanted devotion, I'd buy a dog. Andy agreed to help me because we've known each other since childhood. Also because we share something very important in common."

"What's that?"

"We both despise my father."

She wandered back into the living room, where she spied Regan's 9 mm Walther PPS pistol lying on a table. She slid the gun from its holster and turned, the short, black muzzle leveled at my heart.

"Is this real?"

"Yes, and it's probably loaded."

She smiled. "Good. Take off your clothes."

"Claudia—"

"Come on, Jack, where's your spontaneity? I have twelve-and-a-half million dollars in a Wells Fargo account that requires only one signature. We could hop a plane to Chile, or maybe New Zealand. We could disappear, just like Henri did. Today, this afternoon. Hell, we're a lot smarter than he is. No one would ever find us."

I wasn't smiling as I stepped toward her, advancing until the muzzle was inches from my chest.

"I'm warning you," she said. "I'm mentally unstable. Haven't you heard?"

"I don't think you fully appreciate the gravity of your situation. I've spent the last half hour looking over the D.A.'s latest evidence. You're going to prison, Claudia. If not for murder, then almost certainly for embezzlement. This isn't some parlor game."

Pouting theatrically, she lowered the gun and returned it to its holster, setting both back on the table.

"All right then, we'll play it your way. Attorney and client. All business, and no more messy complications."

She walked to the door and paused there, her hand on the knob, before turning again to face me.

"Somebody killed my brother, Jack. Whoever it was ruined everything I've been planning, and now he's trying to frame me for murder. I understand that perfectly well. But you're wrong about one thing. This *is* a game. It's a game of life and death. And it's a game I have no intention of losing."

The restaurant was called Mustards. It was crowded for a Wednesday evening, the lively voices and laughter a stark contrast to the sepulchral quiet of Pilate's Trattoria, the din magnified by the clink of glasses, the chime and clash of silverware, and the softly muted strains of piped-in music.

"Smoked ribs," said the kid, setting down his menu. "A no-brainer. They're the best in the state."

"You've eaten here before?"

He reached for the ice bucket. "We filmed *Chelsea's Farm* in Sonoma. We used to come over here on weekends. It was Meryl who put me on to the ribs."

My dinner companions were flushed with wine and sun, and collectively we could have passed for any pair of yuppie couples up for a midweek getaway. Except that in our case, half the room was pretending not to stare at Ethan Scott.

The kid had ordered the wine—his treat—one bottle each of Kistler Chardonnay and Spottswoode Cabernet, and he was just topping off our glasses when Regan, impatient with the chit-chat, brought us back to the business at hand.

"We were talking at poolside," she said, addressing me but glancing at the tables around us, "and we have an idea for finding Henri LaBoutin."

"Ethan's going to ask Meryl?"

"It's the check," the kid said, excitement in his voice. "Go on, Marta, you tell him."

Mayday leaned closer, until it looked like we were holding some kind of séance.

"It was something you said earlier that got me to thinking. The cashier's check is just wrong. For one thing, it was issued two weeks before Henri LaBoutin even left Château Giroux. That gave him plenty of time to deposit a regular check and have it clear the bank."

"Exactly," said the kid.

"But here's the key," Mayday continued. "You can't just walk into a bank and cash a check in that amount, even a cashier's check. For one thing, no bank has that kind of money on hand. But more important, I checked the federal banking regulations. If a bank cashes a check for a sum in excess of ten thousand dollars, it has to file what's called a large-transaction currency report with the IRS. It's to prevent money laundering by drug dealers. The person presenting the check has to provide all sorts of information, including his social security number."

"All right, so let's assume he didn't cash the check. That means he either deposited it locally, or he held it for deposit somewhere else."

"Right. But if he was just going to deposit it locally, then why would he ask for a cashier's check?"

Mayday had a point. The purpose of a cashier's check is to assure that funds are available upon presentment—that the check is good. It also precludes the issuer from later stopping payment. Later, that is, after the payee's services have been rendered.

"Okay then, let's assume he held the check for deposit elsewhere. That means he used some other source of funds to buy his plane tickets and whatnot."

Mayday nodded. "Exactly. I checked the flight plans for the corporate jet. It's a Gulfstream IV, part of a shared leasing arrangement through NetJets, and there's been nothing filed by Giroux Beverage since your flights back in June. So either LaBoutin paid for a commercial flight in cash, which itself would raise a red flag with the TSA, or else he booked a commercial flight in advance using a credit card."

"And he didn't have a personal credit card," Regan said.

"So therefore"—the kid threw up his hands—"he used a company card!"

Three shining faces, all watching me with anticipation.

"Not so fast," I told them. "Someone could have booked the flight for him. Probably Philippe."

"Either way," Regan said, "the charge should be somewhere in the Giroux Beverage credit card records. That would give us the airline, and a purchase code, and a direct link to the flight. Problem is, those records were covered by the D.A.'s search warrant, which means that Herrera's already got them."

"Not necessarily. For one thing, he'd have told me as much, and it would have been part of his *Brady* material. So let's think about this. LaBoutin left Château Giroux around August fourteenth. That's according to Philippe, and it's been corroborated both by Lourdes and Larry, Philippe's chauffeur. So if LaBoutin's our killer, then he must have stayed someplace locally until the deed was done on Sunday night. Let's assume he and Philippe cut their deal back in July, shortly before the check was issued on the thirty-first, and at the same time arranged LaBoutin's disappearance. That means the airfare charge would probably appear on the August credit card statement, which may not have arrived as yet."

"That depends on the billing cycle."

"Hold on," Mayday said, removing the iPad from her shoulder bag. "I have those AmEx statements Claudia scanned for us in June. I'll bet the company cards are all billed on the same cycle."

We watched as she poked and swiped, then turned the tablet sideways. She squinted.

"The billing period on Alain's last statement ran from April twenty-sixth to May twenty-fifth, with a past-due date of June fifteenth."

"So the August statement should cover the period from late July to late August, which means the bill wouldn't go out until month's end."

"Or just before."

I lifted my glass. "Which means the August bills should be arriving at Château Giroux right about now."

20

———·———

Lourdes was the first to arrive, in a gleaming white limousine that rolled to a stop at the curb outside the St. Apollinaris Catholic Church in Napa. It was a priest who first alighted when the rear door opened; a handsome young cleric in a Roman collar and cassock. He turned and offered a hand to the grieving widow, whose emergence was heralded by the staccato clacking of a dozen camera shutters as the pack of waiting photographers surged forward from the sidewalk.

But it was the third passenger to step from the Church limousine that really got my attention.

"Holy stromboli," I said to Mayday as the gray eminence in the bright purple beanie ducked under the door frame and into the Thursday morning sunlight.

"A zucchetto," Mayday said.

"You can say that again."

"The skullcap. Purple signifies that he's a bishop."

As the black-clad trio moved past us onto the front steps of the church, Lourdes paused long enough to beam a sheepish smile at Ethan Scott, whom I decided ought to carry one of those take-a-number dispensers with him at all times.

No sooner had the big car moved off toward the parking lot than another, smaller limo took its place. Larry the Driver leaped from behind the wheel and circled to the rear door, holding it open for Philippe Giroux and his buddy Thad Melchior. Both men wore dark suits today, the lawyer going with a charcoal bow tie and Philippe, again with the armband, trading his usual ascot for an understated four-in-hand.

Neither paused to smile in our direction.

"That poor man," Mayday said as the photographers duly recorded Philippe's arrival. "Wasn't today his son's birthday?"

The next of the family cars was Clarkson's silver Beemer, which deposited Claudia at the curb before continuing on to the parking lot. The bereaved sister wore a familiar black dress, today accessorized with a crepe shoulder wrap, and I was pleased to see that I hadn't torn the zipper after all.

"Good morning," she said, stopping to keep us company, or maybe to wait for Clarkson before entering the church.

The kid nudged me aside.

"We haven't been properly introduced," he said, offering his hand to Claudia as the cameras clicked around him. "I'm Ethan Scott. I'm very sorry for your loss."

"That's very kind of you," she said, taking his hand but looking over his shoulder. "Jack, I'm so glad you could make it. And that I could as well, thanks to you."

I looked around. The doorway to the church was empty now, and the photographers had returned to their curbside vigil. Out in the parking lot, Clarkson was just alighting from his car.

I said, "I know this isn't the best time for this, but we think we might have a possible lead on LaBoutin. It involves getting access to the snail mail at Château Giroux."

"The mail? What for?"

"I'll explain later, but could we meet up after the service? Maybe stop by your office for a minute or two?"

She looked past my shoulder toward the parking lot.

"Of course, if you think it's important. I'm hosting the family reception at the Petit Trianon after the Mass." She checked her watch. "Probably around one o'clock. Why don't you all come as my guests, and then we'll try to slip away. With Father in attendance, I'm sure I'll welcome the interruption."

On the outskirts of the legal battlefield camps a shadow army of psychologists, sociologists, behaviorists, coaches, gurus, and self-described experts who, at rates ranging from a few hundred to many thousands of dollars, stand ready to assist trial lawyers like me during the process of jury selection. These so-called jury consultants will sit in the courtroom and analyze prospective jurors for things like dress, grooming, posture, eye contact, facial expression, and sundry other nonverbal ticks and cues in the hope of identifying those who might prove sympathetic to their client's case. Or better still, those who might prove secretly hostile to the opposition's.

While not a convert myself when it comes to the pseudo-science of jury selection, I have developed over the years a heightened awareness of body language, both inside and outside the courtroom. I've become a student, if you will, of the folded arms, the drumming fingers, and the twisted wedding ring. Which is why it occurred to me, as I stood in Claudia Giroux's living room watching the intra-family minuet of stance and gesture, position and personal space, that I ought to be videotaping the proceedings for a graduate-level seminar.

Philippe stood nearest the kitchen, where the bar had been set up, and there received the hushed condolences of guests entering to refresh their drinks. In the opposite corner of the room, Claudia and Andy Clarkson hosted a tight circle of younger mourners, Mayday and Regan among them, while under the archway nearest the front entrance door, Lourdes's clerical contingent provided the third coordinate in what amounted to an equilateral triangle of suspicion, hostility, and estrangement.

I stood at its center. The Mass had ended an hour ago, and the guests, now on their second round of drinks, were just beginning to loosen up. This was, I realized, the first time since Claudia's arraignment that all of the players had assembled together in the same room, but on this occasion, unlike the last, there was no judge present to control the proceedings.

And that meant it was time to stir the pot.

"Mr. MacTaggart." Lourdes gestured with her glass, nearly spilling its contents on the carpet. By my count she was on her third double Scotch, and even behind the veil, I could see her dark eyes growing glassy. "Have you met Bishop Muncie? And this is his colleague, Father Quinn. Father Quinn is a Jesuit and a lawyer, so you have that much in common."

I shook both their hands.

"I'm not really a Jesuit," I told the young priest, whom I'd first seen outside the church, stepping from the limousine. "I'm just angelic by nature."

"That's all right, because I'm not really a lawyer. At least I'm not admitted in California. But I did attend Harvard Law."

"You're the one who's representing Philippe's daughter," the bishop said, his pointed finger completing the accusation. "I saw your picture on television. A most unfortunate situation, if you don't mind my saying."

"Yes, I suppose it is." Your Excellency? Your Holiness? "Remember to keep me in your prayers."

They both politely chuckled.

"If not California," I asked the lawyer, "are you admitted anywhere else?"

"I've never felt the need to sit for a bar exam, since I don't really practice law. At least, not in the traditional sense."

"I've always said, there's nothing traditional about the Catholic Church."

Another chuckle, but less enthusiastic.

"I mostly handle business affairs for the archdiocese."

"Ah."

"Perhaps Mr. MacTaggart could be persuaded to join us for tea sometime soon," the bishop suggested to the priest. "Shall we say Saturday? Perhaps at three? There are . . . issues of mutual interest that have been brought to our attention, and we'd very much like to have your input in the matter."

"Mr. MacTaggart is going to help us find whoever killed Phil," Lourdes said, her dark eyes moving across the room to Philippe. "And then we're gonna sue the pants off the son of a bitch."

The bishop, frowning now, glanced over at Claudia. "But I was under the impression—"

"Judge not lest ye be judged," I said, patting his shoulder. "A wise man told me that a long time ago."

I next crossed the room toward Philippe, who stood with his pal Melchior, both men nodding tersely as I passed them en route to the kitchen. There I topped off my club soda and caught a snippet of the Hollywood war story that Ethan Scott, cornered by the fridge, was telling to a rapt gaggle of middle-aged women. It had something to do with stealing George Clooney's bicycle.

Back in the living room, I stood beside Philippe and sipped, both of us surveying the landscape of milling guests.

"The younger one's Harvard Law," I told him, nodding toward Lourdes. "He handles business affairs for the archdiocese."

Philippe grunted. "I suspected as much. They're like ravens, these Roman Papists. Glossy black scavengers, circling the carcass and trying not to collide. I'm sure Lourdes is telling them all about the trust."

"Last time I checked, that was your duty as trustee."

"Don't presume to advise my client," Melchior snapped, leaning forward to glare, "especially when you're outside your field of competence."

"Said the guy who only does contracts."

"Said the ambulance chaser who—"

"Gentlemen, please." Philippe restrained his friend with a hand. "Today is a day to reflect on Philip." He looked across the room to his daughter, still chatting with Clarkson and the others. "There'll be time enough for recriminations tomorrow."

Claudia smiled as I worked my way toward her through the crowded living room.

"Don't think I haven't been watching you," she said, "skulking behind enemy lines."

I stood beside her, both of us the objects of furtive glances from Philippe and Melchior, the bishop and Father Quinn.

"Is it just me, or are there too many lawyers in this room?"

"It is awkward, isn't it? I don't blame Father for being angry with me, or even for wanting to sue me, but for him to suspect me of killing Phil . . ." She shook her head sadly. "We've grown so far apart. It's like I don't even recognize him anymore."

"He thinks Lourdes is spilling the beans to the bishop. And I suspect he's probably right."

"Good for Lourdes. How much longer do you think we have here at Château Giroux?"

"I don't know. I suppose it depends on whether the church wants to own a winery, or if they're looking for a quick sale. Does your father have eighty-five million stuffed under a mattress somewhere?"

"Even if he could raise that kind of money, it would kill him to buy back what he feels he already owns. Of course, it would also kill him to lose it."

"I'd call that a dilemma."

"I'd call it poetic justice."

"And what about you?" I asked, turning now to face her. "Have you thought about life after Château Giroux?"

"In all honesty, I haven't had time." She sipped at her Diet Coke. "Don't forget, I grew up here. This is where I rode my first bicycle, and wore my first party dress, and I kissed my first boyfriend."

"And then stole his lunch money."

"Don't be unkind. I guess if I can't stay here, then I'd just as soon the Church have it. Anybody but Father. That's become my new motto."

Clarkson, breaking away from another conversation, moved to within earshot, prompting me to check my watch.

"I'm afraid we have to run," I told Claudia. "But if you can spare me a moment, there are some things we need to discuss." I patted Clarkson's arm. "Attorney-client matters. I won't keep her long."

"Of course," she said. "Andy can hold down the fort while I grab my bag and walk you to your car." She leaned closer to Clarkson. "Stay alert, and watch for incoming arrows."

I rounded up Mayday and Regan. We bid our farewells to Lourdes, and I confirmed my Saturday afternoon play-date with the man in the purple beanie. We then followed Claudia out the door and up the car-lined driveway toward the Visitor Center.

It was hotter outside than when we'd arrived, the afternoon temperatures creeping back into the nineties. Somewhere in the distance, a tractor was droning. Regan and Mayday both removed their jackets as we walked.

"Hey! Wait up!"

The kid was trotting after us, a beer bottle in his hand.

As we resumed our uphill march, it occurred to me that we were following the same route Claudia had traveled on the night of her brother's murder. Only she'd been alone then, and still largely anonymous, at least outside of Napa Valley. Today, however, as the Visitor Center parking lot rose into view, a half-dozen news vans were lying in wait.

Which reminded me that Terina Webb had left a message on my cell phone yesterday as we'd driven from the jail.

Claudia removed a key ring from her bag as we approached the rear of the building.

"I haven't been in the office since Sunday," she said, holding the door for us as we filed into the air-conditioned hallway. "There's no telling what it will look like."

The hallway itself was deserted, but we could hear muted voices and laughter beyond the far door leading to the tasting room. Claudia tried the office doorknob, then sorted through her keys.

The room when she'd unlocked it was exactly as I'd seen it on Tuesday, but with a growing volume of paperwork now littering her Louis XIV desk. She fell into the swivel chair and sighed.

"My goodness, what a mess."

"What about mail?"

She lifted a stack of envelopes from her in-box. Most were already slit along their edges, and in some cases the contents were unfolded and fastened with a paper clip.

"What am I looking for?"

"Credit card statements, from American Express."

Her head came up. "You've got to be kidding."

"According to your father, the LaBoutins were issued a company credit card. We're hoping the August statement might give us a lead as to their whereabouts."

She sorted through the rest of the mail, then rolled her chair to the file cabinet behind her. Her breath caught when she opened the empty drawer.

"Search warrant," I reminded her.

"But how am I supposed to run a business without my records?"

"I doubt your father wants you running anything at this point. In fact, I'm surprised he hasn't changed the locks."

"Which is why," Mayday reminded us, "this may be our last chance to access those statements."

Claudia wheeled back to her desk and reexamined the papers. She then picked up the telephone.

"Claire? This is Claudia, in the office. Has today's mail arrived? Uh-huh. Could you bring it down right away? Thank you."

She replaced the receiver, reading her wristwatch as she did.

"Don't worry," I told her. "This shouldn't take long."

A knock sounded, and the receptionist entered with an armful of catalogues, packages, and envelopes. She paused in the doorway, her eyes holding on Ethan Scott.

"Thank you, Claire. You can close your mouth now."

I was standing over Claudia's desk even before Claire had shut the door behind her.

"Here they are." Claudia laid a fan of windowed envelopes in the center of her blotter. She withdrew a letter opener from her drawer.

"Wait!" Mayday said. "Do we want her father to know that we've opened them?"

There were five envelopes in total. They were addressed respectively to Philippe, Phil, Alain, Claudia, and Frederique LaBoutin, each in care of Château Giroux.

The kid drained the last of his beer. "In *Mission to Belgrade*," he said,

"I used a tea kettle to steam open a love letter to my wife from the Habsburg emperor."

"I have an electric kettle in the bathroom." Claudia took the LaBoutin envelope and disappeared through a doorway behind her. We heard the water run, and then, a minute later, a shrill beeping sound.

She returned working her finger under the flap. When it pulled away, she handed the envelope to me.

I unfolded two crisp sheets from inside. Claudia studied my face as I handed the pages to Mayday.

"Whole Foods, Trader Joe's, and the Oakville Grocery," I said, slumping back in my chair. "The last charge was made in July."

Mayday handed the pages to Regan. "What about Philippe's card?"

Claudia gathered all of the remaining envelopes and carried them into the bathroom.

Regan said, "I suppose they could have taken a bus wherever they were going, and used their savings to live on until the check was deposited. Why do we think they flew?"

"Philippe definitely mentioned the airport. He said that Henri had declined a ride. I remember that."

"Except that we don't trust Philippe," Mayday said. "That's why we're here steaming envelopes in the first place."

While we waited for Claudia, I dug my cell phone from my pocket and played Terina's message.

"Jack, you bastard, don't leave me in the pack, chasing after you like a dog! Where are you guys headed? The embezzlement story is going to lead every network broadcast tonight, so why not get out in front of it on my show? I can give you a full ten-minute segment. Twenty, with Ethan Scott. Or how about a thirty-minute special if Claudia will go on camera? Come on, damn it, you owe me this!"

Claudia returned from the bathroom with all of the envelopes opened. She handed her father's to me.

Philippe's credit card statement bore half a dozen entries, all reflecting the purchase of winery or vineyard supplies. DripWorks. True Value Hardware. The Barrel Source. None was an airline charge.

"Well," I said, handing the pages to Mayday. "It was worth a shot."

Claudia sat upright in her chair.

"Oh, my God."

Her face had gone pale, and with an unsteady hand she slid another statement across the desk.

It was three pages in length, reflecting over a dozen credit card charges.

All made by Alain Giroux.

21

The charges began in mid-August. Safeway. AT&T. Costco. Bed Bath & Beyond. Walmart. Charter Cable. Fry's Electronics. Redbox. Save Mart Pharmacy.

Mayday and Regan were behind me now, both reading over my shoulder.

"They're all from around Carmel."

I nodded as the kid moved to stand beside them.

Home Depot. Redbox again. Target Stores. Patisserie Boissiere.

I looked at Claudia. "What became of that replacement card you ordered back in March?"

"I still have it." She lifted her bag from the floor and fumbled around inside. "At least I thought I did."

From her wallet she extracted a gold credit card and laid it on the desktop.

Alain Giroux.

"My God," she said, "you don't think—"

"Here's what I think. I think your father wanted to make Henri LaBoutin disappear. He paid him a hundred grand by cashier's check, with the understanding that LaBoutin would deposit the money later, after he'd reached his destination. But LaBoutin had to hang around for a while until the job was done. So in order to tide him over, your father gave him a credit card. Not Frederique's card, because that one would have to be cancelled. He needed a card he could get in a hurry, but one the accounting people wouldn't be looking to pay. A card your father planned to pay himself, from his own personal account."

Claudia picked up Alain's card and turned it in her hand.

"You think he ordered another replacement?"

"Why not? I think that's a lot more likely than what you're thinking."

We sat for a moment in silence.

"We used to vacation in Carmel as kids," Claudia said. "Before Mother died. For one week every summer we rented a house near the beach. Every day we'd picnic down by Thirteenth Street and watch Alain learning to surf. It was very special to him, that beach."

"But look at the timing," I said, sliding the statement across her desk. "The charges begin in mid-August, right after the LaBoutins left Château Giroux."

"It could still be Alain!"

"There's one way to find out," Regan said. "Let's contact American Express."

I looked at Claudia. "You've done this before. How does it work?"

She picked up the phone and dialed the number off the back of the card. We watched as she keyed her way through a series of voice mail prompts.

"Hello," she finally said. "My name is Claudia Giroux, G-I-R-O-U-X, and I'm the chief financial officer of Giroux Beverage, one of your card members. Yes, hold on."

She read the account number off the face of the card.

"I'd like to know if and when a replacement credit card was ordered for this account."

She frowned, glancing up at us while we waited.

"I see. As of when? All right, thank you for your time."

She hung up.

"What?"

"I'm no longer authorized to receive information on the account."

I stood and started to pace.

Mayday said, "If we could prove that Philippe ordered a replacement credit card just before Henri LaBoutin disappeared, that would go a long way toward creating a reasonable doubt, wouldn't it? There's no legitimate reason for him to have done that. You don't give a departing employee a severance check *and* a company card."

"You could issue a subpoena to American Express," Regan said. "That is, if we don't mind tipping off the D.A."

"Jack?" Mayday turned around to face me. "Have you got a better idea?"

I stopped pacing.

"You remember that probate hearing? At the end, when Judge Mercer said he was keeping the case open pending the outcome of the referral to the D.A.'s office? As far as I know, that case is still open."

Claudia said, "I'm not following."

"If the probate case is still open," Mayday told her, "then we still have subpoena power. That means we could issue a subpoena to American Express in that case. We'd have to give notice to Cameron and Rubenstein, but they won't care, especially since their client is dead."

"We'd have to notice Giroux Beverage as well," I told her, "since these are consumer records."

"We can send that notice to Claudia, who's still the corporate treasurer." She turned to face our client. "The point is, by handling it in the probate action, we can fly under D.A.'s radar. And your father's as well."

"How long will all of this take?"

"At least twenty days," Mayday told her.

"And we're just going to sit around and wait for the results?"

"Heck no," I said. "While we're waiting for proof that your father ordered the card, we're going to track down whoever the hell's been using it."

"Dude, this is getting good," the kid said, leaning his head between the seats as we drove through the maze of news trucks in the Visitor Center parking lot. "What if the brother is still alive? What if, like, the father and the younger brother cut a deal to ice the older brother and make it look like the sister did it? Or better yet, what if the younger brother and the sister are in cahoots and they're using us to implicate the old man? Or, wait! What if the younger brother and his buddy Clarkson are framing the sister so they can keep the twelve mil and run the whole show themselves? Whoa! Now that's what I'd call a plot twist."

"Don't get your hopes too high," I told him, examining the photo Claudia had given us. It showed the ferret-faced chef and her skinhead husband, both standing over a cutting board in what I assumed to be the kitchen of the stone château. "Remember, real life doesn't follow the structure of a screenplay."

"Yeah, but I like the younger-brother-and-Clarkson ending the best so far. I could sell that one to a studio, especially if the truth turns out to be boring."

"But here's the thing, Jack," Regan said. "Those didn't look like the credit card charges of someone who's holed up for a couple of weeks, waiting to do a job. More like someone who's setting up house. AT&T? Charter Cable? If it's LaBoutin, then wouldn't he want to do the deed and get out of Dodge as fast as he could?"

Regan had a point. If LaBoutin did have the credit card, then there'd been no airplane flights and no out-of-town job. Could Claudia possibly be right about Alain? Could one of the kid's Hollywood endings really come to pass? Or did Claudia have another rabbit hidden somewhere, waiting to hop out of her hat?

"Uh-oh, there's Terina," Mayday said, and I looked up in time to spot a familiar blonde coiffure amid the milling gaggle of journalists.

Just as she spotted us.

"Shit."

Terina was shouting, her arms waving like one of those signal guys on the tarmac. Mayday swerved, then swerved again to avoid the other reporters who, following their colleague's lead, had tried to box us in.

"Look out!"

Ethan Scott ducked as a high-heeled shoe glanced off the rear window. Behind us, Terina hopped and shouted, her maledictions lost in the six-cylinder strain of the rental car's revving engine.

. . .

Still in his dark suit from the funeral, Andy Clarkson rested a size-twelve brogan on the edge of my chaise longue.

"Another fifty grand?"

I lowered my sunglasses.

"No, the same fifty, just from a different source. We can't accept funds originating from Claudia's Wells Fargo account. First, it wouldn't be ethical, and second, it wouldn't be smart, since the account's about to be frozen. We'll return your original check."

He grunted, watching Regan and Mayday splashing at the far end of the pool. "Okay, I'll get you a new check tomorrow. Which raises a question. If I'm the one paying your fee, then who are you working for?"

"Claudia. I told you before, you need to hire your own lawyer."

He removed his foot and pulled over an empty chaise.

"Here's the thing," he said, sitting close enough so that we wouldn't be overheard. "Claudia didn't deposit that money directly into the Wells Fargo account. She ran it all over town, through a dozen different accounts. And I'm guessing the D.A. hasn't found it yet, or I'd probably be under subpoena, right? So I was thinking, maybe I wouldn't need to hire my own lawyer if we could make the money disappear again. You know, move it to another bank? Or maybe to a brokerage? Even to Switzerland if we have to. Someplace the D.A. would never think to look."

"You could try," I told him, "but they'll find it eventually. And if I were representing you, I'd tell you you'd be nuts to even think about it."

"Why's that?"

"Because at this point, Andy, the only defense you've got is that you didn't know the money was dirty. Moving it now would be tantamount to an admission of guilt, like fleeing the scene of an accident. If it wasn't your fault, then why did you run when you heard the sirens?"

He nodded, looking again toward the pool. He patted his pockets for cigarettes.

"She can't go back to jail, Jack. I know Claudia, and I tell you she couldn't handle it."

"Let's be honest, Andy. I've seen the D.A.'s evidence. Even if we can beat the murder rap, the embezzlement is a whole 'nother story. Maybe we can plead it down, but given the amounts involved, she'll have to do some time."

He tapped out a cigarette, gazing off to the table where a laughing Ethan Scott and Rachel the bar girl were huddled in conversation.

"Look," I told him, "don't take it so hard. She's a big girl, and she took a big risk. She knew the consequences."

"It's just so fucking unfair. All she wanted is what she had coming. What her brothers were getting anyway, without lifting a finger. And if someone hadn't killed Phil, she'd have gotten it. Now the old man is go-ing to sue her, and the Church is going to take everything she worked so hard to build?" He shook his head at the injustice. "You couldn't begin to appreciate the irony."

I sighed, setting aside my crossword. "Why don't you try me, Andy? You've been dropping these little hints ever since the day we first met. Go ahead and get it off your chest."

"What are you talking about?"

"Okay then, I'll do it for you. Claudia doesn't hate her father because of some clause in her grandfather's trust, or because he never gave credit where credit was due. She hates him because he abused her somehow when she was a girl. Isn't that what you've wanted to tell me?"

He didn't answer, which was answer enough.

"I suppose her mother suspected, and became her protector. That's why the college in Paris. That's why the overdose, and the return home to Château Giroux, and the whole embezzlement scheme. It was the big payback, the best revenge. And at some point after you'd been dating for a while, she confessed it all to you."

"The bastard would get drunk at dinner and come to her room at night. Her allowance, a new bicycle, a new dress—he told her she had to earn them. He said that if she ever told her mother, they'd have to get divorced, and it would all be her fault."

"And you believed all of that?"

"What do you mean?"

"I mean it's a good story, don't get me wrong. And if told to the right guy—a guy, say, with a boyhood crush and a savior's complex—I'll bet that guy would agree to do just about anything to help her."

"You son of a bitch."

"Come on, Andy. Claudia Giroux is a sphinx. I don't know what's fact about her or what's fiction, and if you were being honest you'd admit that neither do you. But don't mind me, I'm a goddamned cynic. Marta will vouch for that. So maybe her story's true, and you're a great big hero, and you're gonna get married and have two-point-two children, and live happily ever after. What the hell do I know? Nothing about women, that's for sure."

"I was only trying to help her."

"Bullshit. You didn't want to help her, you wanted to rescue her. To be her knight in shining armor. If you really wanted to help her, you'd have talked her out of the whole cockeyed scheme in the first place. Now look where your help has gotten her."

"You don't understand."

"You mean I do understand. I understand only too well."

Dripping, Regan and Mayday padded over and wrapped themselves in their towels. Clarkson, his jaw clenched, stood to fish a matchbook from his pocket.

"You're looking for LaBoutin tomorrow?"

I nodded. "That's the plan."

"Where?"

"Carmel."

He lit his smoke. "I guess I don't get it," he said, shaking the match and dropping it into my empty beer bottle. "If LaBoutin's the one who killed Phil, then wouldn't he have left town by now? Maybe gone back to France or something?"

"Thank you," said Regan.

"Tell you what, Andy. If you or anyone else has a better idea for how to defend this case, then now's the time to share it. God knows, we could use the help."

Clarkson took a drag.

"Okay, it's your show. If I can do anything, be sure to let me know."

"You bet we will."

He turned and trudged, like the Little Engine that Couldn't, in the direction of the Clubhouse.

Mayday asked, "What's the matter with him?"

I watched as he stopped to chat with Ethan and Rachel, then shut the iron gate behind him.

"A common affliction," I told her, "for which there's no cure known to medical science."

"What affliction is that?"

I took up my crossword.

"He's in love with the wrong woman."

22

The morning was doubly overcast, the gray mixture of coastal fog and recent cloudburst casting a leaden pall over the rain-slicked parking lot. A fresh breeze cut through the car like an ice pick. I held a fist to my throat as I trained Regan's binoculars through the open passenger window.

The Redbox video rental kiosk snapped into focus. The kiosk was inside the Save Mart Pharmacy building in a strip mall off of Carmel Valley Road—a three-hour drive from Château Giroux but only two miles from the tony coastal tourist village of Carmel-by-the-Sea, California. It stood just inside the pharmacy's glass-front street entrance, enabling us to observe it from where we'd parked our rental car at the adjacent service station.

While we shivered and groused in the elements, Mayday and Ethan Scott, the latter disguised in Ray-Bans and a golfer's floppy bucket hat, monitored the warm and cozy inside entrance off the mall.

"This is crazy," Regan said, gripping her Starbucks cup with both hands. "It could take days."

"Didn't you ever go on stakeouts when you were a cop?"

"In Sierra Madre? We staked out the coffee shop in the morning."

She moved the two photos before leaning back and swinging her tactical boots onto the dashboard, exposing in the process the Walther she wore on her hip. The first photo was the kitchen shot of Frederique and Henri LaBoutin taken at Philippe's château, while the second was the fuzzy blow-up of Alain Giroux that Mayday had downloaded off the Internet nearly two months ago, the last time we'd gone searching for Claudia's ephemeral brother.

"Hold on," I said, raising the glasses. "We have a live one."

A man stood at the kiosk. Medium height, medium build, a dark windbreaker or raincoat draped over his arm. Regan blew warmth into her hand and then keyed the walkie-talkie we'd borrowed from Clarkson's security team.

"You got eyes on this guy?"

After a burst of static, the kid's voice responded, "Yeah, we see him. *The Great Gatsby,* Baz Luhrmann version. Terrible in 3-D, even worse on Blu-ray. Guy's probably trying to get his money back. Over."

I lowered the binoculars, raising my window against the chill.

"Everybody's a film critic."

My cell phone vibrated, the caller ID reading A. CLARKSON. I showed it to Regan, who shrugged.

"MacTaggart."

"Jack? It's Andy. A guy by the name of Garza from the D.A.'s office just came by the club and handed me a subpoena. It says I'm supposed to appear in court on Monday morning at nine. When I asked him what it was about, he said it was a hearing to examine the source of Claudia's bail premium, and that I'd be called as a witness by the district attorney."

"I guess they found your bank account."

"What am I supposed to do?"

"Hire a lawyer. I've told you that twice already. And whatever you do, make sure you're in court on Monday or else the judge will issue a bench warrant for your arrest."

There was silence on the line. Regan swung her boots back under the steering wheel.

"Will they revoke her bail? Send her back to jail?"

"I don't know, Andy. We'll talk about it later."

Regan was reading my face as I ended the call.

"What?"

"Herrera's filed a probable cause declaration on the bail bond."

"Which means what, exactly?"

"It means we're back in court on Monday morning, only now we have the burden of proving that no portion of the bond premium was feloniously obtained."

"Which it was."

"Every penny. If they'd been honest with me from the outset, we could have avoided this."

"So then what? She goes back into custody?"

"Barring a miracle."

The walkie-talkie crackled to life, the kid's voice filling the car.

"Dude, check it out. Dark hair, faded jeans, orange raincoat. Marta thinks it could be him. Over."

I lowered the window. The drizzle had resumed—a swirling gray mist that speckled the binoculars, obscuring my vision.

"I don't see . . . Wait. I've got him."

The figure was bent at the kiosk, punching buttons. He had Alain Giroux's general build and coloring, and he wore what might have been a ski jacket. I traded Regan for the handheld.

"We can't see shit in this weather. If you really think it's him, then I'll meet you inside."

"Roger that. I'll be by the condoms, chillin' like a villain. Over and out."

"If I strangled that kid, no court would ever convict me."

"What is it?"

"Sasquatch sighting." I turned up my collar. "Wait here, but start the engine and keep it running, just in case."

The mall's driveway entrance—fifty feet of landscaping and blacktop— was all that separated the gas station where we'd parked from the street entrance to the pharmacy. I covered it at a run. A bell above the door tinkled as I entered.

The guy was still at the kiosk, his nose pressed to the glass. That and the bunched nylon hood of his jacket obscured my view of his face. Mayday and the kid had already entered the store and were crossing the center aisle, angling for a better view. In his shades and goofy hat, the kid looked like a Hollywood movie star trying not to be recognized.

"Did you get a good look at him?" I whispered to Mayday, who carried copies of both photos on a clipboard. She pretended to sort through a rack of toothbrushes.

"Fleeting. Right age, same general bone structure, but hard to tell for sure."

As I turned back to the kiosk, our target was moving out the street door and into the parking lot, raising the hood as he walked.

"Come on."

He was twenty yards away from us and jogging toward a black Lexus that stood by itself near the main entrance to the mall. We jogged as well, our feet splashing in the puddles, when a silver Range Rover screeched to a halt behind us, the driver laying on the horn.

"Assholes!" a voice called.

The passenger door to the Lexus slammed shut. We picked up our pace.

Mayday, the first of us to reach it, knocked on the Lexus's passenger-side window while the kid and I circled to the driver's side. A smiling young woman lowered her window. There were children, two of them, squirming in the backseat.

"Can I help you?" the woman asked. As I opened my mouth to answer, I heard Mayday addressing the husband.

". . . a survey for Redbox on customer satisfaction." She lifted a pen to her clipboard. "Starting with what you've rented from us today?"

I could see the guy in profile now, his hood pulled all the way back. I straightened and caught Mayday's eye over the roof of the car. I shook my head.

"We've got *Chelsea's Farm,* and *Mission to Belgrade,* and *Training Day.* The wife's a big Ethan Scott fan."

"Excuse me," the kid said, leaning into the driver's window. "Ethan Scott wasn't in *Training Day.* That was Ethan Hawke."

The guy ducked his head. "Ethan Hawke? Are you sure?"

The kid removed his shades. "Trust me," he said.

The rain had all but stopped, and celestial sunbeams were piercing the haze, spotlighting the gleaming blacktop. We walked together as far as the gas station, where the rental car caught my attention.

The fact that it wasn't running. The fact that it was empty.

"What's the matter?"

"Regan. She was supposed to wait for us."

We all looked around. I tried the door, which was unlocked. The walkie-talkie rested in the plastic cup-holder. The photos were missing from the dashboard.

"Let's check inside."

By the time we'd reached the door to the pharmacy, steam was rising off the sunlit asphalt. The bell tinkled. The Redbox kiosk stood unattended.

The store itself appeared deserted until, like a furtive prairie dog, Regan popped her head above the shelving. She stood mid aisle, around halfway toward the mall-side entrance. She saw us and made a gesture with her hands—a finger pointing into her upraised palm.

We followed the finger to the pharmacy counter, where a guy stood with his back to the store. He wore jeans and a dirty camouflage jacket.

Regan held a photo aloft. She nodded urgently and pointed again.

The guy turned from the counter and started for the door to the parking lot. I bent to examine a shelf of laxatives as his gaze swept over us. The bell tinkled, and he was gone.

"Can I help you?" the pharmacist called, but we were already moving.

Outside, we saw him pause to study the sky. He carried his little white pharmacy bag in a clenched fist. He started walking again, faster now, heading toward the silver Range Rover.

"Regan, get to the car. You guys, too. We'll call you on the handheld."

We split—Mayday and Ethan toward the mall entrance, Regan and I toward the gas station. By the time we'd buckled up and backed the rental car and lurched forward into the driveway, the Range Rover was passing us in the opposite direction. We swung a U-turn in the parking lot in time to catch the temporary dealer license plate taped to the rear window.

I toggled the handheld.

"It's Jack, can you hear me?"

Static.

The Range Rover had turned onto Carmel Valley Road. We had to wait for three cars to pass, and then we followed.

"This is Jack, do you guys read me, over?"

"We read you." Mayday was breathless. "Where are you now?"

"West out of the parking lot onto Carmel Valley Road. Now he's turning north on Highway One, heading toward Carmel."

"Roger that," she said. "We're right behind you."

As the Range Rover turned, we signaled to follow. Of the three cars between us, only one was turning right. We waited for it to find a gap in the traffic and we squeezed in right behind. Now there were six cars between us and the Range Rover.

"Don't lose him," I said to Regan as I twisted in my seat. If Mayday was behind us, I couldn't see her.

In less than a mile, the Range Rover signaled a left-hand turn onto Ocean Avenue, the clogged main artery leading straight to the beating heart of Carmel's downtown shopping district. Two of the cars between us did likewise. We slowed again and signaled.

"I see you now," crackled Mayday's voice on the handheld. "We're four . . . make that five cars back."

By the time we'd turned onto the pine-studded avenue, the Range Rover was far enough ahead that we saw it only in flashes. It continued straight, descending through downtown—past the boutiques and art galleries, past the bistros and the quaint little inns—all the way to the public beach parking, where it turned to the right.

The street sign read San Antonio Avenue.

"This place is beautiful," Regan said, her attention wandering to the sidewalks choked with tourists. "It's like some quaint little European village."

"I think that's the general idea."

We made the turn. The Range Rover was dead ahead of us, gliding through the high-rent district of oceanfront homes overlooking Carmel Bay. Regan slowed to put some space between us. I saw Mayday's car make the turn directly behind us.

"Hang back," I said.

We followed as the Range Rover made a little left-right jog onto a street called North San Antonio. At the end of the block stood the guard gate to Pebble Beach and the fabled 17-Mile Drive.

"Where the heck are you going?" I said aloud and then, as if in answer, the driver slowed mid-block and signaled a right-hand turn into a drive-way. Regan pulled hard to the curb.

"Don't stop," I told her. "Do a drive-by."

I lowered my window as she inched the car forward. With an open hand shielding my temple, I watched through spread fingers as our quarry emerged from a garage, the pharmacy bag still swinging at his side. Regan ducked her head to look, and for a fleeting moment both of us had an unobstructed view of the face of the burr-headed man in the dirty camouflage jacket.

The face of Henri LaBoutin.

23

W hat now?" Regan asked.

We'd circled the block and parked both cars at the bottom of Ocean Avenue, a quarter mile from the house on North San Antonio with its million-dollar views of twisted Monterey pines and rocky outcroppings framing the glowing crescent of Carmel Bay. Around us, panting dogs strained at leashes, while a mixed assortment of locals and tourists, kids and geezers, stood by their cars or strode forth with pant legs rolled for a stroll on the world famous beach.

"We should call Ronaldo Herrera," Mayday said, "and not do anything rash."

"Why, so he can waterboard him?"

"What?"

"He doesn't give a hang about LaBoutin. He's already got his suspect, and his fingerprints, and now he's got his motive. If we called him, he'd laugh in our faces."

My phone vibrated. It was Claudia calling. I raised a finger.

"MacTaggart."

"Jack, thank God. A young man was just here—"

"Carlos Garza."

"That's right. He—"

"Served you with a subpoena requiring your appearance in court on Monday morning."

"How did you—?"

"Andy just called me. They served him, too. The D.A. plans to call him as a witness."

There was a pause.

"Is this to revoke my bail?"

"I'm afraid so. We'll discuss it later, okay? Meanwhile, I think we've found Henri LaBoutin."

"In Carmel?"

"Yeah. He's holed up in a rental house near the beach."

"You mean on North San Antonio?"

"Yeah. How did you—?"

"That's the house Father used to rent when we were kids! Near the Carmel gate to Pebble Beach?"

"That's the one."

"Is Alain . . . ?"

"I'm afraid not."

Another pause.

"What are you going to do?"

"We're not sure yet, but I'll tell you what. Call Andy, and let's all have dinner tonight. Maybe around eight. How does that sound?"

"All right," she said. "Call me when you get back to the Valley. And Jack?"

"Yeah?"

"Be careful. Henri LaBoutin can be unpredictable."

"Don't worry," I told her, "I can be unpredictable myself."

I ended the call and turned to Mayday.

"Got your iPad with you?"

"In the car."

"Can you download court forms off the Internet with that thing?"

"Sure," she said, "but I can't print them."

"Shit."

"Why? What are you thinking?"

"That we could serve LaBoutin with a subpoena for Monday's hearing. That way we can put the whole can of worms—the severance payment, LaBoutin's disappearance, the credit card—before the court and see what happens. Shake things up a little. It's a long shot, but it's the only shot we have at keeping Claudia out of jail."

"There was a Kinko's back at that mall," Mayday said. "I could download the form while Ethan drives, and maybe we could print it there."

"Go," I said. "If we're not here waiting, we'll be at the house. Hurry!"

They went. We could see Mayday hunched over her iPad as the kid pulled a U-turn and accelerated up the hill.

"Well," Regan said, hands in pockets. "We could shop, or walk on the beach. Have a cup of tea. Or else we could reconnoiter."

"Still got your gun?"

She flashed me her hip under her windbreaker.

"Let's reconnoiter."

And so we walked. The sun was all the way out now, the coastal fog having receded like a melting glacier into a grayish smudge a half mile out to sea. Shorebirds streaked and cartwheeled, their wings flashing, while an onshore breeze carried the timeless aromas of kelp and whitecap, tide pool and warming sand.

Two blocks later, we stopped on the roadside path with our backs to the house, pretending to take in the view. I glanced over my shoulder.

"I'll bet we could follow that wall on the north side of the house and not be seen," I told her. "Maybe take a peek in the windows."

"And why would we want to do that, exactly?"

"Because we're reconnoitering. And besides, I'm easily bored. Come on."

I took her hand. We strolled for another twenty yards or so, then crossed the street and doubled back. As we approached the house from the north, we watched for signs of life—shut-ins, kids, nosy Neighborhood Watch types—inside the adjoining homes. All appeared deserted.

I bent at the curb to tie my shoelace.

"Ready? Here goes nothing."

Crouching, we followed a four-foot retaining wall up the neighbor's lawn to the north side of the house. There we vaulted over and squatted in the bushes, quietly listening, waiting for our breathing to quiet.

Well, my breathing anyway.

I put a finger to my lips and jerked my head. Still hunching, we duck-walked through some foliage to the first window and took up positions on either side, our backs pressed flat to the house. We each took a furtive peek. Seeing no one, we pivoted for a better look.

This was the front room, its blue-and-white striped sofa and chairs arranged to face the ocean-view windows. The décor was nautical in theme, with sailboat paintings adorning the walls and model sailboats in oversized bottles stashed amid the built-in bookshelves. A new flat-screen television—a real sports bar monstrosity—stood on the floor at the room's center, its wires running off in all directions.

I moved my head again, and we tiptoed up the slope through an over-grown shade garden to the next side-window. This was a bedroom—likewise vacant—but furnished with a crib and playpen, its walls freshly painted in bright baby blue.

Beside the crib was an open door that looked onto a hallway. We heard a toilet flush, and we ducked our heads just as a figure went shuffling past.

We returned to the first window. Frederique LaBoutin, a hand on her enormous belly, sank into one of the armchairs facing the ocean, her le-mur eyes blinking in the bright sunlight. She lifted her bare feet, one at a time, onto a striped ottoman.

I hooked a thumb at Regan and pointed it over the wall. She nodded. We each hopped over onto the adjoining property and slunk back down to the street.

"That was the wife, Frederique," I told her.

"She looks like she's ready to burst."

"I didn't see Henri. Maybe he—"

We both looked up at the sound of the sputtering engine. It came from a green Subaru that slowed as it approached the driveway in front of us. I took Regan's hand, and we turned our faces toward the ocean. The car kept slowing, then it turned into the driveway.

We shared a look.

"Who the hell?"

We walked, still hand-in-hand, both of us watching as a gray-haired matron stepped from the Subaru with what looked like a yoga mat under her arm. She knocked on the door that Henri LaBoutin had entered. We heard voices raised in greeting as the woman stepped into the house.

We stopped and turned around.

"Now what?"

"I don't know about you, but I've got to see this."

This time we sneaked up the driveway side of the house, using the Subaru to shield our approach. The old hatchback was rusted in places, with a faded bumper sticker that read AT LEAST THE WAR ON THE ENVI-RONMENT IS GOING WELL. The front door to the house had a single high window, and I signaled Regan to wait as I slipped past the front end of the car.

The window afforded an oblique angle into the living room, where the new arrival steadied Frederique's arm as she lowered herself to a knee on the rolled-out yoga mat. I turned to Regan and beckoned with my head.

At five-foot-five in her lug-sole boots, Regan tried standing on tiptoes, but still couldn't see in the window. I knelt, lacing my hands into a step.

And that's when I heard something behind me.

In hindsight, the sound of Regan's shout and the concussive force of the blow—a meaty thump to the back of my skull—seemed simultaneous. I recalled toppling sideways, seeming to lose the force of gravity, as the world around me darkened.

And that's all I remembered.

When I opened my eyes again, they were all standing over me—both LaBoutins, the gray-haired midwife, and Regan Fife. Even Mayday and the kid were there, the latter bent forward with his Ray-Bans low on his nose.

The midwife seemed to be speaking.

". . . but I think he'll be all right. Look, his eyes are opening now."

Henri LaBoutin stepped forward, an object held at his side.

"What the hell do you want?" he demanded, his Gallic accent heavy.

I propped myself on an elbow, touching a hand to my head. No blood.

"Name's MacTaggart," I said. "I'm a lawyer, for the Giroux family."

The Frenchman backed a step. "You work with Melchior?"

"No." As I struggled to stand, he raised what turned out to be a wooden rolling pin, which met the muzzle of Regan's Walther somewhere near his right earlobe. The Frenchman's eyes slid to confirm his worst suspicion. He lowered the club, which hit the concrete with a *thunk*.

Ethan Scott proffered a hand, hauling me to my feet. The driveway tilted slightly, and I steadied myself against the house, battling a wave of nausea.

"There's a hearing on Monday," I told LaBoutin, pinching the bridge of my nose. "At the criminal courthouse in Napa. It pertains to Phil Giroux's murder. The court will want to ask you some questions about your arrangement with Philippe."

Frederique grabbed for her husband's arm, but Henri shook her off.

"I don't work for Giroux, and I'm not going back to fucking Napa, so fuck you. And get your ass off my driveway before I throw it off, you hear me?"

He grabbed his wife by the arm and marched her to the door.

"Wait!" I said, my voice stopping him in the driveway. I opened my hand to Mayday, who filled it with a folded sheet of paper. I stepped up to LaBoutin and tugged at his cammo jacket and stuffed the subpoena inside.

"You'll be in court on Monday morning," I told him, my weight backing him against the door, "or you'll be in jail on Monday afternoon."

24

You were unpredictable all right. Who could have predicted you'd vomit all over his shoes?"

Mayday grinned over the steering wheel as she piloted our car back toward Napa. Regan and the kid were in the car behind us, while the flat infinity of the great blue Pacific filled the windshield dead ahead. I tilted the seat back and half-turned toward the center console to shield my skull from the headrest.

"When I serve process—ouch!—I like to include a little extra."

"Here," Mayday said, folding her jacket and offering it as a pillow. "I still think you should have gone to the hospital."

"And had my head examined."

"You suffered a concussion. Just thank your lucky stars Regan was there."

"And that I wasn't standing over a vat of pinot noir."

Mayday lowered the rear windows. We were on Highway 1 north-bound out of Monterey, and the fluttering roar of ocean air filled the conversational lull. Mayday, when she spoke again, had to shout to be heard.

"He'll contact Melchior, you know. And Philippe."

I said, "If he hasn't already."

"I'd pay to see the look on their faces when he calls."

My phone vibrated, and I eyeballed the caller ID.

"It's Bernie."

I put the call on speaker, resting the phone in the plastic cup holder between us.

"MacTaggart."

"What, are you skydiving? It sounds like you're in a friggin' wind tunnel."

Mayday held a button, raising the windows.

"I've got you on speaker. Marta's driving. I'm coagulating."

"Coagulating?"

"Or maybe I'm congealing."

"I don't know what you're talking about, but is Ethan Scott still with you?"

"He's with Regan. They're in the car behind us."

"God, what I wouldn't give. Is he a dreamboat or what?"

"I'm afraid you're asking the wrong people." I adjusted my pillow. "What's on your mind, Bernadette?"

"I thought you should know that a fax just came in. It's a pleading in *People v. Giroux*. The title is 'Notice of Motion and Motion to Revoke Bail; Probable Cause Declaration of Ronaldo Herrera.' There's a hearing set for Monday morning at nine o'clock in the Napa County courthouse. There's also a bunch of exhibits. The thing's like forty pages long."

Mayday said, "Can you scan it and send it to my personal account? I can get it on my iPad."

"Does that mean you're not coming home for the weekend?"

Mayday and I shared a look. "Are you okay with Sam until Tuesday?"

"Are you kidding? Tonight we're watching *Sleepless in Seattle* and doing our nails. But has Ethan mentioned the script at all? Or wanting to meet me?"

"Last I heard, he was still working on the ending," I told her. "I think he's counting on a big surprise."

We'd stopped for a bite in San Francisco, but still made Napa Valley ahead of the weekend tourist traffic. Claudia called to say that dinner would be at her place, and that Clarkson would pick us up at seven-thirty, which left us time to shower and change. And because Ethan Scott's presence would raise confidentiality issues, I was relieved—if somewhat peeved—to learn that our resident celebrity had made dinner plans of his own, with Rachel the bar girl.

Regan stood at the mirror fiddling with an earring as I emerged fully dressed from my bedroom.

"Where's Marta?"

"She went to the business center to print that document. How's your head?"

"Better, thanks." I felt the bump under my hair. "At least the phone's quit ringing."

When Mayday finally returned, she was paging through the D.A.'s motion.

"It's about what we expected," she said. "There are bank records attached, and a copy of the Giroux Family Trust. The basic argument is that Claudia embezzled over twelve million from her father as payback for being disinherited, and that she used part of the illicit proceeds to fund her bail premium."

"That all sounds vaguely familiar."

"There's no mention of the proposed sale of the vineyard, but it looks like they're planning to call Clarkson anyway, since he's a cosignatory on the account. Also the bail bondsman, and Philippe Giroux, and a records custodian from Wells Fargo." She looked up from her reading. "How the heck are we going to oppose this?"

"The same way that porcupines make babies," I told her.

"You mean carefully?"

"Hell no. I mean we're gonna find some way to sneak up on them and stab them in the back."

Regan and Mayday were busy in the dining room, helping to set the table, while Claudia stood in her kitchen stirring a bubbling pot of mushroom risotto. She was also paging through the D.A.'s motion where it lay on the counter next to the stovetop.

"He makes three basic arguments," I told her, leaning my weight on the fridge. "First, that because the bail premium was feloniously obtained, your bail should be revoked and you should be remanded to custody."

Hovering in the doorway behind us, Clarkson said, "Can't I just substitute a new premium from my personal savings? Won't that cure the goddamn problem?"

"I'm afraid it's not that simple. The D.A.'s second argument is that because we made a knowing misrepresentation to the court as to the source of the bond premium, that alone is grounds to disqualify Claudia from bail."

"She didn't make any misrepresentation. She didn't even speak."

Clarkson's protectiveness—his looming, tutelary presence—was starting to wear on my nerves.

"I spoke on her behalf, Andy. And when Herrera raised the issue, I said that the bail premium was coming out of your pocket."

"There you go. You said it, not her."

I turned to face him. "What are you suggesting? Should I tell the court that the reason I said what I did is because my client and her boyfriend both lied to me, so please don't hold it against them?"

Claudia lowered the heat on the stovetop. "What's his third argument?"

"His third argument is that because the embezzlement provides a financial motive for your brother's murder, this is now a capital case for which no bail is warranted in any event."

She stopped stirring.

"You mean the death penalty."

"I'm afraid so. They haven't filed as yet, but that's clearly their intention."

"Shit," Clarkson said, patting at his pockets.

"Don't you dare smoke in this house, Andy." Claudia turned from the stove and arranged five bowls on the counter. "We wouldn't want to deprive the district attorney by shortening my life expectancy."

"I don't mean to be an alarmist," I told Claudia, "but we need to start thinking about worst-case scenarios. If bail is revoked on Monday, and if the D.A. files a superseding indictment on either the embezzlement count or the capital murder charge, then there's a good chance you'll be in custody for a while. At least until the trial is over."

"Jesus Christ!" Clarkson was pacing now, doing the hand-rake thing with his hair.

Claudia asked, "When will the trial be held?"

"I don't know. With a prelim set for October, we could be looking at spring of next year."

"Spring?" Clarkson stopped and turned. "What about LaBoutin? Won't his testimony help us?"

"I'm not sure," I admitted. "Philippe and Melchior went to a lot of trouble to make him disappear, so no matter what LaBoutin says about the so-called severance payment, I think I can make them all look dirty."

"And how will that help Claudia?"

"I can't guarantee that it will. But the problem we've had until now is that the court has been focused exclusively on Claudia, because that's where the D.A. keeps pointing. If we can't divert the D.A.'s attention, then maybe we can divert the court's. But I need to be honest with both of you. This embezzlement business is making the murder case extremely difficult to defend."

While it wasn't the cheeriest dinner party I've ever attended, it was definitely one of the tastiest. Claudia had grated fresh Parmesan onto the risotto, and she'd served it with two bottles of the 1992 Château Giroux Cabernet, the last dregs of which she emptied into Clarkson's glass while answering Mayday's questions about Melchior.

"Thad went into partnership with his father-in-law, Bernard Moore, in the early nineteen-seventies," Claudia told her. "Moore had been a sole practitioner, back when Napa was a quiet farming town. He'd represented Grandfather for years, going all the way back to Prohibition. It was Moore who prepared Grandfather's trust, although he was very old by then. He died in nineteen seventy-nine or eighty, I believe."

"Was he an estate-planning attorney?"

"I think he was more of a general practitioner, back before lawyers really specialized. When Moore died, Thad took over his practice."

Mayday turned to where I sat beside Clarkson. "I've checked up on Melchior, and he's no country bumpkin. He's a Stanford Law graduate who practiced at Pillsbury, Madison and Sutro for over a decade before coming up to Napa."

Clarkson asked me, "What will Melchior do when he hears that Henri is going to testify?"

"We were speculating about that earlier. He could counsel Henri to ignore the subpoena, but that would be unethical, and it would only result in a bench warrant for Henri's arrest, which is probably the last thing they want. And it's not likely that Henri will run again, not after just getting settled."

Mayday added, "And not with his wife about to give birth."

"My guess is he'll show. He really has no other choice."

"Then what?"

I looked at Mayday. "Then we'll see if we can't sneak up on him from behind."

It was ten o'clock by the time we'd helped Claudia dry the last of the dinner dishes. Mayday and Regan were both stifling yawns, the three of us having departed for Carmel at dawn, over seventeen hours earlier. And from the looks Clarkson was giving Claudia, I could tell he regretted having volunteered to drive us from Napa Springs Spa—and that he'd have to drive us home again.

Claudia dried her hands on a towel. "Thank you for helping, and for everything you've done today. I'm sorry if I've appeared frustrated at times, but I want you all to know how very grateful I am. I really mean that. Whatever happens to me on Monday."

Regan gave her a hug, while Mayday, I noticed, did not. When she turned to face me, I offered her my hand.

"Stay positive," I told her. "If there's one thing I've learned in this business, it's to expect the unexpected."

"Would it be all right if I keep that?" She nodded to the bail motion, still resting on the countertop. "I'd like to read it more carefully. Maybe I'll remember something useful from law school."

"Of course," Mayday told her. "I can always print another."

We all stood looking at Clarkson, who appeared to be rooted in place.

"Hey," I said. "Here's an idea. What if I drive Andy's car back to the club and leave it in the parking lot out front?"

"That won't be—"

"Thanks," Clarkson said, digging into his pocket. "Just leave the keys under the floor mat."

In the darkness outside the Petit Trianon, where the stone château's turrets stood in black silhouette against the blue ink of the sky, the chirping of frogs and crickets were the evening's only sounds. I fumbled for the UNLOCK button on Clarkson's key fob, and the parking lights of his Beemer flashed to confirm that I'd found it. I powered on my cell phone as I circled to the driver's side door. It chimed to announce a text message.

"What is it?" Regan asked, reading the look on my face.

"A text. I never get texts."

The message appeared in a little green word balloon, like the kind you'd see in a comic strip. It read:

It's high time we had a talk. Tomorrow, Silverado Country Club, 8:30 A.M. Hope you're a gambler. Thad Melchior.

25

We stood on the first tee of the North Course looking down the barrel of a narrow par four with a gentle dogleg right. Beyond the oak trees crowding the left side of the fairway stood condos or hotel units—an unbroken line of whitewashed two-story duplexes with balconies overlooking the golf course. Melchior squatted behind our cart, a cigar clamped in his teeth, rummaging his bag for a lighter, while I stood on the tee box in my rented golf shoes warming up with my rented three-wood.

The old lawyer suspended his search long enough to observe, "That might be the ugliest golf swing I've ever seen."

Okay, so I'm not a golfer. Truth is, I'd only played a few rounds in my life, and the last of those was over a dozen years ago. Moreover, I'd learned my swing technique from watching my uncle Louis—a public-course hustler for whom I'd occasionally caddied—and Uncle Louis had honed it with the specific goal of disguising his three-handicap.

I, on the other hand, had nothing to hide.

"Show us the way," Melchior said, leaning on the cart and gesturing with his stogie as I teed up a brand-new Titleist. I'd bought five sleeves of new balls—fifteen balls in total—in anticipation of inventory shrinkage.

I gave my three-wood a waggle as I addressed the first victim.

"Oh, and about that bet," Melchior said as I began my backswing.

I turned to glare at him. "What bet?"

"Skins. Ten dollars a hole, ties carry over. How does that sound?"

I resumed my stance. "Let's make it twenty."

Aiming for the left side of the fairway, I hit a sweeping banana slice that landed deep in the right-hand rough, maybe two hundred yards away. I feigned pique, but was actually quite pleased.

Melchior rested his cigar on the hood of the cart. He was thin and bandy-legged, and he approached the tee box with his driver. After a few practice swings, he stepped to his ball and rapped it straight down the middle, maybe 175, the ball coming to rest in the center-left fairway.

"That's a peach," I told him. "Does your husband play as well?"

Melchior drove the cart.

"I take it you don't get out to play very much," he said as we hurtled down the cart path, his silver hair fluttering in the breeze.

"What was your first clue?"

He removed the cigar from his mouth and spat. "Yet you pressed my bet without quibbling or asking for strokes. That tells me something."

"What's it tell you?"

"That you're cocky, for one thing. But I already knew that."

Melchior's ball had found a perfect lie maybe two hundred seventy yards from a target green flanked by sand traps left and right. Either by luck or design, he'd left himself a straight, line-of-sight angle to the flagstick. He chose a five iron.

"Too much real estate for me," he said, pausing and grooving his swing. "When I was your age I'd have gone for it, but today I'm laying up."

He took a three-quarter swing, lifting a high fade that carried maybe one-forty, again finding the center of the fairway. He had, as I was starting to appreciate, a classic old-man's game—short, straight, and always in the right position.

I, on the other hand, found Redwood National Forest blocking my view of the green-side bunkers.

"You should play it safe," Melchior suggested. He gestured with his cigar to the open fairway to my left. "Live to fight another day."

"Is that golf advice or legal advice?"

Again I drew the three-wood from my bag. With my ball sitting down in the second cut of rough, the shot I had in mind should play perfectly to my slice.

"Christ, watch those condos," Melchior said as he backed the cart, whirring and beeping, out of harm's way. "I have clients who live over there."

I swung with all my might. With a grassy *thwack,* my ball started left, heading toward the condos, then faded into the center of the fairway, bouncing and rolling to a halt just short of the bunkers, maybe forty feet from the flag. It was a hell of a shot.

"Better to be lucky than good," I told Melchior.

"Is that a golf aphorism," he said, disengaging the foot brake, "or a legal one?"

I managed to get up and down in three strokes, carding a bogie five. Melchior hit his approach to within ten feet, then made his putt for par.

I was down a skin.

"Not to rush things," I said as we waited for the twosome ahead of us to finish on the par-three second hole, "but your text message said something about a talk."

He examined the lit end of his cigar.

"A little birdie tells me you served a subpoena yesterday. I have to say, I'm impressed with your resourcefulness. It's your discretion that gives me pause."

"I can be as discreet as the next guy, Thad. Go home and ask your wife."

"You see that? That's exactly what I'm talking about. There's no profit in antagonizing me. We can help each other, you and I, but all this public grandstanding is distressing to my client who, need I remind you, used to be your client as well."

I turned to face him. "I represented Philippe Giroux in a very limited capacity. Our attorney client relationship ended in July, when he lied to me about some credit card records and got his ascot caught in a ringer."

"Nonetheless, he respects you. I dare say, he even likes you. Plus he has a keen interest in the matter of his daughter's prosecution. Surely you can appreciate that."

The twosome on the green ahead of us replaced the flagstick and moved off to their cart. The distance on the card read 195 from the blue tees. I pulled a four-iron from my bag.

"He's interested all right. Interested enough to spend a hundred grand and counting to make his gardener disappear. Stuff like that, Thad, it piques my curiosity. For example, why would the gardener, when I told him I was representing the Giroux family, ask me whether I worked for you?"

"He'd probably heard my name mentioned around the house, that's all. You're not one of these conspiracy-theory types, are you? Black helicopters and chemical trails?"

A creek bordered the right-hand side of the fairway, while houses loomed large on the left. It was a narrow, nasty little hole for golfers like me who are prone to asymmetrical play.

"You go ahead," Melchior said, bending to relight his cigar. "We'll play ready golf."

I found a broken tee and pressed my lucky ball into the ground.

"So what is it, exactly, you wanted to discuss?"

He waited while I hit my four-iron long and right, the ball sailing over the treetops and landing in the creek, the splash visible from where we both stood leaning our bodies in silent telekinesis.

Melchior went back to his bag and switched his iron for a hybrid.

"Discretion, Mr. MacTaggart. That's what we were talking about. My client is a public figure. When all is said and done, he'll have lost both his sons, and his daughter will be in prison. If not for murder, then almost certainly for embezzlement. Which was a nasty piece of business, by the way, even for a spoiled brat like Claudia. So while he has no control over what's already happened, my client is keen to see his life returned to some semblance of normalcy. That means no more press coverage, and no more legal proceedings than are absolutely necessary. And no parading his household staff before the cameras like show ponies."

Melchior teed his ball and stepped back to consider his approach. He then stepped up and hit a low draw that bounced twice and trickled onto the front edge of the green.

"Nice shot."

He nodded. "Discretion. It's like club selection. The right choice in the right situation can make all the difference in the world."

"Okay, so Philippe doesn't want Henri LaBoutin to testify on Monday, is that your point?"

"That's one of my points," he said as he returned his club and resumed his place behind the wheel. "The other is sparing his daughter any unnecessary pain or humiliation."

"That's very thoughtful of him. How does he propose to do that?"

We zipped across the fairway, then wended our way through a cluster of trees until we came to the spot where my ball had entered the lateral hazard. With a one-stroke penalty, I'd take a drop and be lying two. But I still wasn't out of the woods.

"Despite what you might have heard to the contrary, MacTaggart, my client has no control over the district attorney's investigation or his prosecutorial decision-making. Would that it were otherwise. So while there's nothing Philippe can do about the murder charge, he might be in a position to steer the embezzlement investigation in a manner that's advantageous to your client. If, that is, she's willing to reciprocate."

I climbed from the cart and fished another golf ball from my bag. Holding it at arm's length, I dropped it onto a flat patch of grass beside the creek.

"I failed circumlocution in law school, Thad, so maybe you could just tell me what it is you have in mind."

Like Rodin's statue of *The Thinker,* Melchior sat sideways in the cart with his elbow on his knee and his fuzzy chin resting on his fist. He looked around, up and down the fairway, as though leery of being overheard.

"Our proposition is this. If Claudia withdraws the subpoena you served on Henri LaBoutin and promises never to bother him again, then her father will take the stand on Monday and testify that all of the withdrawals made by Claudia from the various corporate accounts were known to and fully authorized by him. Bonuses, we'll call them. With both her brothers gone, there's nobody left to contradict him. In short, Mr. MacTaggart, we'll make the embezzlement case go away."

"And let her keep the money?"

He chuckled. "That, I'm afraid, is a bridge too far. Think of this as a one-time amnesty. If she returns the money, then Philippe will accept it and let bygones be bygones."

I chose a sand wedge, which was the only club in my bag theoretically capable of lifting a ball over the trees and the bunker without flying the green beyond. I took a practice swing, and then another. Then I stepped up to my ball and swung as hard as I could.

Whack!

I'd skulled it, the blade of the club rocketing the ball low across the pine straw. Like a running rabbit, it disappeared among the trees and then scooted into the green-side bunker, from which it flew up the opposite lip, like a kid on a skateboard ramp, landing two feet from the flagstick.

Melchior was shaking his head.

"Setting aside for a moment the ethical and legal ramifications of your proposal," I told him, giving my sand wedge a twirl, "there are practical issues as well. Taxes, for one thing. Plus if I quash the subpoena to Henri, then how do I know Philippe will hold up his end of the bargain?"

"You'll have our word on that."

We were back in the cart, retracing our path across the fairway. Both balls dotted the green to starboard, while the tee box to port stood empty.

"Allow me to reframe your proposal," I told him. "Philippe, who authorized various loans to Claudia over the years from the corporate bank accounts, will gladly so testify on Monday. Henri LaBoutin will be present in court to witness that testimony pursuant to my subpoena. Once Philippe so testifies, then Henri will be released from his obligation to appear, and will never be called as a witness. Claudia, meanwhile, in anticipation of her forthcoming trial, will repay her corporate loans in full. Is that what you meant to say?"

We marked our balls and stood with our putters in hand. Melchior was away. He replaced his ball and squatted to reread the fifteen feet of sloping green that lay between his ball and the cup. He rose to stand over his putt.

"How do we know she'll repay the money?"

"I suppose we could set up some sort of escrow."

He thought for a moment, then lightly tapped at his ball. It gathered speed as it moved, breaking hard left-to-right, coming to rest three feet past the cup.

Melchior was still away. This time he circled the green, assessing the putt—and my proposition—from every possible angle.

"She'll bring a cashier's check to court," he finally said. "I'll trust you to hold it."

"Funny how you'd think of that."

Again he stood over his ball. The putt was uphill now, and he stroked it firmly, but his ball died a half inch short of its target.

Never up, never in.

"That's good," I told him, conceding the bogie. I replaced my ball and pocketed my marker.

Melchior said, "And how do I know that if Philippe testifies as we've discussed, you won't go ahead and call Mr. LaBoutin anyway?"

I stroked my two-footer for bogie, tying the hole.

"Trust me, Thad. I'm a lawyer."

26

Y ou can't do it."

Mayday set her iPad down just as Regan executed a graceful flip off the diving board, twisting and tucking and entering without a splash. That girl was full of surprises.

"First of all, you'd be suborning perjured testimony. Secondly, you'd be foreclosing our only line of defense in the murder trial."

"But the murder case is winnable even without LaBoutin's testimony. Remember, I didn't agree not to bring up the severance payment or the new credit card. We can still use those to cross-examine Philippe and raise a reasonable doubt. Especially if the AmEx records show what we think they'll show."

She was still shaking her head.

"Think of it this way," I told her. "We're no worse off than if we hadn't located Henri. Only now we can make the embezzlement case go away, and almost certainly keep Claudia out on bail. Besides, I lost three hundred and twenty bucks in skins to get this deal. You think Clarkson will question that as a line item on our cost bill?"

Mayday didn't smile, and she still wasn't buying it, which is exactly what I'd expected. In fact, I'd have been disappointed otherwise.

"Okay then, let's consider the alternative. We've received what amounts to a settlement offer. Aren't we obligated to communicate that to our client? And if she wants to accept it, are we representing her best interests if we tell her she can't? Or that she'll have to fire us first? Because that won't make the problem go away. She'll just hire another lawyer, and then she and Melchior will do the deal anyway behind her new lawyer's back. The result will be the same."

"Yes," Mayday said, "except that it won't be our result. You're proposing to join in a conspiracy to obstruct justice."

Regan had climbed from the pool and was padding over to join us. She and Mayday had obviously been shopping, since both wore new one-piece racing suits that, in Regan's case, looked to have been freshly painted onto her body.

"Who's conspiring to do what?" she asked, sitting on Mayday's chaise and draping a towel over her shoulders.

We used Regan as a neutral sounding board, each of us arguing our case. She listened to both sides, then stood to shake water from her ear and render her verdict.

"I think you at least need to tell Claudia. If you don't, and if she finds out later, she'll be pissed. I know I would. Especially if I was in jail."

Mayday said, "And what if she wants to take the deal? We can't just sit there with our mouths shut and let Philippe lie to the court."

"Why not?" I said. "We're not the ones calling him as a witness. Besides, all I ever do is sit in court and listen to people lie. That's pretty much my job description."

"No, your job is to expose lies and seek the truth. That's your ethical obligation as a lawyer. Here you'd be doing the polar opposite."

"While keeping our client out of jail."

"Our guilty client."

"Whom we've agreed to zealously defend."

Mayday threw up her hands as she stood.

"How, exactly? By tying a hand behind your back? Because that's what you're doing. There's a *reason* Philippe doesn't want Henri LaBoutin to testify, and it has nothing to do with discretion or adverse publicity or saving his daughter from embarrassment."

"We both know that," I told her. "But Regan's right. It's Claudia's call to make, not ours. She's the one going to trial. And if we lose, she's the one who'll be serving the time."

Mayday wriggled out of her shorts and started for the pool.

"Wait, there's one other thing."

She stopped and turned, her arms folded.

"When I accused Philippe of having lied to me about Alain, Melchior didn't deny it. 'Nonetheless,' is what he said. That's pretty significant."

"Why?" Regan asked.

"Because," Mayday told her, "that means Philippe's been lying to Jack from day one. So what else is he lying about?"

Claudia rose from her dining table and crossed to the window, where she parted the curtains and looked out toward the stone château.

"If Father testifies that the withdrawals were loans, then there's no longer an issue about the source of my bond premium, or misrepresentations having been made to the court, or a financial motive for wanting my brother dead. Is that what you're saying?"

"That's exactly what I'm saying. In all likelihood, you remain free on bond."

"That's essential," she said, turning to face us. "I can't go back to that jail."

"But there's a trade-off," Mayday told her. "Your father has gone to great lengths to shield Henri LaBoutin, and it's obvious he doesn't want Henri to testify. By agreeing not to call Henri as a witness, you're playing right into his hands. You're compromising what might be your best defense to the murder charge."

"I don't care about that," she said.

Mayday and I shared a look.

"What I mean," Claudia said, her tone softening, "is that we need to take this one step at a time. Once we get past this bail revocation hearing, then we can worry about the trial. You said that will be months away, right?"

"Right."

"And Father's testimony will prevent the district attorney from making this into a capital case?"

"For now, anyway."

"Then that settles it. Even if I am hindering my own defense, at least it won't be a capital charge I'm defending. That alone makes the deal worth taking."

I looked first to Mayday and then to the clock on the wall. "In that case, you have two hours to get to the bank. Let's just hope they haven't frozen the account."

"It has to be a cashier's check?"

I nodded. "I hold the check until after the hearing on Monday. If your father testifies as promised, then I tender it to Melchior."

I could see in Claudia's face a flock of C-notes as they flapped out the door like bats departing a cave at sunset. She sighed.

"At least returning the money will help poor Andy."

"You mean he'll no longer be an accessory to a charge of embezzlement."

She looked at Mayday. "I mean that after you left last night, he told me that he planned to testify it was all his idea. That he'd threatened me, or blackmailed me somehow into stealing the money in order to fund his golf course expansion."

"That's why he hasn't hired a lawyer," Mayday said.

I said, "That's why he ought to hire a shrink."

As we turned south on Silverado Trail toward the Napa Springs Spa, I dialed the private number Melchior had given me.

"Good afternoon," he answered, sounding wary. As though fearing, as I was, that the conversation might be recorded.

"And to you. I was mulling over our round this morning, and I want you to know that I like your suggestion very much."

"I'm glad to hear that. You've cleared it with your playing partner?"

"I have. She wasn't thrilled with the penalty strokes, but what can you do?"

"Exactly. They'd have been assessed in any event."

"That's what I told her."

"And you'll be holding the bet?"

"As we agreed."

"Excellent. Well then, so glad we had a chance to play together. I guess I'll see you in court on Monday."

"Right. Oh, and Thad? Are you sure your friend can't help me solve my other problem?"

He chuckled at that. "I'm afraid not. My friend makes his wine from grapes, Mr. MacTaggart. Not from water."

There's a unique odor—an oleaginous mingling of dust and wood polish, incense and candle wax—that's instantly familiar to anyone, anywhere, who was raised in the Catholic faith. I'm thinking they must manufacture it in the basement of the Vatican and ship it out to the various dioceses in fifty-gallon drums. If they were smart, they'd bottle the stuff and sell it as perfume, or maybe as aftershave.

They could call it *Guilt*. They'd make a fortune.

I recognized that smell as I followed a secretary from the reception area down a silent corridor to an oak door on which she knocked once and then opened without awaiting a reply. The two men in black arose from where they'd been sitting at a small conference table in the middle of a wood-paneled room. The bishop's office was spacious and subdued, and could have passed for a judge's chambers but for absence of law books and the presence of a heavy bronze statue of the crucified Christ hanging over his empty desk.

"Mr. MacTaggart. So good of you to come," said the man in the purple zucchetto, gesturing to the chair opposite his lawyer. Blueprints or building plans—oversized sheets of architectural schematics—blanketed the table between them.

We settled into our seats while the secretary crossed to a silver tea service that had been laid out on a sideboard. The bishop waited in silence until she'd delivered a tray heaping with all the accoutrements, including a three-tiered serving dish laden with delicate pastries, setting the whole thing carefully at the bishop's right hand.

The bishop smiled, and the secretary withdrew.

"Lemon? Or just sugar, perhaps," the bishop inquired, filling the cups as Father Quinn, the Harvard man, dealt out saucers and napkins.

"I'll take mine straight," I told them, tilting for a better look at the drawings and recognizing in their blue-line geometry the distinctive glass façade of the Château Giroux Visitor Center.

"We received them this morning," Quinn explained, noting my interest. "From Lourdes Giroux. Luckily, her husband had a set. Also a copy of his grandfather's trust."

"Ah."

"You're familiar, I'm told, with the latter document," the bishop said, blowing gently into the teacup he lifted with his pinkie extended. "Needless to say, we're delighted with the late Monsieur Giroux's generosity and foresight."

"Just as you're saddened, I'm sure, by the intervening circumstances."

"Of course." The bishop nodded gravely. "A tragic series of events for all concerned."

Not all, I thought, helping myself to one of the little éclairs.

"This business of finding the real killer," the bishop continued, turning to face me. "Is that wishful thinking on Lourdes's part, or is there really a question as to your client's innocence? Speaking in strictest confidence, of course."

"Since we're speaking in confidence, you wouldn't happen to have a cold Budweiser stashed away in a fridge somewhere? I'm afraid I'm not much of a tea man."

The clerics shared a look.

"I don't believe we do. But perhaps we could open a bottle of wine?"

"Never mind. To answer your question, Claudia Giroux didn't kill her brother. To answer your next question, I don't know who did, but I'm toying with the idea that it might have been someone with an interest in seeing that the Church inherits the Château Giroux winery. I don't suppose any suspects leap to mind? Confidentially, of course."

"That's very amusing, Mr. MacTaggart. Very amusing indeed."

"Yeah, I'm a funny guy. So far I've been seduced, lied to, threatened, flipped off, set up, cold-cocked, propositioned, and double-crossed, and here I sit no closer to finding Phil Giroux's killer than I was when I stepped off the plane on Monday morning. So if I seem less than my usual cheery self, chalk it up to frustration." I pinched another éclair. "But enough about me. What's up with the blueprints?"

"Lourdes and her husband had plans for expansion," Father Quinn explained, pointing to a blank area behind the Visitor Center. "A barracks of some sort over here, and a schoolhouse and health clinic there. She wanted to be sure we knew about that."

"Which begs the question, is the diocese planning to run the place, or to flip it for a quick infusion of cash?"

The bishop's eyes lifting to the crucifix over his desk.

"I don't know if you realize this, Mr. MacTaggart, but the Catholic Church has a storied tradition of winemaking in this part of the world. It was a Jesuit missionary, in fact, who planted the first grapevines in what is now California, back in the seventeenth century. And of course the great Franciscan, Junípero Serra, planted vineyards at all of the California missions he established in his travels. In the modern era, the Institute of the Brothers of the Christian Schools established a winery in Martinez in 1882 before moving their operations to Napa Valley in the 1920s. While Prohibition was decimating California's nascent commercial wine-making industry, the Christian Brothers continued making sacramental wine, enabling them to emerge as industry leaders following Repeal."

"Seizing opportunity in the face of tragedy," I said, raising my teacup. "Another storied Church tradition."

Neither man thought that was funny.

"The Christian Brothers winery was sold in 1989," Quinn said, taking up the narrative, "and for a quarter century, the Church has had no real presence in an industry it all but established." He gestured to the blueprints. "But now, all of that is about to change."

"Have you talked to Philippe about any of this?"

The two priests shared a look.

"Actually," Quinn said, "that's why we've been so looking forward to this meeting. You see, we've tried reaching out to Mr. Giroux, and also to his lawyer, Mr. Melchior, but they haven't returned our calls. Technically, the Giroux family are squatters at this point. We thought perhaps that you, having represented both father and daughter, might be in a position to help us."

"Help you with what? You own the place. If they're squatters, have them evicted."

"Yes, but it's not that simple. To insure a smooth transition, we'll need to work with either Philippe or Claudia. Moreover, we'd like to retain the family name and its attendant goodwill. That means having a family member as part of our team going forward. Lourdes can fill that role at least, but she's never had an active hand in management."

The bishop leaned forward, his gold ring glinting in the overhead lights.

"We'd like your help, Mr. MacTaggart, in bringing one of them— either father or daughter—to the bargaining table. We're prepared to offer a generous consulting contract to whoever's the first to accept it. To be perfectly candid, we'd prefer to work with Philippe, given his daughter's— how shall we say it?—recent notoriety. We do have an image to think of. But Claudia will do in a pinch, since time is of the essence, and since our consulting arrangement need never become public."

"Ravens" is how Philippe had described them, but to me they recalled characters from a medieval costume drama—*Becket*, or maybe *A Man for All Seasons*—scheming powers behind the throne who profess piety while plotting regicide from the dark cloister of their torchlit dungeon lair.

Then again, maybe I'd spent too much time with Bernadette.

"I can't actually speak for Philippe," I told them, returning my cup to its saucer, "but I'll be very surprised if he's interested. As for Claudia, her availability depends on a hearing that's scheduled for court on Monday morning."

"Rest assured that we'd make it worth her while," the bishop persisted, and as I wiped the chocolate from my fingertips onto my napkin, I pictured Claudia at that very moment, standing at a teller's window at a bank in San Francisco.

"I'll communicate your offer," I told them. "Who knows, she's having an expensive weekend, so maybe she'd welcome the gig."

27

Claudia Giroux laughed.

"Helping the Catholic Church assume ownership of Château Giroux? If Father found out, he'd have a thrombosis. Come to think of it, that's as good a reason as any to accept."

I think she was a little tipsy. We were on our second glass of bubbly, both of us seated at a round patio table under a huge umbrella on a concrete terrace so vast that it made the one at Pilate's Trattoria look like a narrow widow's walk. Our view to the east was onto a manicured formal garden with the parking lot beyond, while behind us, a three-story pile of stone and slate called Domaine Carneros—the American outpost of the Taittinger Champagne empire—rose like Walt Disney's version of the Élysée Palace.

When Claudia had called me to suggest a Sunday-morning picnic, I'd envisioned a blanket under a shade tree beside a rocky, babbling brook. Instead she'd driven me south beyond Napa to the Highway 121 split—the fork in the road at which northbound visitors chose between the Sonoma and Napa Valleys. We had entered, she explained, the Los Carneros AVA—a viticultural region hard by the shore of San Pablo Bay whose cooling breezes created ideal conditions for growing pinot noir and

Chardonnay grapes, the dross from which California's golden sparkling wines—never call them champagnes, Claudia had admonished—was spun.

"I can't imagine Father living anywhere but Château Giroux," Claudia continued, lifting our bottle from the ice bucket and topping off our glasses. "Did you know that he was born there? Right in the master bedroom of the château. And except for the years he spent in Bordeaux after high school, he's lived in that house his entire life."

"Maybe they'll let him stay on."

"Oh, no, he's much too proud for that. Imagine a former president keeping a room in the White House—being physically present at the seat of power, but having no power to exercise." She shook her head. "If I were the new owners, I'd never let it happen. And if I did sign on as a consultant, his eviction would be the first condition of my employment."

When the waitress returned to check on us, Claudia ordered a cheese plate and a tasting flight of caviar. I ordered a Budweiser. The waitress thought that was funny.

"So where do you think he'll go?"

Claudia's brow furrowed. "That's the thing—I can't imagine him going anywhere. I mean that literally. His DNA is imprinted on Château Giroux. It's like, I don't know . . . Apple without Steve Jobs. Only Steve Jobs wasn't born in Cupertino, and his name wasn't on the product, and he didn't sleep every night of his life in a bed on the Apple campus."

"What are you saying?"

She shrugged, taking up her glass. "I'm saying I'm not convinced. I'm saying that Father has always found a way both to get what he wants and to keep what he has. Speaking of which."

She twisted in her seat to unhook her bag from the chair-back. She removed a folded envelope from inside and slid it across the table.

The check was payable to Giroux Beverage, Inc. The memo line read "Loan Repayment."

Meanwhile, a woman in a dark business suit and a brass name badge had emerged from the building and was approaching our table with long, confident strides. Claudia stood, and the two women embraced.

"Sylvia Bennett, this is Jack MacTaggart. Jack's a friend from L.A."

I stood to shake hands. Sylvia, whom I surmised to be Claudia's counterpart at Domaine Carneros, gave me the once-over.

"Pleased to make your acquaintance," she said to me, and to Claudia, "If you have any more like him, would you send one my way?"

The ladies chatted about the wine, and the weather, and about some marketing conference they were both scheduled to attend, and when they'd run out of small talk they exchanged an awkward air kiss, both having avoided the elephant on the terrace.

Sylvia gave a little wave, and we watched her disappear back into the building.

"Sylvia is a dear, and much too polite to mention my legal woes, but you can see what life will be like for me here, whether or not I'm actually acquitted."

"If you don't go to work for the Church, then what else would you do?"

"That's a good question. I have a few thousand in savings," she said, "and my car. The clothes in my closet, some good jewelry, and a few pieces of art. I never imagined having to worry about what I'd do for work, or where I'd live. I always assumed I'd be at Château Giroux until I could open my own winery. I was going to call it Morel Vineyards, by the way. Mother's maiden name was Morel, spelled like the mushroom. I'd even reserved the domain name, and had some preliminary sketches done for the label. Stupid of me, counting chickens like that."

She sighed, reaching for her glass.

"I guess Father and I aren't so different after all. Neither of us appears to have had a viable plan B."

The food appeared with another bottle of wine, both compliments of Sylvia Bennett. We finished both while watching the tourists arrive and depart, posing for pictures with the garden or with the rolling acres of vineyard as a backdrop.

Neither of us should have been driving, but since I outweighed her by a hundred pounds, I was the one behind the wheel of her Porsche as we zoomed back into Napa Valley, bypassing the entrance to the Napa Springs Spa and Golf Resort and roaring over the hill to the gates of Château Giroux.

There were no news vans in the Visitor Center parking lot. Outside the Petit Trianon, where I pulled to a stop behind my rental car, Claudia turned in the passenger seat to face me.

"Does twelve million buy me a little more of your time?"

"At my hourly rate it should buy you approximately . . . three years."

"I'll settle for an hour."

I sat on a couch in her living room—the same room that she'd cleared of furniture for her brother Phil's post-funeral reception. With all the furnishings restored, the room exuded a kind of Middle Eastern exoticism—kilim textiles and dark, intricately carved woods. There was an abstract canvas on the wall above the fireplace that I hadn't noticed on Thursday, rendered in the same reds and blues as the geometrical carpet.

From the kitchen, she called for my drink order. It was ice water.

She returned with two tall glasses and set them on the coffee table. She crossed to the stereo cabinet. Norah Jones—all soft and breathy—caressed the room as Claudia eased onto the leather couch beside me, lifting her water glass in a toast.

"Thank you for sharing what might have been my final day of freedom. If I have to survive on prison fare for the rest of my life, I'll always remember my last taste of champagne and caviar."

"Sparkling wine," I told her, touching my glass to hers.

Her body brushed against me as she returned her glass to the table. Her hand came to rest on my knee, and the kiss that followed was long and tender and sent my brain for a swim. Not a quick dip, but a Diana Nyad marathon that brought to mind a story Claudia had told me at brunch, about the seventeenth-century Benedictine monk who, as the cellar master of a small abbey in Reims, had made the mistake of bottling the order's altar wine before fermentation was complete. In spring, when the bottles warmed again and fermentation resumed, the result was a sparkling beverage that would make the Champagne region of France famous throughout the world. Upon sampling his creation, the old monk—whose name, of course, was Dom Pérignon—was alleged to have exclaimed, "I am drinking the stars!"

Claudia pulled away, but the stars still sparkled.

"I'm sorry," she said, breathless, her hands fumbling for the buttons on my shirt. "I know I promised to behave myself, but . . ."

I stood, mentally slapping my face with a rolled up copy of the Rules of Professional Responsibility. I crossed the room toward the painting. It was, I realized then, a nude—soft hips and breasts emerging from the abstract swirls of red and blue.

I wondered if Alain had painted it. I wondered if Claudia had posed.

"Where's Andy today?" I said, just to say something. "I would have thought you'd need a restraining order to keep him away."

She was sitting forward now, hugging herself.

"I told him I had affairs to put in order."

"Which I'm sure you do, so I shouldn't keep you any longer." I looked at my watch. "Thank you again for the picnic. I'll see you at the court-house tomorrow morning at eight forty-five. You probably shouldn't drive, by the way, just in case—"

"My car ends up in the parking lot for the next thirty years?"

She reached for her water glass. She had begun to cry.

"Where were you?" Regan demanded as I returned to our little apartment above the spa and made a bee line for the fridge.

"Collecting debts for Philippe Giroux. Where's Marta?"

"She went to church. I've broken her of several habits, but that's one I'm still working on. I expect her back shortly."

"If she comes back tall, maybe I'll start going."

I sniffed at the milk carton and took a slug, wiping my mouth on my sleeve.

"That's disgusting."

"You haven't tried fish eggs for breakfast."

I offered her the carton but she shook her head. She laid her newspaper aside and sat up on the couch. "Are you in Marta's doghouse for some reason?"

"Uh-oh. Why do you ask?"

"I don't know, but I know something's been bothering her."

"That's usually me. Did she drop any hints?"

She shook her head again. "This may come as a shock, but we don't actually talk about work all that much. Not if I can help it. And don't forget, we're having dinner with Ethan tonight."

I returned the milk to the fridge and snatched the sports section off the table.

"In that case, I think I'll grab a little nap. If I'm not up by four, send up a flare."

I got as far as the bedroom when I stopped at the threshold and turned around to face her.

"Hey, Regan. You ever seen the film *Pretty Woman*?"

"Of course."

"You know at the end, when Richard Gere climbs up the fire escape?"

"Yeah?"

"Do you think they lived happily ever after?"

28

———◆———

"Hearsay," the kid said, frowning at Mayday's iPad. "I still don't get it."

"It's complicated," she told him, lifting the Chardonnay bottle and topping off Regan's glass, "especially all the exceptions. Just focus on the basic rule. Hearsay is evidence of a statement made by someone other than the witness who's testifying in court, and that's being offered to prove the truth of the matter stated."

"This wine sucks," I told him.

"Dude, you're not even drinking."

"Exactly. So if you were to testify that I said the wine at Meadowood sucks, that would be hearsay if offered to prove that the wine is no good."

His brow furrowed.

"Think of it this way. A statement of fact shouldn't be allowed in court unless the person making the statement is there to be cross-examined. So if you're the witness, and you say the wine sucks, then that's okay. They can cross-examine you and ask you why. But if you testify that MacTaggart said the wine sucks, then that would be hearsay because I'm the one who made the statement, not you, and I'm not there in court to be cross-examined. And if they ever did cross-examine me, they'd find out that I never tasted the wine to begin with, thus proving the wisdom of the rule."

"I guess that makes sense."

"Then you're in worse shape than I thought, and you should have a glass of wine."

It was Sunday evening, an hour before our eight o'clock dinner reservation, and Mayday, Regan, and I were sprawled on the plush white sofas of Ethan Scott's three-grand-per-night estate suite at the Meadowood resort in St. Helena where our host, looking purposely studious—or was it studiously purposeful?—in a pair of Clark Kent eyeglasses, struggled to learn the rules of evidence from a Web site Mayday had located for his benefit.

All of which reminded me of a story I'd once read, about the actor Dustin Hoffman. He and the legendary Sir Laurence Olivier were filming *Marathon Man* in New York in the mid-seventies. When a scene called for Hoffman's character to have been awake for three days, Hoffman, a scrupulous method actor, himself stayed awake for three days in order to get the feeling right. When told of his costar's dedication to the craft, Olivier drolly replied, "Why doesn't he just try acting?"

Mayday returned the dripping bottle to the ice bucket. "Will Claudia be joining us?" she asked me.

"She said she wanted to get her affairs in order. I have a feeling she just wanted to be alone."

Regan looked up from her magazine. "What about Rachel?" she asked the kid. "She's a beautiful girl, and you two seem to be hitting it off."

"Nah."

That got my attention. "What happened?"

He shrugged. "*Res ipsa loquitur.*"

"Exactly."

"No, dude, what does it mean?"

"It's Latin," Mayday told him. "It means 'the thing speaks for itself.' But it's a rule of tort liability, not a rule of evidence."

"Then when does a document speak for itself?"

I sighed. "Do you really need to know this stuff? I'm betting Raymond Burr never studied the rules of evidence."

"Who's Raymond Burr?"

I covered my face with a pillow.

Mayday asked, "Do you remember we talked about the best evidence rule?"

The kid consulted his notes. "Secondary evidence of a document may not be admitted to prove its contents unless the document is unavailable."

"Right. The corollary is that if a document is available, then the terms of the document are what govern and not, for example, what a witness says he thinks the document means. In that case, the document is said to speak for itself."

"Speaking only for myself," I said, swinging my feet to the floor, "I need to stretch my legs. I'll be back before dinner."

"Wait up," Mayday said, bending to gather her shoes from the floor. "I'll walk with you."

After descending a ziggurat of outdoor decks and staircases, we found ourselves on a wooded path leading in the general direction of the resort's tennis courts. We'd been walking in silence, enjoying the sunset and the pine scent and the sylvan quiet broken only by the distant *pock* of tennis balls, when Mayday finally broke the ice.

"I have a bad feeling about tomorrow."

"I know that, but we've already—"

"No, that's not what I mean. I'm talking about Claudia."

"What about her?"

She didn't answer at first, which gave me the sinking feeling that I knew exactly where this was heading.

"I know it's late in the game to be saying this, but I'm really regretting our decision to represent her."

"You mean my decision."

"I meant our decision. Especially knowing what we do now, about the embezzlement scheme and her whole inheritance plan. In furtherance of which she's lied to us, and used us to perpetrate a fraud on the court. Not once, but twice. And now she's doing it again, only this time with our full knowledge and complicity."

"She didn't murder her brother."

"Let me finish. So as far as I'm concerned, she already has three strikes against her, and it seems like every time we walk into a courtroom on her behalf, she throws us another curve."

When Mayday dusts off the sporting allusions, you know there's a lecture coming. There was a bench on the path ahead of us, and I sat.

"But that's not the worst of it," she continued. "I have no doubt that if Melchior hadn't offered us this deal, then Claudia would have allowed Andy Clarkson to throw himself under the bus on her behalf. It's astounding, really. I don't think I've ever seen a man more tightly wrapped around a woman's little finger. Or a woman less reluctant to twist."

She sat down beside me, her body angled toward mine, our knees almost touching.

"And that's what concerns me most of all. Claudia's ability to charm people, to charm men, into overlooking the obvious. Namely that she's a conniver, and a liar, and a world-class manipulator."

"Let's don't beat around the bush."

"That's an interesting word choice, Jack."

So there it was. I stood.

"Do you know what Clarkson told me the other day? He said that when Claudia was a girl, Philippe used to come to her bedroom at night and bribe her into having sex. He'd offer to buy her things, like bicycles and clothes. He also threatened that if she told anyone, her mother would have to leave, and it would all be her fault."

"That's horrible, if it's true."

"That's exactly what I said. If it's true."

I sat down again beside her.

"Listen to us. If it's true? My God, we've become jaded."

"We've become realists," she said. "And from one realist to another, here's something else to think about. Even if Claudia's story were true, then there's the further question of who was actually bribing whom."

"Wow. You really don't like her, do you?"

"It's not a question of like or dislike. The point is, I don't trust her, not for a minute. And with that being said, is there anything else you'd like to tell me?"

"Yeah. Aren't you the one who once told me that your personal life was none of my business?"

"That was different," she said. "I wasn't sleeping with a client."

"Neither am I."

"Good, I'm glad to hear that. Especially since the client is probably a murderer."

I turned to look at her.

"What do you mean?"

"Come on, Jack. She's the one who's been pulling all the strings. She's the one who was vulnerable to exposure, the one with everything to lose. It was her fingerprints on the murder weapon. She has no credible alibi, and she has a history of mental instability, whatever the alleged cause. The list goes on and on."

"We've been over this a dozen times. Why would she kill her brother?"

"I don't know. Maybe Phil did threaten to expose her. Or maybe her father did, and she killed Phil as revenge, so the Church would get Château Giroux. Or maybe she has some side-deal with the bishop. Who the heck knows? The point is, we haven't been focused on Claudia because we've been too busy listening to her stories about how horrible her father is, and how Alain might still be alive."

"Me, you mean. I'm the one who's been listening."

This time she didn't respond.

"What about Henri LaBoutin?"

"What about him? If he were the killer, would he still be around? Regan is right about that. Maybe Philippe is just a generous employer. It was Claudia, don't forget, who told us otherwise. And it was Claudia who practically jumped at the deal to keep LaBoutin off the witness stand."

By now the tennis game had ended, and the only sounds in the woods were the gentle trilling of crickets.

"So what are you saying, that I should renege on my deal with Melchior and put LaBoutin on the witness stand?"

She shook her head. "I don't know. I guess what I'm saying is that if we're ever going to solve this thing, then we need to start looking at it from a different angle. Not just through the frame provided to us by Claudia Giroux."

At our corner window table, Ethan Scott raised his wineglass in a toast.

"Okay you guys, listen up. I'm heading back to L.A. after the hearing tomorrow, so I just want to take this opportunity to say that it's been really real, and that if any of you are ever out Malibu way, you'd damn well better look me up, and I mean that. You've given me some really great stuff to work with, and I'm warning you right now that if my career as an actor ever goes sideways, I just might enroll in law school."

"In that case," I told him, "we're all going to hell."

We touched glasses.

Regan, with two glasses of Chardonnay already under her belt, demanded, "Tell us about this film project of yours. What is it, like, another Grisham novel?"

"Nah, it's just a concept in development. I have this production company, see, and we're thinking about optioning a screenplay. I haven't read it yet. In fact, I'm not even sure that it's finished yet, but it's loosely based on this case."

"And you're going to pattern your character after this guy?" She hooked a thumb in my direction. "You're sure it isn't a horror film?"

"Objection," the kid said. "Leading."

"And what about us? Is there a part for a lesbian cop and her brilliant, beautiful partner who do all the dirty work and keep the lawyer out of trouble?"

"I believe that would make it a fantasy," I told her.

"Actually," the kid said, "I've been thinking about the casting. Who do you think should play Marta?"

"Bearing in mind," I said, "that Natalie Wood is dead."

"Who?"

"Never mind. How about Penélope Cruz?"

"Too old," Regan said. "What about Eva Mendes?"

"Dude, she's even older. I was thinking Selena Gomez."

"Good idea. Then Justin Bieber can play Regan."

"Shut up, Jack."

"Objection," the kid said, joining in the laughter. "Excessively harsh."

29

As we rolled to a stop in the courthouse parking lot, I spied Herrera and Walker in the aisle directly ahead of us. They were bent over the open trunk of their official county vehicle, hefting heavy banker's boxes onto a folding luggage cart.

"Looks like they're loaded for bear," I told the kid, who, in his navy suit and striped rep tie, looked every inch the bright young lawyer he aspired to portray.

"Dude, how come we don't have any boxes?"

"Boxes are for sissies. And besides, we have something better."

"What's that?"

"An overconfident prosecutor."

The kid craned his neck, searching for the rental car in which Mayday and Regan had gone, at Claudia's request, to fetch her to the courthouse. She'd specifically asked, in fact, that I not be the one to pick her up.

"Dude, they should have been here by now."

No sooner had the words left his mouth than the blue Ford Fusion swung into the parking lot. The kid alighted to wave it over while, in the aisle ahead of us, Walker slammed the trunk and grabbed the cart handle,

trailing the district attorney up the pedestrian mall toward the courthouse entrance.

Regan pulled into the space beside us, then unbuckled her seat belt
and reached across the console to stow her Walther in the glove compart-
ment. As Mayday emerged from the backseat with her briefcase, I circled
both vehicles and opened the passenger door for Claudia, who swung her
legs onto the blacktop.

"I appreciate the show of confidence," I told her, taking hold of her hand.

"What do you mean?"

"Your watch. A pessimist might have gone with plastic."

She looked at the gold bracelet on her wrist, which, were she to be remanded into custody after the hearing, would wind up in a storage room
at the jail.

"This is my lucky charm," she said, rising to her full height. "Mother
bought it for my high school graduation."

Other vehicles were arriving as we spoke. Andy Clarkson's BMW. The
church's white limousine, from which Lourdes emerged in the company
of Father Quinn. A battered Mercedes sedan driven by the ponytailed
bail bondsman who today, with a subpoena in his pocket, wore notice-
ably less jewelry than at the previous hearing.

Clarkson hurried to join us, and while he and Claudia huddled, I
watched as Larry the Driver piloted Philippe's gleaming Town Car to a
halt. Philippe, then Melchior, and then Henri LaBoutin each stepped to
the curb, where I was relieved to see the gardener sporting a striped soc-
cer jersey over jeans and ratty sneakers.

Relieved, because it meant he had no plans to testify.

My eyes followed Claudia as we made our way up the long pedestrian
mall toward the courthouse. She'd worn a black business suit with matching black pumps, and her hair glowed like poppies in a summer morning
meadow. She appeared especially nervous—fidgeting with her jacket, tug-
ging at the ends of her sleeves—and I wondered how I'd comport myself
if I were the one staring into the business end of a long prison stretch.

Lourdes had waited for her sister-in-law by the courthouse entrance,
and the two women embraced.

I had a flashback then—a gauzy déjà vu in which Claudia stood back-lit by a fireplace. I glanced at Mayday who, like me, had been watching our client. My hand went to my pocket—the one that held a folded ca-shier's check for twelve-and-a-half-million dollars. Enough money, I thought, for two to live comfortable lifetimes in a place like Chile or New Zealand.

"It's not too late," Mayday said, sidling up beside me.

"What?"

"To change your mind about LaBoutin. The reason Claudia wanted to ride with us was to ask us in confidence if doing the Melchior deal was going to get you into trouble. She said if it was, then you had her permis-sion to back out. So you see, it's not too late."

"Why didn't she mention that yesterday?"

"I don't know. Maybe she's having an eleventh-hour outbreak of con-science."

Claudia held the heavy glass door, and the six of us—Regan and the kid, me and Mayday, Clarkson and then Claudia—all entered the court-house together.

There was a line for the metal detectors, and when we finally reached the front, I removed my phone and my belt and laid my briefcase on the conveyor belt. Behind me, Claudia let out a startled sound.

"My purse!"

"Do you need it?" Clarkson stood on the other side of the security checkpoint, his belt still in his hands. "I can run back to the car."

"No," she said. "I'll go. I have time, don't I?"

"Sure," I told her, "but you'd better hurry."

She accepted the keys from Regan, and with the *klack klack* of her heels on the marble floor tiles, disappeared back into the sunlight.

"All rise!"

The Honorable Walter Saxby, his black robes flapping, alighted on the bench. The courtroom was nearly empty this morning, word of the un-scheduled hearing having failed to reach either the local or national media,

most of which, like our own Terina Webb, had returned over the weekend to their regular regional beats.

As the judge sat, so did the witnesses, leaving me with an unobstructed view of the closed door to the courtroom.

"In the matter of *People versus Giroux*," the judge read from his file,
"we have a motion by the people to rescind the defendant's bail. All counsel are present, and the defendant—"

Here the judge paused, realizing that the defense table was one-third
short of a trio.

"Mr. MacTaggart? Where's the defendant?"

I stood. "She's here, Your Honor. She went back to the car for her purse."

While the judge scowled at the clock, I caught Regan's eye and gestured
with my head. She stood and moved toward the door.

"Very well," said the judge, "we can give her another minute. Meanwhile, I've read the people's motion. Has the defense filed any written
opposition?"

"We have not, Your Honor, but we obviously oppose the motion. We'll
take the People's witnesses on cross."

The judge nodded. He eyed the clock again, which now read 9:05. He
drummed his fingers on the bench.

"Mr. Herrera? Any objection to starting without the defendant being
present, assuming Mr. MacTaggart concurs?"

Herrera and Walker huddled, and the D.A. raised his head.

"No objection."

"Mr. MacTaggart?"

I stood again. "The defense has no objection."

"Very well. Mr. Herrera, this is your motion. Call your first witness."

Herrera turned to the gallery. "The People call Sandra Portman, a records custodian from Wells Fargo Bank."

A nervous young woman, birdlike in her manner, rose from her seat
and flitted through the gate that the bailiff held open. After she'd been
sworn and answered some preliminary questions from Herrera about her
background and job duties, the D.A. placed a tall stack of bank statements on the witness stand before her.

"Calling your attention to the joint savings account maintained by the accused and Andrew Clarkson at the Pacific Heights branch . . ." Herrera began his next question, just as Regan returned to the courtroom. I rolled backward in my chair.

"She's gone," Regan whispered over the bar. "The car's gone. My fucking gun is gone."

"Mr. MacTaggart?" the judge interrupted.

"A moment, Your Honor."

I handed her my keys. "Take the other car and go to Château Giroux. Check the house and the Visitor Center. Call me when you get there."

I stood again as Regan hurried for the door.

"It seems, Your Honor, that Miss Giroux is missing. My investigator, Ms. Fife, is going to look for her."

The judge's eyes narrowed.

"Missing?"

"She was here a moment ago, but we think she may have left her purse at home. With any luck, she'll be back in a jiff."

"Mr. Herrera?" the judge asked without moving his flinty gaze from me.

"A jiff?" the D.A. said, hands in pockets. "Is that longer or shorter than a tricc?"

The judge drummed his fingers. Again he looked at the clock.

"All right, we have witnesses in the courtroom with better things to do than sit around waiting for Miss Giroux. Let's keep going."

It took another forty minutes for Herrera to complete his examination of the records custodian, during which he established the timing, amounts, and sources of the many deposits made to the Wells Fargo account. It was a dreary exercise that ended with a bang when the witness, unbidden, informed both the court and the district attorney that the account had been closed on Saturday afternoon.

"Are you saying the funds were *withdrawn*?" the D.A. yelped, cutting an accusing look toward our table. "Withdrawn how?"

"Apparently Miss Giroux requested a cashier's check over the counter."

"Hearsay," Ethan Scott stage-whispered over the railing from behind me. I waved a shushing hand behind my back.

"Mr. MacTaggart?" the judge demanded, as if I were the one under oath. As if he expected me to offer testimony against my client. As if it was my fault the D.A. hadn't frozen the account when he'd had the chance.

I stood.

"No objection," I said, sitting again as both men glared in my direction.

"Your Honor," the D.A. pleaded. "In light of this testimony, and the fact of the defendant's failure to appear—"

"Now I'll object," I said, again finding my feet. "If that's a question, then the form is improper. If it's an argument, then it's a little early in the day."

The judge pursed his lips. After a moment, he nodded. "Sustained. Any further questions for this witness, Mr. Herrera?"

There were not, and I didn't bother to cross-examine. As Sandra Portman stepped down from the witness stand, the judge looked at the clock, the D.A. looked at his watch, and I looked at my cell phone. We all looked at the door to the courtroom.

"The people next call Philippe Giroux."

As Herrera announced his name, Philippe leaned to have a word to Melchior before standing and squaring his shoulders. He sidestepped past LaBoutin as he made his way to the center aisle.

"Do you solemnly swear that the testimony you are about to give in the cause now pending before this court shall be the truth, the whole truth, and nothing but the truth, so help you God?"

"I do," Philippe answered in a quiet voice before lowering his hand and settling in the witness chair.

I turned to look at Melchior, who gave an imperceptible nod as Herrera rose to examine.

"What is your relationship, Mr. Giroux, to the defendant Claudia Giroux?"

"Claudia is my daughter."

"Your only daughter?"

"That is correct."

"And what is your present affiliation with the winery known as Château Giroux?"

"Château Giroux is owned by a corporation, Giroux Beverage. I am the president of that corporation. I am also the chairman of its board of directors."

"Are you also a shareholder in Giroux Beverage?"

Philippe looked at the judge. "I'm afraid it's a bit complicated. The capital stock of Giroux Beverage is owned by a testamentary trust of which I am the sole trustee."

Herrera laid a familiar document on our table before approaching the witness.

"Do you recognize what's been marked for identification as people's exhibit one-seventeen to be a true and correct copy of the instrument establishing the testamentary trust you've just described?"

Philippe removed his cheaters from an inside pocket. Knowing where this was heading, I flipped ahead to the relevant trust language, which appeared at paragraph twelve:

> When the youngest living son of Philippe Giroux attains the age of forty (40) years, this Trust shall terminate and the corpus thereof shall be distributed to the living male issue of Philippe Giroux in equal shares. If all of the male issue of Philippe Giroux should die before attaining the age of forty (40) years, then this Trust shall terminate and the corpus thereof shall be distributed to the Roman Catholic Diocese of Santa Rosa, California.

"Yes, this is the trust document."

Herrera approached the clerk. "Offer exhibit one-seventeen."

"No objection," I said, just as my cell phone vibrated.

I knew the caller was Regan. I also knew that Philippe was five minutes away from exonerating Claudia on the embezzlement charge. I glanced over at Mayday. My hand went to my phone, then came away again. I let it vibrate.

"Calling your attention to paragraph twelve of the trust instrument," Herrera continued, his voice rising, "is it your understanding that Claudia

Giroux, your only daughter, had been disinherited by her grandfather, and that the Château Giroux winery was to pass to one or both of her brothers?"

"Best evidence," came the kid's whispered voice from behind me. He had the right idea—Philippe's understanding of the trust language was irrelevant in this context, as the document spoke for itself—but it would have made for a nuisance objection, and so I let it slide.

"Yes," Philippe replied. "That is my understanding."

"And is it also true that your daughter's sole source of income was her salary as an employee of Giroux Beverage?"

"To my knowledge, yes."

"She'd inherited nothing else, as far as you know?"

"That is correct."

"What is her position at Giroux Beverage?"

"Claudia was, or perhaps still is, the chief financial officer. She's also a director."

"How long has she held the position of chief financial officer?"

"Approximately eight years."

"And her annual salary is what?"

He considered it. "I believe her current annual salary is one hundred and twenty thousand dollars."

Herrera moved a step closer to the witness.

"Is it true, Mr. Giroux, that in her position as chief financial officer of Giroux Beverage, your daughter Claudia was entrusted to pay the corporation's bills and payroll and to balance the corporate bank accounts?"

"Yes, that is correct. Claudia was in charge of every aspect of the company's finances."

"And were you aware of a personal relationship between your daughter Claudia and a gentleman named Andrew Clarkson, whom I believe is present in the courtroom this morning?"

Philippe stiffened ever so slightly, his eyes finding Clarkson in the gallery.

"No, I was not. Not until last week."

Herrera crossed to the clerk's desk. He hefted the stack of Wells Fargo bank statements already in evidence, and he set them before the witness.

"Mr. Giroux, were you present in the courtroom when Miss Portman of Wells Fargo Bank testified?"

"Yes."

"Let the record reflect that I have placed before the witness people's exhibits one through one-eleven. Directing your attention to these bank statements, Mr. Giroux, will you please tell the court whether you were aware of the fact that your daughter Claudia had, over the course of the past seven-plus years, transferred some twelve-and-a-half-million dollars from the corporate bank accounts of Giroux Beverage to a personal account she shared with Mr. Clarkson at Wells Fargo Bank?"

Silence hung over the courtroom. Philippe shifted in his chair. He glanced over Herrera's shoulder, to where Henri LaBoutin sat beside Melchior.

"I wasn't aware of Clarkson's involvement, but yes, I was aware of these transactions. They were loans to my daughter that I, as the corporation's president, had personally approved."

You don't spend a decade in L.A. courtrooms without witnessing a little drama now and again. I, for example, had seen witnesses cry, and lawyers brawl, and a bailiff tackle a prisoner. I'd once watched a judge throw a book at a lawyer in mid-argument. I'd seen a prosecutor taken out of a courtroom in handcuffs.

Until that day, however, I'd never seen a lawyer rendered speechless.

Ronaldo Herrera stared at the witness for close to twenty seconds. He gestured to the bank statements, his mouth opening to speak, but no words came. He turned a pleading look to Yolanda Walker at the table behind him. He looked to the judge.

"Mr. Herrera? Anything further of this witness?"

"I . . . yes, Your Honor. If these were loans, Mr. Giroux, then where are the promissory notes? Where are the corporate resolutions approving the loans?"

"Compound," the kid whispered, and again he was right. Again I didn't object.

"We're a small family company, Mr. Herrera," Philippe explained. "We don't always observe those kinds of corporate formalities, especially in transactions involving my children."

Again the district attorney stood mute.

"Mr. Herrera? Anything more from this witness?"

Herrera's shoulders sagged. He shook his head. He shuffled back to the prosecution table.

I used the lull to check the voice mail screen on my cell phone. I stood.

"No questions of this witness, Your Honor, but might this be a good time for the morning recess? Because I just had a phone call from my investigator, Ms. Fife."

His gears suddenly meshing, Herrera jumped to his feet.

"Regardless of this morning's testimony, Your Honor, the defendant's failure to appear is itself grounds for revoking her bail. She has twelve million dollars, for God's sake! The people request that a bench warrant issue immediately."

The judge looked first to the D.A., and then at the clock on the wall. He sighed.

"Very well. We'll stand in recess, and I'll see counsel in chambers."

30

While the spectators stood and stretched and Herrera followed the judge through the door behind the bench, I tapped the voice mail icon on my cell phone. Mayday moved closer to listen.

"Jack, it's Regan. Nobody in the tasting room has seen Claudia, and the office door is locked. Her car is at the house, but nobody answered my knock, so I let myself in. The house is empty. I don't think she came back. I'll sit tight here and wait for your call."

"What should we do?"

I looked to the door behind the bench. "What we shouldn't do is keep the judge waiting. You go ahead. Tell him I'll be there in a minute."

I tapped the CALL BACK button, and Regan answered before the first ring had ended.

"Jack?"

"Yeah, I just got your message. What's your status?"

"Nothing new to report. Wherever she went, it wasn't back here. I'm in her bedroom right now. Her car keys are on the dresser, but her purse is gone. Bed's made. Looks like she really was doing homework last night."

"What do you mean?"

"The trust thing, that document you guys left her, is on the nightstand. And so is a textbook."

"What book?"

"Wait a minute. Hold on. It's called *Estate Planning Principles and Problems*."

My eyes fell to the Giroux Family Trust, still open on the table before me.

"What do you want me to do next? I could run over to the spa, but I think it'd be a waste of . . ."

Whatever Regan said next, I didn't hear it over the grinding sound of my own gears starting to mesh.

"Second chances."

"What?"

"Philippe." I turned to where the old man stood in the center aisle, quietly conferring with Melchior. "Philippe said he saluted me for believing in second chances."

"What has that got to do with—"

"Never mind. I have to go."

I pushed through the gate and brushed past Philippe and Melchior, the lawyer's voice calling after me as I slammed through the courtroom door to the hallway.

A crowd milled by the elevators. I shoved past them to the stairwell door, where I took the two flights down to the lobby in flying leaps and bounds.

In less than a minute, I was outside.

Still trotting, I raised a hand to scan the curb and the parking lot beyond. After a moment, I saw what I was looking for.

"Larry!" I called, approaching him at a run. The chauffer was leaning on the shaded fender of Philippe's limousine. He was reading a newspaper.

I doubled over, breathless, when I reached him.

"Larry, do you trust me?"

"Sure I trust—"

"I need to borrow your car."

"The car? No, I can't—"

"Sure you can. Here."

I took the cashier's check from my pocket and pressed it into his hand.

"That's for your boss. Tell him he can buy a fleet of limos, but I need the keys to this one right now."

Larry examined the check. He whistled. His hand went into his pocket.

"Thanks," I said, snatching the keys. I slammed the driver's door and turned the ignition, the big eight-cylinder engine roaring to life. "Don't worry, I'll bring it back in one piece!"

The limo handled like an aircraft carrier, slow to get going and sluggish to turn. I'd swung it in a wide loop around the parking lot and pointed it toward Third Street when I glimpsed a navy-blue blur in my side view mirror. Ethan Scott was yelling and chasing after the car.

"Get in!" I shouted, slowing just enough for him to execute a hobo's running clamber into the backseat as I accelerated toward the highway.

"Dude, what's the hurry? What's going on?"

I eyed him in the mirror. "Hang on, junior. This may be a wild ride."

The traffic on Third Street was sparse, and I slowed only slightly before blowing through each of the traffic lights. Not until we were safely southbound on Highway 29 did I punch up Mayday on my cell.

"Jack?" Her voice was a whisper. "Jack, where are you?"

I put the phone on speaker, setting it in a cup holder in the center console. The kid leaned forward to listen.

"I'm in a borrowed car on Highway twenty-nine heading toward Carmel. Ethan is with me. By the way, I gave the cashier's check to Larry, Philippe's driver. You might want to tell that to Melchior."

There was silence on the line as I pictured Mayday excusing herself from the confab in Saxby's chambers. After a moment, she returned in a normal voice.

"Carmel? What's going on? The judge is issuing a bench warrant for Claudia's arrest."

"Good. She has an hour's lead on us, but this boat should easily do a hundred once I open her up."

"Will you stop talking in riddles and tell me what you're doing?"

"I'm going after Claudia. It's the motive, Marta, I finally figured it out. I know who killed Phil Giroux, and I know why."

"Are you saying it was Claudia?"

The needle on the speedometer showed eighty-five and rising, and the gas gauge read three-quarters full. I was sliding left and right, weaving through southbound traffic and using my horn to run interference.

"No, not Claudia. Listen carefully. Go all the way back to the beginning, after the avalanche killed Alain in February. It was Philippe's idea to stall the ownership transfer, by making it appear that Alain was still alive. He approached Claudia, probably with the same save-the-winery bullshit he fed to me. Little did he know that Claudia had her own agenda. She had a plan already in motion to buy her one-third of the vineyard with her father's own money, using Clarkson as a front. So she played right along with Philippe. She ordered the replacement credit card, and she took it on trips, and she forged Alain's signature. Philippe thought they were in cahoots—that he was manipulating her. In fact, it was the other way around."

"We already know all that. She was setting him up for the probate hearing."

"Right. She and Clarkson pestered Phil into bringing the probate action and having Alain declared dead. That would clear the path for Phil to sell the fifty acres to Clarkson. Then once we were hired by Philippe and the credit card statements were filed with the court, she made a false confession to her brother. Something like, 'Daddy made me do it. Check my old appointments calendar on the computer.'"

"Revealing the credit card scheme."

"And double-crossing Philippe in the process. So at that point, everything was Jake. Alain was declared dead, Phil was set to inherit, and he'd agreed to sell the acreage to Clarkson. Claudia would finally have her one-third share of the estate, and Lourdes and Phil could use the sale proceeds to build their workers' paradise."

"But then Phil was murdered. By LaBoutin?"

We were doing a hundred now, hewing to the left-hand lane and flashing our brights at the cars up ahead. They all moved aside.

"No, not by LaBoutin. Think about motive. That's what's been missing this whole goddamned case. And then it hit me in the courtroom this morning. First when Ethan said 'best evidence' and then later, as I was talking to Regan. When I reread the trust language."

"What are you talking about?"

"The trust instrument. *Tabellae pro ipsa loquitur*—the language speaks for itself. It doesn't matter what Maxine Cameron thought it meant, or what Ronaldo Herrera thought it meant, or what Father Quinn thought it meant. It doesn't even matter what Moore intended. The language means what it says—nothing more, nothing less."

"Come on, Jack. You're not making sense."

"Think, Marta. The trust was drafted by Bernard Moore, Melchior's father-in-law. He was an old man, and a general practitioner, and a sloppy draftsman. At some point while Alain was still alive, Philippe must have shown the trust instrument to Melchior, the contract specialist. Melchior realized what it really meant, and he explained it to Philippe. And that's what set the whole plan in motion."

"What plan? What are you even talking about?"

"Philippe's plan—to keep control of the winery. Stop for a minute and put yourself in his shoes. He'd worked his whole life building the business, all without a single word of thanks from his father. Instead he wound up being a placeholder, a bookmark, just waiting for his sons to grow up and inherit everything. That devastated him, and it gnawed at him for decades. But then Melchior gave him the key."

"What key?"

"The key to the castle. A way that Philippe could keep Château Giroux for the rest of his life. It's right there in the language of the trust. Do you have it handy? I left it sitting on our table in the courtroom."

"Wait a minute . . . Okay, I've got it."

"Read paragraph twelve. It's only two sentences, but don't read them together as a whole. That was my mistake. Read them separately."

"Hold on . . ."

"The first one describes what will happen when Philippe's youngest living son reaches age forty."

She read the language aloud. "'. . . the Trust shall terminate and the corpus thereof shall be distributed to the living male issue of Philippe Giroux.'"

"Right. So after Alain died, that's what would have happened on Phil's birthday. The trust would have ended, and Phil would have gotten everything. Okay, now read the second sentence. It describes what will cause the trust to fail and the corpus to be distributed to the Church."

Again she read out loud. "'If all of the male issue of Philippe Giroux should die before obtaining the age of forty years—'"

"Stop. That's it. That's the key."

"I still don't—"

"*All* the male issue. Not just Phil or Alain."

Silence. Then, "Oh, my God."

"You see? Philippe could retain control of Château Giroux for the rest of his life. All he had to do was father another son."

There was a longer silence as Mayday moved the final pieces into place. "Frederique."

"Right again. Philippe wasn't hiding Henri LaBoutin—he didn't give a shit about Henri LaBoutin. He was hiding Frederique. After Melchior explained the trust language, back when Alain was still alive, Philippe must have approached the LaBoutins with a proposition. Something like, if Frederique will have my baby, and if the baby is a boy, then I'll make you both rich. Melchior would have drafted some kind of surrogacy contract. I'm guessing the hundred grand was a down payment, probably dependent on the amniocentesis, to determine the baby's sex."

"But can a man his age—"

"I guess he could, the old rascal. Remind me to drink more wine."

I saw blue lights in the mirror behind me. Cursing, I slowed and changed lanes. Two Highway Patrol units zoomed past without slowing. I charged lanes and fell in behind them.

"Okay," Mayday said, "but that still doesn't tell us who killed Phil."

"Yes it does. Follow the motive. Frederique was already pregnant at the time of the avalanche. She'd been scheduled to bear Philippe his fourth child at a time when Alain would still have been only thirty-nine years old. When the trust would still be in place."

"But then Alain died."

"And that changed everything. It screwed up the timetable, and it placed all of Philippe's eggs in one basket. Luckily for him, the baby was a boy. But he still had to keep Alain alive until the baby was born, in order to forestall termination of the trust."

"Which would have happened automatically on Phil's fortieth birthday."

"And so he hired us. But then Claudia, who knew nothing about Philippe's real plan, put a stick in his spokes at the probate hearing."

"Leaving Philippe with only one option to stop the trust from distributing."

"The terminal option. He had to stop Phil from reaching forty. That would leave the trust in limbo until Frederique had her baby. At that point, with another male heir in the picture, he could fight the Catholic Church over the estate, and almost certainly win."

She fell silent again, thinking it backward and forward.

"But wouldn't news of the baby's birth make Philippe the prime suspect?"

"Yes it would. But not if he kept the baby a secret until someone else has been charged, tried, and convicted. Which is why he went to such pains to make Frederique disappear."

"And to set Claudia up for her own brother's murder."

"Exactly."

"But how? How did he do it?"

"I'm not sure, but here's what I think. Philippe was livid at Claudia. For reasons he still didn't understand, she'd double-crossed him in probate court, leaving him with a terrible dilemma. He went into seclusion— alone, and brooding, and maybe drinking too much—and he thought about life after Château Giroux. About Phil selling acreage to Andy Clarkson. About Lourdes and Phil in control of whatever was left. And if he couldn't live with that, then he knew there was only one solution. He'd always blamed his father for the trust, but now he blamed his daughter for forcing him to contemplate something as terrible as murder."

"Worse than murder."

"And then one evening, as the deadline to act was approaching, he made up his mind. He somehow knew that Claudia had gone into the winery building, so he watched from the laboratory. When he saw Claudia leave, he slipped on a pair of rubber gloves. He climbed onto the ladder, hit Phil from behind, forced his head under the surface, and left the punch-down tool with Claudia's prints on the floor to be found."

"Killing two birds with one stone."

"And to his warped way of thinking, giving himself a second chance in life. Both as a parent, and as the owner of Château Giroux."

We were in Vallejo now, approaching the on-ramp to Interstate 80. There'd been an accident—a pickup and a white stretch limo—and five CHP units were already on the scene with their light-bars flashing. I slowed again to change lanes.

"All right, I'll buy it," Mayday said. "But there's one thing I still don't understand."

"What's that?"

"Why is Claudia heading to Carmel?"

We took the on-ramp with four tires squealing. At last on the open freeway, I put the pedal all the way to the floor.

"Because Claudia figured it out before we did. That's why she wanted you and Regan to give her a ride to the courthouse. To where she knew Henri LaBoutin would be waiting, leaving Frederique alone at home. In the car where she knew Regan would have to stash her gun."

"Are you saying—"

"Yes, damn it. Claudia's gone to Carmel to kill Frederique's baby."

31

It was high noon when I made the final turn onto North San Antonio Avenue. I'd been anticipating police cars and commotion, flashing lights and shouting paramedics, but I never expected what the kid and I witnessed through the windshield of Philippe Giroux's limousine.

A quiet, empty street.

The kid leaned forward between the seats. "Do you think we got here first?"

"I don't see how."

We pulled to the curb, where I killed the engine and stepped into the drifting coastal fog. The only sounds to greet us were the keening of seagulls and the distant crashing of surf.

"There's a car," the kid said, and I saw it then as well, in the shade of the open garage—a battered green Subaru.

"Come on."

We hustled up the driveway. As the kid banged on the entry door, I cupped my hands to the window glass that looked into the living room.

The house appeared to be empty.

We stood listening. After a minute of anxious waiting, I tried the knob.

The door swung inward.

"Hello? Frederique! Is anybody home?"

We stood in the foyer. Then, after a moment, we both heard it.

"Down here," I said, running past the nursery and the bathroom and into a master bedroom at the back of the house where a figure on the bed lay writhing and grunting in the semidarkness.

"Open the blinds!"

I moved through the slatted gloom to where a woman—the gray-haired midwife—was facedown in the covers, her wrists and ankles heavily wrapped in tape.

"Jeez," said the kid as grayish sunlight flooded onto the bed. I turned the woman over and tore the tape from her mouth.

"Ah. Thank God. Are you the police?"

I tucked a pillow under her head.

"Get scissors from the kitchen," I told the kid, and to the woman I said, "What happened? Where's Frederique?"

"There was a lady. She came to the house. She had a gun."

"How long ago did they leave?"

"Ten minutes, maybe less."

"Any idea where they went?"

She shook her head. "They were speaking in French."

The kid returned with a knife, and as I stood to make room, he sat and sawed at the tape.

"You stay here," I told him. "Call her an ambulance."

I was moving again, down the hallway and back into the dull sunlight.

The limo roared to life. It took me no more than a minute to round the block onto Second Avenue, then onto Camino Real. I was bobbing my head, ducking to read the street signs, and when I hit Fourth Avenue, I knew I was heading in the right direction.

I punched up Mayday on speed dial.

"Jack? What's going on?"

"Listen carefully and don't talk. I'm in Carmel, and I just left Ethan at the rental house. Claudia's kidnapped Frederique. I don't know where she's taken her, but I'm playing a hunch. Call the local police and tell them I'm heading for the beach at Thirteenth Street, or Avenue, or whatever the hell they call it. Explain the whole situation. I don't have time."

My horn sent the pedestrians on Ocean Avenue scattering. Next came Ninth Avenue, Tenth Avenue, Twelfth. I hung a right at the next street and followed it down to the ocean.

The road curved to the left, following the shoreline. After a block or so it widened into a small parking lot where a lone vehicle—a blue Ford Fusion—was angled against the curb.

I stood on the brakes. Then I was out of the car and running.

The fog along the shoreline seemed heavier somehow, forming a low ceiling over a seascape rendered in mute watercolor. The beach was wide and white and sparsely dotted with blankets. Down by the water's edge, children ran shrieking and laughing ahead of the incoming waves.

I paused with hands on knees, scanning the beach. North to south I saw nothing but the children and the blankets and a wedge of pelicans gliding over the waves in silent formation.

And then I saw them. Far to the south, two small figures in silhouette. They were waist-deep in the frigid water amid a foaming jumble of rocks. They appeared to sway drunkenly in the surf, both figures stumbling, struggling against a heavy undertow.

I was running again, my legs churning in the soft, heavy sand. Past the children, past the blankets, then through a crusted band of kelp and fleas and broken shells, the sand filling my shoes and my shoes growing heavier, splashing now, my footfalls sending seagulls flapping and shrieking in angry protest.

Ahead of me, the silhouettes became people, and the people became Claudia Giroux and Frederique LaBoutin, their clothes drenched and their hair wet and matted. Frederique's housedress clung to her beachball belly while Claudia, in her black suit and with a white towel draped over her arm, looked like some lunatic valet who'd waded out to serve her.

It was Claudia who noticed my approach.

"Get back!" she shouted.

She took a grip on Frederique's collar as her towel-hand swung toward the shore.

"Claudia! Don't do this. It isn't necessary."

"Stay back or I'll shoot!"

"Listen to me! We know your father did it, and we know why he did it. He can be prosecuted. You can help us bring him to justice."

Both women stumbled sideways as a breaker hit the rocks, showering them in spume.

"Justice? Did you say *justice*? Go tell that to my brother!"

"Phil wouldn't want this, Claudia! Just drop the gun and come back to shore. Here."

I started into the water, but again she leveled the towel.

"Stop!"

"Come on, Claudia, think! Think what you're doing! Frederique is a witness. She's the one witness who can put your father in jail!"

"She's the one who can keep him in power! If this baby lives, then Father wins! I'm sorry, but I can't let that happen! Alain and Phil are gone, and I'm the only one left who can stop him!"

Frederique reached a trembling hand to shore, shouting something in French.

I tried a different tack.

"That baby is innocent, Claudia! And so is Frederique! Your father used her, just like he used you and everybody else!"

Claudia's gaze, I noticed then, had moved over my head. I turned to see two patrol cars, their grill lights flashing, roll to a stop on the roadway.

"Listen to me, Claudia! If you kill Frederique, you'll go to prison. I know you don't want that."

"I'll go to prison anyway!"

"No you won't! You're in the clear now! Just drop the gun and walk toward me."

She shed the towel then, exposing Regan's Walther. She tightened her grip on Frederique's collar—yanking her, standing her upright.

"Don't do it, Claudia!"

Shorebirds were settling on the beach around me. They fluttered and landed, strutting and scampering ahead of the lapping waves. Behind me, four uniformed officers, hands on holsters, were running onto the beach.

"Come on, Claudia, let her go! Let her testify against your father! Between the two of you, we'll put him away where he belongs!"

Claudia shook her sodden head.

"He'll never go to jail. You know that. And neither will I."

Behind me, shouted commands.

"We should have gone to Chile, Jack."

And with that she shoved Frederique, sending her tumbling into the surf. Claudia raised the gun in both hands, aiming directly at the officers.

"No! Don't shoot!"

Four guns exploded, the reports like summer thunder echoing down the beach.

All the shorebirds flew.

32

The invitation arrived in October of the following year.

It came in a creamy white envelope whose return address, with its familiar 94558 zip code, was embossed in satin gold.

Some debate ensued, and no little histrionics, but at the end of the day we agreed both to put the matter to a ballot, and that all would be bound by the outcome.

The vote was three-to-one.

"Okay, I'll come," Bernie had said before slamming the conference room door, "but I can't promise I'll behave."

And so it was that on the second weekend in November the law offices of MacTaggart & Suarez shuttered its doors on Thursday afternoon to decamp, kit and caboodle, for the climatic and cultural cool of the Fifth Annual Napa Valley Film Festival.

"This brings back memories," Regan observed as our airport rental car made the transition from Highway 29 onto Trancas Street in Napa. "None of which are fond."

Our three-bedroom suite at the Silverado Resort and Spa overlooked the golf course on which Thaddeus Melchior had, some fifteen months earlier, dipped his liver-spotted hand into my knickers to extract over three hundred dollars in skins. From the window of my bedroom I could see the very spot where my tee shot had found the creek on the par-three second hole, and I wondered if my ball was still there.

Shaved and showered, dressed and perfumed, we drove for twenty minutes to the historic Cameo Cinema in St. Helena, where Bernadette elbowed her way through the milling crowd and proceeded to inflict carpal tunnel syndrome on the bartender. Adopting a somewhat lower profile, Mayday, Regan, and I sipped our Chardonnay and watched the guests arrive.

"Who do you think will be here?" Mayday asked me.

"I don't know. But I know who won't."

We witnessed the arrival of Lourdes Giroux, darkly resplendent in the company of a taller, older gentleman whose smiling face I recognized, but couldn't quite place.

"Mark Rubenstein," Mayday reminded me. "Remember? He was Phil Giroux's probate lawyer."

With our laminated VIP passes hanging from our necks, we were approached several times by total strangers and questioned as to our affiliations with the event, the film, and the entertainment industry in general. We denied any association with such a ruthless, cutthroat, and mercenary enterprise. We told them we were lawyers.

It was only as the house lights dimmed and brightened and dimmed again that we caught a glimpse of Ethan Scott sweeping through the lobby, his blinding starlight reflecting on a swirling nebula of publicists and press, handlers and hangers-on, all of them orbiting just beyond the pull of our feeble gravity.

We poured Bernie into her seat in time for the opening credits.

The title they'd settled on was *The Grape Estate*. The director, of course, was Ethan Scott. It was a Great Scott Production, in association with Scott Free Films, Ltd.

The movie opened with a soaring aerial view of vineyards bathed in the russet hues of sunset. Pan in on the French Laundry restaurant. Cut to Ethan Scott and the estimable Christopher Plummer facing off across a table crowded with wineglasses. The older man reaches into his pocket for a newspaper clipping.

"Oh, for fuck sake," Bernie muttered.

She was loudly shushed.

By the time the house lights brightened and the stage was set for the post-preview Q and A, Bernadette had returned to the lobby bar.

"Ladies and gentlemen," a disembodied voice announced, "please welcome to our St. Helena village stage the executive producer, director, and star of *The Grape Estate*, the dashing and multitalented Ethan Scott!"

We clapped. The kid appeared from the wings in a baggy turtleneck sweater and his Clark Kent eyeglasses, carrying a coffee mug. He sat in an upholstered chair alongside a film critic in a tweed jacket. They bumped fists.

Twenty minutes or so into the hour-long program, the crowd was briefly distracted by a fussing child in the front row whose mother finally scooped him up and carried him up the aisle on her hip. Frederique LaBoutin wore textured leggings and high-heeled boots under a stylish black dress. According to Mayday, she carried a Birkin bag on her shoulder.

Up on stage, Ethan Scott was answering a question about inspiration.

"When Antonio Silva first approached me with the concept, I was leery of undertaking a story like this, ripped from the headlines," the kid explained. "But then I thought, wait a minute. It's the artist's duty to hold a mirror to the issues of his day, right? Sure, I could have played it safer for my directorial debut, but that's not my style. Life doesn't follow the structure of a screenplay, you know what I mean? Besides, I'd always wanted to play a lawyer, ever since I saw *To Kill a Mockingbird* in film school. And then when I read Antonio's script, well, I knew that the Nick McCoy character was my Atticus, and that this was the film I was destined to direct."

Somewhere in the lobby, a glass shattered.

The screening at Cameo Cinema was followed by a VIP-only reception at a restaurant call Tra Vigne where a hundred or more of the Valley's best-connected cinephiles gathered to munch and mingle in theoretical proximity to the evening's guest of honor. It was there that I saw Ronaldo Herrera holding court at a center table.

"What do you know," the former district attorney said as he rose from his chair. "I was wondering if you'd show up."

We shook hands and repaired to the bar.

"Thank you again for testifying." He touched his highball glass to mine. "It meant a lot."

"I'm sorry it wasn't enough."

"You and me both." He sighed heavily. "Nothing like having my O.J. moment immortalized on film."

He was referring, of course, to his failed prosecution of Philippe Giroux for murder—a sensational acquittal made doubly humiliating by Lourdes Giroux's subsequent civil verdict against her father-in-law for the wrongful death of her husband. As lawyers we understood the difference between proving guilt beyond a reasonable doubt—as the law requires in a criminal prosecution—and the lower civil threshold of awarding damages based on a mere preponderance of the evidence.

The voters of Napa County, alas, were less understanding.

We leaned with our backs to the bar and surveyed the roiling multitude. Regan and Mayday still lingered by the restaurant's curtained front entrance. They were keeping an eye on Bernadette, who, at the far end of the bar, was balancing a martini glass on her head.

"Whatever happened to Henri LaBoutin?"

Herrera grunted. "Deported to France, I think. Frederique divorced him as soon as the ink was dry on the death certificate."

This was a reference to the fact that, under the California Probate Code, a person cannot profit from causing the death of another. Which meant that Philippe, thanks to Lourdes's verdict—and despite his acquittal on the charge of capital murder—could no longer serve as trustee of the Giroux Family Trust. According to the suicide note they'd found in his bedroom, it was Lourdes's appointment as successor trustee—more so than her forty-five-million-dollar wrongful death award against him—that had been the final, fatal straw.

The note, I'd heard, had made no mention of either Phil's or Claudia's death.

"And Melchior walked away unscathed?"

Herrera shook his head. "Between Philippe's suicide and the attorney-client privilege, there was no way we could prosecute him. He's still practicing in Napa. Matter of fact, he's in line to head up the Napa County Bar Association next year."

"And how are Frederique and Lourdes getting along?"

Herrera looked to the far side of the room where the two women, each with a grip on one of baby Alain's hands, were swinging the now-giggling child like a pendulum.

"Like red wine and steak. Philippe, ironically enough, died without a will. As his sole heir, the baby inherited whatever crumbs were left after Lourdes collected her verdict. Enough to keep mother and child in silk underpants until the baby turns forty and inherits the winery. I hear that Frederique volunteers in the health clinic, and the baby's enrolled in the new daycare center. They're all living together in the stone château."

"And the Catholic Church?"

He shook his head. "They squawked, but nothing ever came of it. It was the publicity, I think, that finally backed them down. Even they didn't relish the prospect of suing an infant."

I wandered for a while—first through the room, and then to the patio out back. It was cold out there, and mostly empty save for a few tight clutches of smokers.

And one smoker standing alone, apart from the others.

"Hello, MacTaggart," he said before I'd noticed him. He was leaning against a tree that was wrapped in twinkling white lights.

"Hello, Andy."

I moved to stand before him, our breath making frost in the crisp evening air.

"Enjoy the movie?"

I shrugged.

"Tell me something. Is that really how it went down?"

"You mean the scene at the end, on the beach?"

He nodded.

"More or less. Not the exact dialogue, but . . ."

"But the same ending."

"Yeah, the same ending."

His eyes drifted across the patio.

"I heard you sold the club."

He laughed.

"If foreclosure is selling, then yeah, I guess I sold." He dropped his cigarette and crushed it underfoot. "What the hell. I never liked golf that much to begin with."

"So what are you working on now?"

"Oh, you know. A little of this, a little of that."

We stood for a while in awkward silence, stamping our feet in the cold.

"Well. Best of luck to you."

His voice stopped me again at the rear door to the restaurant.

"Hey, MacTaggart."

I turned. "Yeah?"

"You ever been in love?"

It wasn't the question I'd been expecting, and it took me a moment to think about it. I'd been infatuated, certainly, and I'd been intrigued. I'd had my head turned and my heart lightly bruised. I'd even used the L-word once, several years ago, on a rainy afternoon in Pasadena. But I'd never altered my life, or erected a temple, or risked prison for the love of a woman.

"No," I told him. "No, I guess I haven't."

"Too bad. It's all there is, really. Everything else is just waiting."

By the time I'd reentered the restaurant, the guest of honor had arrived. Like the eye of his own hurricane, Ethan Scott was surrounded by a crush of fans and well-wishers, groupies and glad-handers, all of them jostling, crowding in close for a fleeting ray of his golden sunshine.

"There you are," Mayday said, appearing beside me. "Bernie looks like she's had enough, and we're pretty tired ourselves. But we should probably say hello to Ethan before we go."

She and Regan, I noticed, were holding hands. Regan stifled a yawn and rested her head on Mayday's shoulder.

"Forget it," I said. "Bernie's drunk, and Ethan's busy, and if it's all the same with you, I'd rather not waste another minute."

ACKNOWLEDGMENTS

For this, my third foray into the fictional world of attorney Jack MacTaggart, I had the help of several guides and porters, most of whom will be familiar to readers of the series. They include, first and foremost, my wife, Lynda; my agent, Antonella Iannarino, of the David Black Agency; and my editor, Peter Joseph, of Thomas Dunne Books. Also my brother, Dan Greaves, and his daughter, Katie, both of whom were kind enough to read and critique the initial draft of the manuscript. Vallejo attorney Mike Vlaming helped fact-check some of my Napa County scenes—any errors or embellishments are mine alone—while Pasadena super-lawyer Susan House helped me to craft what she aptly described as "the worst trust provision in the history of estate planning." General thanks go to Hector DeJean, and Melanie Fried of St. Martin's Press, to Luke Thomas of the David Black Agency, to Jon Cassir of CAA, to copyeditor Jane Liddle, to my friends and coconspirators Steve Madison and Todd Moore, and above all to those faithful readers who've helped to sustain and inspire me on this crazy, exhilarating journey. I am indebted to all of you.